PRAISE FOR *THE RATTLED BONES*

"The feminist ghost story you've been waiting for." —Bustle

"Equal parts beautiful and chilling, Shannon M. Parker's sophomore novel will sweep you away to the icy waters and small coastal towns of Maine, where the past refuses to be ignored and family secrets are dredged to the surface with the day's catch. Unputdownable, and like the roar of the sea once you've heard it, unforgettable."
—Sarah Glenn Marsh, author of *Fear the Drowning Deep*

"A beautiful, mournful tale of a grieving young woman who faces, with courage and empathy, the dark secrets of her family's history and the unknown terrain of her future. *The Rattled Bones* is utterly steeped in the atmosphere and hardships of life on the Maine coast, exploring a shameful and little-known episode of American history with unflinching honesty and obvious respect."
—Kali Wallace, author of *The Memory Trees*

"*The Rattled Bones* is like a ghost story told around a bonfire on a cold northern beach. This exquisite, stormy mystery and its seafaring heroine will keep you reading long into the night."
—Rebecca Podos, author of *The Mystery of Hollow Places*

"In *The Girl Who Fell*, Shannon Parker established herself as a master at weaving a compelling story in a high stakes, thrilling ride of a read. She does it again, superbly, in *The Rattled Bones*, where a haunting on the Maine coastline blurs the line between sanity and madness." —Karen Fortunati, author of *The Weight of Zero*

ALSO BY S. M. PARKER

The Girl Who Fell

THE
RATTLED
BONES

S. M. PARKER

SIMON PULSE

NEW YORK   LONDON   TORONTO   SYDNEY   NEW DELHI

SIMON PULSE

An imprint of Simon & Schuster Children's Publishing Division

1230 Avenue of the Americas, New York, New York 10020

First Simon Pulse hardcover edition August 2017

Text copyright © 2017 by Shannon M. Parker

Jacket photograph copyright © 2017 by Stephen Carroll/Arcangel Images

For information about special discounts for bulk purchases, please contact Simon & Schuster Special Sales at 1-866-506-1949 or business@simonandschuster.com.

The Simon & Schuster Speakers Bureau can bring authors to your live event. For more information or to book an event contact the Simon & Schuster Speakers Bureau at 1-866-248-3049 or visit our website at www.simonspeakers.com.

Jacket designed by Regina Flath

Interior designed by Mike Rosamilia

The text of this book was set in Adobe Caslon Pro.

Manufactured in the United States of America

2 4 6 8 10 9 7 5 3 1

Library of Congress Cataloging-in-Publication Data

Names: Parker, S. M., author.

Title: The rattled bones / by S. M. Parker.

Description: First Simon Pulse hardcover edition. | New York : Simon Pulse, 2017. | Summary: After her father's death, Rilla Brae puts off thoughts of college to take over his lobstering business, while helping an archaeology student excavate nearby Malaga, an uninhabited island with a ghost that beckons her. | Includes bibliographical references.

Identifiers: LCCN 2016056047| ISBN 9781481482042 (hardcover) | ISBN 9781481482066 (eBook)

Subjects: | CYAC: Lobster fishers—Fiction. | Ghosts—Fiction. | Archaeology—Fiction. | Islands—Fiction. | Racism—Fiction. | Maine—Fiction. |

BISAC: JUVENILE FICTION / Legends, Myths, Fables / General. | JUVENILE FICTION / Horror & Ghost Stories. | JUVENILE FICTION / Love & Romance.

Classification: LCC PZ7.1.P366 Rat 2017 | DDC [Fic]—dc23

LC record available at https://lccn.loc.gov/2016056047

For my sons.
The story of how you walked into my life
will always be the greatest story I could ever tell.

THE
RATTLED
BONES

BEFORE

My mother had been pacing the lip of the ocean for hours, talking to the Water People the way she did. They tended to visit when the fog rose high, and the fog always rose high when my mother neared the sea.

On the back deck, I leaned against my gram's chest as we watched my mother patrol the slice of shore where the waves met our backyard. Her long yellow skirt was wet at the bottom, the waterline crawling up the cloth as she walked back and forth and then back again. Her skirt held the brightest glow under the stars, and the light made six-year-old me wonder if my mother carried the moon tucked under her heart.

I didn't tell Gram how I squinted my eyes to try to see the Water People. I didn't tell her how much I wanted to run to my mother on nights like this, pull her away from the spell of the people who visited with the mist.

I wanted to talk to the people who lived in the ocean and I wanted to hear the words they spoke in whispers carried on waves. Because then I could tell them to go away, that my mother didn't need them.

But no one ever heard their voices.

No one but my mother.

I watched her pluck small stones from the band of foamy sea spit, collecting jewels from the deep. My blood ran with excitement, wanting her to come to the deck and show me all the rocks made glossy from the lick of seawater, give them to me like gifts. She'd tell me of their origin and how they were millions of years old, once trampled on by dinosaurs, squeezed by continents of ice. Sometimes we would find broken glass, pieces soft at the edges thanks to time and the rolling current. We would talk about the story of the glass, how a great ship lost an exotic perfume container to the sea, its purple shell shattering into treasure of a different kind.

Then there were the broken bits of potter's clay my mother would tuck against her breast, as if holding these shards could make the pottery whole again. She told me tales of how the Water People left their pots behind. She knew everything about the Water People, and I was both jealous and frightened.

But my mother never showed me the rocks that day. As I waited, Gram's body went rigid behind me. It felt as if her heart had stopped, as if she froze still. I wondered if she finally saw the Water People too. But Gram rose too quickly, dumping me from her lap. I knew then that my world was turning over. My gram didn't bend to me to see if I was okay. She only said one word. Tossed into the ocean, a skipping stone.

No!

Just that one word, but it seemed so loud over the waves, over the breathing of the sea. The small lonely word thumped inside of me, replacing my heartbeat. *No. No. No.* I didn't chase after Gram as she darted into the house. I heard the frantic hum of her words spoken into the phone in our kitchen.

I stayed watching my mother hunt for larger rocks to add to the pockets of her long skirt. How my mother bunched the skirt at her waist as the elastic band began to slide at her hips. I could see the weight of the rocks was almost too much to bear. And I watched her walk straight into the waves with all that weight on her body, with so much purpose in her every step. I thought she might go into the sea and bring the Water People back for me.

But it was Gram who brought my mother back. She ran out of our house, across the lawn. Gram dove into the midnight water and drew my mother from the grip of the deep. She wrestled her to shore and rocked her daughter's wet limbs in the cradle of her own body. My mother curled her long legs so tightly to her chest, as if she wanted them to disappear. My mother still called to the sea from the safety of Gram's arms, her words wet and distant.

My mother and Gram stayed locked together like that for so long I thought the sun might have enough time to rise, push away the moon. But I couldn't watch for the sun. I kept my eyes on my mother as she eyed the sea. Knowing, without anyone telling me, that she wanted to be with the Water People more than she wanted to be with me. Fear crept inside of me then, a dark eel slicking through my veins.

After Gram walked my mother to the ambulance, she came to hold me once again, wrapping me close enough to sync our fears. I pressed into the thundering wail of her heartbeat.

I told Gram I would never need the people from the deep.

Gram promised she would never leave me.

I latched tight to her promise.

As the sirens faded in the distance, I burrowed hard against my gram so that no one could climb between us, separate my heart from hers.

CHAPTER ONE

There is no name for what I am.

Boys have their choice of titles—lobsterman, sternman, fisherman—but since I'm a girl, I am none of these. My gender isn't welcome at sea, which is ridiculous since no one is more tied to the moon and the ocean than a female. But maritime lore has always claimed that a girl on a ship is bad luck, even though nearly every sailor in the history of braving the ocean has named his boat after a girl. Men even invented the mermaid to feel safer at sea.

I'll always defend my right to fish the water.

But today I don't want to be here.

I nudge my wrist forward, pressing against the throttle to make the *Rilla Brae* quicken. My lobster boat—the one Dad named for me—cuts a certain path through the rough, curling Maine water. The morning fog parts as I push against its thickness, the displaced mist twisting into thin gray fingers, beckoning me toward deeper waters.

I go because I have to.

Because it's what my father would have wanted.

I steer toward the swath of ocean my family has fished for generations while the GPS bleeps out navigation points. I silence the machine and its piercing electronic pulses because I don't need technology to find the string of lobster traps my father set into the deep three days ago—his last day on earth. The watery pathway leading to the Gulf of Maine is an artery I've traveled since before I could crawl. Its inlets are as recognizable—as memorable—as the laugh lines that track around my father's eyes.

Tracked.

The VHF radio above my head wakes with static before I hear Reed's voice. "All in, *Rilla Brae*?"

I pull down the mouthpiece and press the side button to talk. "All in." It's the same response I always give Reed when he checks in on my fishing. All in. These two words let him know I'm on the water. That I'm all right and that I love him—things you need a code for when talking over a public channel.

A wave of static and then, "*Charlotte Anne*, out at Lip Gulley, watching for you, *Rilla Brae*." The voice is Billy Benson's, captain of the *Charlotte Anne*—a vessel named for his wife—and I'm not sure if he's watching for me or my boat or both. I don't have time to respond before Emmet Teale's call comes across the wire: "*Maddie Jean*, good to hear ya on the line, *Rilla Brae*."

"Heavy seas today. Keep beam to." George Mank, telling me to keep my boat perpendicular to the swells, even though I know what he's really telling me. How all the fishermen are using their own kind of code to say the hard things.

I press the VHF button and ask: "You boys gonna tie up this channel all day with this lovefest?"

Being a wiseass might be the most sacred language among us on the water. It tells the men that I'm okay, even if I'm not.

The radio chirps with a lighter chatter about weather and bait prices as I slow near a green-and-orange buoy bobbing with our family's fishing colors. Dad, Gram, and I spent the winter painting all eight hundred of our Styrofoam buoys—a thick horizontal stripe of orange crossed with a thin vertical strip of green. The specific colors and design mark our traps. My traps now. Every fishing family knows each other by the colored pattern of their buoys. Just as every fishing family knows it's forbidden to set one's traps in another family's fishing grounds. It's a hard thing to think I'm a fishing family of one now. Well, me and Gram. But Gram doesn't go out on the water anymore.

I flick the throttle to neutral and step outside the wheelhouse to cast my hook, spearing the buoy rope on the first try. I pull the lobster line manually—old-school—straining the muscles in my arms and back to coax the metal crate from the bottom of the sea. It rises inch by inch through the layers of water as I work the wet rope through my hands.

My arms tire quickly.

The soggy, slack rope curls into a sleeping snake behind my feet as the corner of the first lobster trap breaks the water. Its green metal edge winks against the gray waves as it sloughs off excess water. My heart stutters as I hold the trap at the waterline, unable to let it fully break the surface.

"This is the moment," he'd say, and I'd watch my dad's frame swell with hope for the catch, each trap a new gift. "What treasure will the sea bestow upon us?"

I want to hold the trap suspended like this for the rest of time, feel my father's enthusiasm here with me. But of course I can't. I reach for the trap, insert my gloved fingers into the wire mesh, and wrestle the cage onto the deck.

And then a smile crests on my lips. A pop of laughter jumps from inside of me.

Because the trap is full and it feels like a gift from my dad.

I cast my eyes to the sky to thank him, even if I wasn't raised to believe in heaven or happily ever afters.

*   *   *

By the time I reset my string of a hundred pots and deliver my catch to the fisheries co-op, the sun has bullied away the fog and swallowed every drop of cool air. I shed my heavy rubber overalls and strip down to my everyday uniform of leggings and a plain white tee. I turn my course toward home, where Gram will be waiting.

Only Gram.

I raise my face to the sun to let its warmth reach inside of me, stretch into my bones. I keep my hips pressed against the boat's steering wheel, coasting in the sea that has calmed now. My reliable engine hums as I watch the sleek missile dive of an oil-black cormorant. The bird retrieves a fish from the water and spreads her wings against the blue-and-white marble sky as she flies off with her breakfast.

Life and death in a heartbeat.

The bird disappears into the thick green tree line of a nearby island just as my boat lurches to a violent stop, pitching me forward. My hip bone slams against the corner of the instrument panel and pain sears along the length of my body, hot as fire. At the back of the boat, my engine misfires with a shotgun blast that raises thunder in my heart. Then the engine dies.

Leaving me bobbing, alone at sea without power.

Every mariner's nightmare.

I scan the console, but it's darkened to black. No electricity. No VHF. I throw the motor into neutral and crank the key. The engine doesn't speak. The boat tumbles with the sway of the waves. I try the key again. Nothing. And no cell reception along this waterway.

I draw in a deep breath. I know this boat. I've got this.

Except, maybe I don't.

I move to the engine at the back. I run my fingers along the fuel lines, testing every valve, every connection. The fuel filter's clean. No broken belts, no blown hoses. I straighten, mystified. And that is when Malaga Island draws my full attention—or rather, the small wooden boat resting at its shore. The empty skiff is old, its paint beaten bare from Maine's harsh seasons. But who does it belong to? And can they give me help if I need it?

Help. Something I've never been good at asking for.

The current pushes me closer to the uninhabited island, which isn't much more than a rough mound of stone. The island's trees are thick green spruce, with pointed, triangle tips that gobble up the sunlight. Tufts of fennel grass cling for life along the rough, small beach. And then, a figure.

A girl.

Maybe my age.

She is bent and focused as if rubbing something against the

rocks. Her dark braids slip over her sharp shoulders as she leans forward, pulls back. Rhythmically. Expertly.

I wave, but the girl doesn't look up.

I call to her, my hands cupped around my cry. "Hello!" I fan my arm again, cutting a single arc through the air. The girl doesn't respond. I stare at her too-long dress, its white lace seeming so out of place.

The air buckles, allowing a cold current to sweep across the water. The wind has the bite of winter in its breath, too icy for June. My skin blooms with gooseflesh.

Then I hear her.

The girl raises a song over the pounding waves, a low and mournful melody that lifts louder as she presses forward and back, her eyes never leaving her task. Her tune sounds like a lullaby from my childhood. Maybe something Gram would hum as she cradled me in her rocking-chair lap. Or is it from the forgotten depths of days when my mother lived here? Did my mother know this song? Sing it to me?

My memory can't pull up the words, but it doesn't matter.

Because it feels like the girl is singing for my loss.

I call to her again. "Hello!" My yell is primal, and I'm not entirely sure it has anything to do with my need to be rescued. When she looks up I see her brown face, her large eyes finding me. Do I know this girl? A word forms on her wide mouth, but the shrill bleat of an air horn devours all other sound. I startle and turn.

Old Man Benner's slick new lobster boat—appropriately named *Pretty Penny*—putters beside mine, dwarfing the *Rilla Brae*. He cups one hand around his mouth and calls, "Ya's all right, Rilla?"

"Fine." The lie is quick and spiteful. I'd rather swim home than accept help from Reed's grandfather, but I hear my dad's words: "You get farther with sugar than you do with spice, sunfish." I throw a forced smile.

"Glad ta see ya pulling them pots." Now it's his turn to lie. Only one morning after Dad's death, Old Man Benner called Gram to bully me off our fishing grounds. I listened with my head pressed to hers, our ears tented over the kitchen wall's landline receiver. When I heard Old Man Benner's dense Maine accent spit out the words "Ayuh. Ocean's no place for a girl," I hung up on him, leaving me alone with Gram and her stern stare. I set twice as many traps into the deep that day.

"Sorry again 'bout ya father." Old Man Benner's tongue is thick with Maine, making *father* sound like *fath-ah*. It's the regional accent Dad trained out of me from the first words I spoke. Not because he was ashamed of our roots, but because he knew it would mark me, and he wanted me to make my mark on the world instead.

"Need anything?" Old Man Benner calls.

A tow. My father. I need to believe I didn't fail Dad on his last day, the way his heart did. I slide my dignity down where I can't hear its protest and move to the rail. A request for help sits on my lips, but my pride won't give it sound. "I'm all set." Another lie.

"Ya shouldn't be out he-ah, Rilla." Benner sucks on a toothpick, teetering it between his teeth. "No sayin' what could happen to a girl alone."

The threat smacks me hard enough to rattle my head. My blood thickens with hate. "I'll keep that in mind." I stretch my arm toward him, hold up my open palm when I want to hold up my middle finger. He laughs at my fisherman's—fishergirl's?—wave, jimmying that gnawed toothpick deep in his bite.

My wave is enough to make him move on, and I flip him the bird once he's passed. His boat stirs a wake that leaves me bobbing in giant man-made swells. When the sea settles, I try the key again. Nothing. *It's okay,* I tell myself. *I'll ask the girl for help. It'll be easy. People ask for assistance all the time.* I reach for a rag under the console, find a white square of torn sheet and raise it over my head, readying to wave the international distress signal.

But the girl is gone. I trade the SOS cloth for my binoculars and scan the island.

She is nowhere.

I settle into the captain's chair—my chair now.

I search Malaga with a strange disappointment swelling my heart. I don't know why I feel solidarity with the girl; maybe because she's not supposed to be out here. Same as me.

I stand quickly, feeling trapped. My binoculars catch the edge of the key as they fall from my lap. The electronic gauges light up. "Well, hello," I say, bringing my fingers to the dashboard. I turn the key fully and the motor turns over with a smooth rumble, shimmying the boat to life.

"Good girl." I pet her console before I set the *Rilla Brae* in gear and ease nearer to the island. I stop before the sea becomes too shallow. I look for the girl and her boat, but there are no signs of either. I press the heels of my palms against my eyes and know I need more sleep. Could I have imagined her? How else could she be here one minute and not the next?

Because a boat can't just disappear.

Unless she pulled the skiff ashore and it's resting in an island inlet I can't see. I decide that's what's happened before turning the helm toward home. I set my course to Fairtide Cottage, the only home I've ever known.

And I see our flag at half-mast.

All the flags on our fishing peninsula ripple at half-mast.

When I dock the *Rilla Brae*, Gram greets me, barefoot as

always. She's made of sturdy Downeast stock and tries to hide the grief that slumps her shoulders as she marches across the yard, intent on inspecting the cooler filled with a sampling of today's catch. Tonight's dinner.

With each of Gram's steps, the melody of the girl's song returns, rising as Gram gets closer. It feels new and old all at once. Like I know it, but I'm also discovering it. My ears fill with the tune. My heart swells for it. My memory reaches for it. The song wraps me in the safety of my past and promises the same for my future. *Come here, come here. My dear, my dear*, it says.

"What's that song?" My words sound weak, as if I were too afraid to speak them.

"Song?" Gram bends to tug on my dock lines to make sure they're secure.

I clear my throat. "The one you were singing."

"Wasn't me singing this time," Gram says. She's been the world's biggest fan of The Who since forever ago. It's not uncommon to hear her belting out "Pinball Wizard" while she's beating eggs or glazing a pie. But today Gram puts her hand on my shoulder, like she knows maybe the song I'm asking about is in my head. Like she knows my head is crammed with too much noise. She gives my shoulder a gentle squeeze and the music stops.

We're left to the beat of lapping waves and the chorus of brawling seabirds hovering always at the shore.

Gram boards the *Rilla Brae* as I study the rise of granite and trees that make up the forty acres of Malaga Island. I'm searching still for the girl, even from here. Listening for her song. Gram watches me carefully, an unasked question in her eyes. "Maybe Hattie's singing." She nods up at the house. "She's waiting for ya."

Hattie. The last girl I want to see.

CHAPTER TWO

Hattie is up by Gram's medicinal garden, picking tiny blue petals off a forget-me-not as if she's counting *he loves me, he loves me not*. I almost want Gram to reprimand her for this gardening offense and ban her from the property.

Hattie meets me in the middle of the lawn that holds the divots of our cartwheels, the scars of our bonfires—the wounds of all eleven years of our friendship.

"Hey," she says, testing the waters.

"Hey." I let the silence gather between us.

"So you won't answer my texts."

"There's a lot going on."

"Too busy to let me know how you're holding up?"

"I'm fine." Lie. I shift my feet in the grass and envy the stability of the ground.

"Do you wanna hang out? Keep your mind off stuff?"

I bristle, my back straightening. "My father's death isn't 'stuff.'"

"Of course not." Hattie retreats a step, a concession so against her bold nature. "I didn't mean it like that. I just thought you might want to go somewhere. You know, get away."

Like Senior Celebration Day, the day after graduation? Hattie dragged me there even though I'd told her a hundred times that I didn't want to go to another predictable quarry party.

"I can't." Maybe if I'd been working on the boat that day I could have radioed for help. Or maybe my father's heart wouldn't have had to work so hard if I'd been hauling traps with him.

"You can't or you won't?"

Can't. Won't. It's hard to see the difference. "Both. I don't know, Hattie." I realize it's not rational to blame her; I was the one who abandoned my dad. Still.

She casts her eyes to her feet. "Maybe I should go."

I nod as if that's even an answer. Because the last thing I can do is explain any of my actions to her. All I know is that forgiving her means forgiving myself for leaving my dad alone to die at sea. How can I ever be ready to do that?

Hattie turns, and I immediately feel a pull to run to her, get swallowed in her hug. But my feet are too grounded now. Stuck.

I focus on Gram's blooming lilac bushes, their branches bending with the weight of their own beauty. The air is filled with the smell of the warm lilac compresses Gram would make to soothe my childhood cuts, calm suspicious rashes. Is there any combination of flowers that have properties powerful enough to quiet the agony of loss?

Hattie twists before disappearing around Gram's garden. She fixes her eyes, hangs them on me with regret. "Losing you to Rhode Island next year scares the shit out of me, Rills. I just wanted one more day with you. An afternoon when we didn't have to think about a future without each other." Her plea now is so similar to the one that swayed me to ditch work on Senior Celebration Day, a lifetime ago. "If I'd known any of this would have gone down this way . . . I would have done it all differently and you know that. You know me, Rilla."

I'm not sure what I know anymore. I turn and head back to the boat.

Filled with resentment toward Hattie.

And forgiveness.

And everything in between.

My father owned exactly one dress jacket, but I wanted him buried in his favorite sweater, the one with frayed cuffs and a high fisherman's neck. I found his suit jacket at the back of his closet. It is navy blue and stubborn. It refuses to let go of my father's smell, so I wear it over my dress as we return home from his funeral the following day.

The jacket's interior lining is silk and slips off my shoulders when I move. I pull the front of the blazer tighter across my middle as if the fabric is strong enough to keep the liquid spill of my heart from drowning our kitchen table.

"It was the finest kind of service." Gram doesn't turn from the stove, where she is literally watching a pot that won't boil. "I can't think of a soul who wasn't there."

I don't point out the obvious.

Gram adjusts the mesh silver tea ball steadied over one of the two waiting mugs, her small, practiced movements too much like his. "Your father would have been some touched by the speech ya gave today, Rilla."

A hiccup of grief jumps high in my chest, and suddenly it's hard to breathe. I turn to the window, toward Gram's flowers. My eyes cloud as they watch a bumblebee hover over the cone of a deep purple lupine. The insect's bright color and free wings beam in direct contrast to the black wall of suits that stood in the church today, the straight broad shoulders of the fishermen who carried Jonathan Brae's casket out of the church and across the cemetery green.

I watch the bee crawl into the bloom, depositing a story, Gram would say. Bees sew stories through the earth, leaving one tale while raising up another. They carry the stories on the whisper of their wings, Gram says.

I pull my eyes from the bee emerging from the lupine. "What do we do now?"

The snake hiss of the kettle builds. "Now we get on with the business of living, hard as that may be." The teapot screams.

Gram sets my mug in front of me, and lemon steams the air. Gram uses fresh lemon rind, shaved into thinness before she adds it to her tea leaves. I hadn't grown past her knees when she first taught me about how the citrus skin would soothe my sore throat, how ancient healers believed inhaling the zest would improve a person's mood. Today, though, I'm calling bullshit.

Gram settles her mug onto the opposite side of the table before taking her seat. Even this small act reminds me how off-balance our family is now. We are a tripod missing a leg.

"I think I have to notify the University of Rhode Island, let them know I won't be coming."

"Is that what ya want?"

"It doesn't seem like the universe is particularly interested in what I want."

"Maybe so." Gram rounds her gnarled fingers around the curve of her cup. "But I'm not asking the universe. I'm asking ya, Rilla."

I shift in my seat just to feel the cool silk of my father's jacket slide across my skin. "I need to stay here. Someone has to fish." And Gram is too old to lobster. "If I don't keep lobstering, you know Old Man Benner will claim our grounds before my bags are even packed for school." I fail to mention that my bags have been packed for the University of Rhode Island for weeks.

"And would that be the worst thing?"

We both know the worst thing has already happened. I bring my fist to my chest to keep the sadness from rising, too late. A sob escapes. "Dad wouldn't want to forfeit our legacy."

"No." Gram stirs honey into her tea. "He wouldn't want that *for him*. But he certainly wouldn't want ya sacrificing your future for his past either." She *tink*s her spoon against the edge of her cup before her gaze challenges mine, forces me to look away. "From where I'm sitting, it feels wholly possible for ya to go to college and fish the summers. We'll manage."

My head screams: How? How could we manage? Who will pay the bills? Watch out for Gram? Leaving is absurd; it's no longer an option.

I'm grateful when the doorbell announces Brenda Sherfey on the step offering tuna casserole and condolences. I abandon Brenda's food to the counter because the fridge is already crammed with sorrow. Then I leave Gram to the soothing words of her bridge partner and disappear upstairs to my room.

I'm not surprised to see Reed there, at the dormered window seat that overlooks the water. Reed Benner, the only good Benner. Old Man Benner and my dad hated when we started dating, and maybe that's why we did it. At first. Reed's been using the rose trellis to climb into my bedroom for the last two years, like our time together is a secret even if everyone knows about us. He turns when he hears me enter my room, pats the window seat cushion next to him. He is mere feet away, but it takes so long to reach him. My steps seem too slow, like time and my body are being dragged forward against my will.

Dorm room cubes wait against the front wall of my room. They hold strangely normal items, like flip-flops and an extra-long twin sheet set. The sheets are sun yellow. The shower shoes are a size too big. I'd planned to exchange both, except now I can't. How can I surrender the gifts my father presented waiter-style, a platter of sheets and shoes with an oversize hoodie from the University of Rhode Island perched on top? And his smile then, how it welled with pride for the first Brae to attend college. I dust my fingers over the edge of the sheet square as I pass and I'm surprised by how these insignificant items scream with importance now. It wasn't like this with my mother, who has stayed away for years by choice, who left before making memories for me to miss.

But my dad is everywhere.

At the window, I let Reed gather me in his arms. He rests my head against his side as I tuck my knees into a ball, my body turned toward the water, the sea breeze. Dad's dress jacket drapes over me, a blanket.

"You're stoned," I tell him, like he doesn't already know. It's a familiar fog that covers Reed's eyes lately.

Reed twists a curl at my temple, lets the soft hair wrap around his finger like an eager vine. "Ayuh."

"At the funeral too."

"Had to be."

The funeral took years, each moment stretching itself into a day. "Did you have to smoke? It felt"—feels—"disrespectful."

"It's a heavy day, Rill." His words make a bullet of anger rise in me. Like I don't know today is weighted with loss? But then he takes my hand and my fury gets pulled down, pushed away. If I don't know how to deal with this kind of grief, how can I be mad at Reed for dealing in his own way?

"Rill?"

"I'm here." I close my eyes to Reed's rhythmic stroking of my temple, the way his fingers draw precise lines around my features. Memorizing me, he says. For when we can't be together.

"Maybe today. Maybe all this happened—"

"Don't." My quick warning is a whisper, a plea. "Please." Don't tell me there's reason in this.

I can't hear again how much Reed wants me to stay in Maine, turn down my scholarship. He's never understood that I need to study harder, work harder than the men here. Reed left high school midway through our junior year to get his GED because he was already making good money catching bugs. Fishing's all he's ever wanted to do, which is fine. I just don't have the energy to fight over our future again.

"Okay." Reed pulls me closer, his arm wrapped around my waist. "Let's just sit here in the quiet."

Yes. Quiet. "Quiet is good."

He leans his head back against the window, exhales softly. Outside, the *Rilla Brae* bobs at the dock. The water is calm for the entire stretch of the inlet, as far as Malaga Island and beyond. These are the days my father wouldn't fish. "Never trust a quiet sea, sunfish," he'd say—each time sounding like the first time he was bestowing this bit of advice.

I feel my father here with us as I fix my eyes on the sea and watch an impossible tidal wave begin to grow off the shores of Malaga. The water rises, becomes a wall reaching for the sky. Higher, stronger, its frothed cliff edge as white as the clouds. My back straightens. The rogue wave builds. Hurries toward my house. Its blue swell charges at us as if we are its target. I bolt upright and press my palms against the window, try to push back the water. The enormous wave slaps at the lawn, lunges toward the house.

I claw at Reed.

A scream rips from my throat, fills my ears.

The pelting spray crashes against my second-story window,

hard as hail. The bullets of water drive me backward as wind squeals through the window's frame. I trip to the floor, screaming. The gust carries a northeast chill that traps ice in my bones.

The air is as cold as death.

Then there is Reed's voice, his strong arms shaking me. "Rilla?" His eyes are wide, so alert now. "What's wrong?"

Reed. I scramble to my feet. "You're okay." My words mumble with disbelief. I dash to the window. "The wave, the—" The aftermath steals my thoughts.

The *Rilla Brae* buoys gently in the sleeping current. Unharmed.

I press my hand to the windowpanes, matching my fingers to the prints I left only seconds ago. The glass shimmers in the mid-June sun. Dry. "The water. It rose up over the lawn."

Reed's hand meets my back in a way that suggests he's holding me upright. "Water?"

I point as Reed gazes out over our quiet yard. Our dry lawn. "Didn't you . . . ?"

My memory hears my dad answer before my question can fully pass my lips: "It's been a longer day than any twenty-four hours has a right, Rilla. A mind can bend with exhaustion."

My father's right. Even now, he's right.

"Everything's okay." Reed presses his hand against the small of my back. "Everything's gonna be okay." But I sense how he's trying to make sense of this strangeness in me. And I feel his distance, how he doesn't gather me to his side.

"Tomorrows always arrive lighter," my father says. *Said.*

It's the first time I don't believe him.

CHAPTER THREE

I fear I'll never know deep sleep again.

Reed convinced me that yesterday's vision was the fallout of insomnia: nightmares visiting in full view of the sun. I can't shake the fear that it was something more. I should have asked him to stay with me last night—for protection or comfort. Or both. But independence was drilled into me early. I have a hard time asking anyone for help, even if it is Reed and I really needed it.

I crawl out of bed and layer for the sea. T-shirt. Leggings. Fleece. My bright orange Grundens are on a hook upon the *Rilla Brae*, like always, even though I won't need my rubber overalls or my all-weather jacket today. It'll be different this winter. I won't be able to pull on enough layers. If I stay.

In the kitchen, I pack my lunch. I make Dad a sandwich too. Out of habit.

Gram squeezes through the patio doors, joins me in the kitchen. Her sigh is heavy and foreign; Gram never complains.

"Everything all right?" I suspend my knife in the peanut butter jar and hear the absurdity of my question only after it passes my lips.

"Ayuh." She wrestles her dirt-caked gardening gloves from her fingers and abandons them to the table. Tiny pebbles of earth skitter across its worn wood surface. Gram looks out at her back gardens, clean hands planted on her sturdy hips. "I've got grubs, Rilla."

I almost laugh. Insects? Insects are a solvable problem. "Grubs, huh?" I paint the peanut butter onto my bread, all the way to the very edges the way my father liked.

"Those devils have got some moxie being so close to my peonies." Gram huffs past me and dips her head into the fridge. She draws in a small gasp when she opens the door. "There's more food in here than stars in the sky."

"What do you need? I'll get it for you." I place the knife onto the cutting board and join Gram at the open fridge.

"Beer." She says it like it's not six o'clock in the morning.

"Beer?"

She fans her twisted fingers to hurry me along. "Well, I'm not gonna drink it, Rilla. It's for the grubs. Give me as much as we've got."

"Right." I remove the casserole dishes and pass each one to

Gram. I reach into the back and grab four bottles. I tuck the fifth deeper into the corner. It feels wrong to give the last of my father's beer to garden pests.

Gram packs the casserole dishes into the freezer with impressive economy, then scans my outfit. "Looks like you're dressed for buggin'."

"Not today. The traps haven't soaked long enough. I'll haul tomorrow."

Her side glance tells me she's waiting for more.

"I just need to be on the water."

She nods, covers my hand with hers. "You're just like him, Rilla. Two seals always needing their ocean."

I don't tell her I'm headed for land.

It takes only minutes to reach the lee side of Malaga Island, the protected side. I tell myself that I'm here for a new perspective— to see my surroundings in a new light. And if I'm being honest, I need to put some distance between me and Reed and his choice to check out when I don't have that luxury. And Hattie's voice mails. I don't know what to say to her yet, and I can't hurt her more. But it's when I idle my engine in front of the exact spot where I saw the girl two days ago that I know my motivations are singular: I'm looking for the singing girl.

The beach is empty, which should be zero surprise. Still, a

part of me hoped she'd be here, waiting for me or something. It's been impossible to shake the memory of her and her disappearing skiff, not to mention the tidal wave growing from Malaga's shores. But I'm not willing to chalk these things up to hallucinations just yet. I refuse to let my brain slip into the space of madness that stole my mother.

I thrust my anchor overboard and the water swallows its weight. I strip off my layers and toss them into the tiny rowboat tied to *Rilla*'s stern. On another day, I would row the short distance to shore, but today I want the bite of water to wash over me. Through me. I climb onto the starboard ledge wearing only my bra and underwear. My toes hug the cool fiberglass rail as my eyes measure depth the way Dad taught me.

Black at the deep.

Green at the shallows.

The water before me swirls with a jeweled color that's between black and green.

I jump.

The icy water swallows me as I plummet, feet first. Bubbles crowd around me, the water making room for my shape. I thrust my arms up, pressing deeper into the sea despite the shock to my lungs, the cold squeezing me. I open my eyes, the salt stinging as I stare at the black. In the depth of this water there is no loss. In the ice of this sea there is only numbness.

And a song.

I hear it over the weight of the water pushing against my ears.

Come here, come here, my dear, my dear.

I spin around, search the deep. Cold fear rips through me.

Come here, come here, my dear, my dear.

I hear the words too clearly. Here, underneath millions of years of ocean, I hear the song meet me. *Come here, come here . . .*

I bullet to the surface. My ears pop and then the voice of the ocean rushes all around me. The waves explode as they crash against the side of my boat. My mouth takes in seawater and I spit it free. The salt bites against my tongue. My fingers work to free the skiff rope from the *Rilla Brae*, but they are wet and fumbling. I kick my feet below the surface of the thrashing water, to stay upright, but also to push away the song rising from the deep. My fingers are cold and cramping as they rip at the knot, too clumsy. Too wet. Too slick. I look over my shoulder, into the sea of waves, my heart thundering for what I might see surface from the spraying waves.

When the knot opens, I slip the rope around my wrist and swim to shore. I scramble onto land, dress quickly.

The air on the island is still, quiet. The breeze holds its breath. I stumble back from the beach, waiting for something— someone—to rise. The singer. The girl? But the sea holds its secrets. The waves roil unfazed. I squeeze my palms to my temples, pressing them hard against my skull. Did I imagine the song? I shake my hands free. No. I heard the singing. Impossible, maybe. But I heard it. I take a few steps back, putting distance between me and the deep. When nothing emerges from the surf, I turn and quickly hike to the highest slab of granite. I sit against the rock's heat, pulling my legs to my chest as if they are some kind of protection.

My breath steadies, but only some. There has never been a time when I feared the water. Any water. Is that what this is? Me, afraid of the sea in the wake of my father's death? I shake the thought from my head. I hear the chanting verse in my memory, *Come here, come here, my dear, my dear*, and I know this isn't about me being frightened of the sea; this is me fearing my brain could be too much like my mother's. Because what if my mother didn't just talk to the Water People? What if they answered her? What if they sang to her?

Come here, come here, my dear, my dear. The verse taunts me now, begs me to call it real or imagined. How is it the same song that soothed me when I heard it only days before? I tuck my chin to my knees and rock the way Gram rocked me for so many of my childhood years.

A shrill cry sounds from behind me and I whip around. Stand. Expecting the girl. But it is only an osprey calling from atop a high tree gray with death. Her massive nest is fat and round, crafted expertly with woven twigs and flotsam. Bits of bright yellow buoy rope and sun-dried seaweed jut out of the sides. My heart relaxes. I know this environment. The high-hanging sun. The surrounding saltwater blue. The silver-gray outcroppings of rock. I pull in a calming breath and let it fill me. Then another.

Then I hear the sound again.

This time it's not a bird. The scream starts as a stutter until it builds into a deafening screech. The infant's shrill cry packs my ears, forces every thought to evacuate my brain. I press my hands over my ears and crouch against the rising hopelessness in this baby's scream. I fall to my knees just as I see a flash of the girl, the unmistakable black braids, her flowing dress. She darts into the trees, clutching a bundle to her chest. Her long yellow-ing dress sways out behind her, its skirt floating until it frays into strips of cloth that swim like tendrils before disappearing. No, fading. The hem of her dress dies away like the edges of smoke, undefinable and vaporous.

When the last pale wisps of the fabric disappear into the tree line, soundlessness fills the air.

I shake my head, clear my ears. The wailing has stopped. All is quiet until there's the thrum of an engine announcing an approaching boat. I will it to be Reed, here to tell me that this is a normal island. That nothing is strange. But no. If

Reed tells me everything is okay here, then I'm the strange thing on this island.

I focus only on the infant. The cry that carried too much fear. I push my own fear down and head into the stand of trees, darting under their dark canopy of shade. My heavy steps crack twigs, the sharp edges of wood tearing at my soles. Spruce pitch is everywhere, clinging to the bark of the trees, cramming the air with its Christmas scent. I search the forest for the girl and the infant, the pair that is somehow surviving in this cut-off place.

I call for them.

"Hello? Can you hear me?" The breeze answers me, combing through the high boughs with its whistle. I duck around the lowest branches. "Hello!" I yell this once or maybe a dozen times before the answer I both want and dread reaches me from beyond the woods.

"Hello?" It is a male voice, his tone deep and bellowing. His greeting a question.

I go still, a tickle of dread climbing my spine. Because I'm in the woods and I'm not alone, and for the first time since arriving on this uninhabited island, it occurs to me that this may not be a good thing.

I make my way beyond the tree line and see the *Rilla Brae* safely bobbing over her anchor. I walk toward the shore, wincing at the slicing cuts on my feet, trying to steady my fear.

"Hello!" the voice calls again, and now I see the dark-haired boy and his eager wave. I recognize the logo on the starboard side of his boat: UNIVERSITY OF SOUTHERN MAINE. The familiar institution drives away some of my anxiety.

Some.

I return his wave with a small flick of my hand at my hip.

He bends over his rowboat, tugging it onto land, away from the hungry mouth of the ocean and over the spot where I first saw the girl laboring only days ago. I watch him. This visitor isn't a seaman; he's uneasy with his knots and he's awkward in his command of the small boat that is white and spotless. Virgin fiberglass. So different from the weather-beaten wooden skiff I thought belonged to the girl.

By the time I reach the beach, the boy is all smiles and eager words. "Hey. I thought I might have company today." He flicks his thumb in the *Rilla Brae*'s direction in explanation. He extends his hand. "I'm Sam."

"Rilla." I link my fingers behind my back. "What are you doing out here?"

His hand retreats. "Direct. I like that about Mainers."

His words confirm that he's "from away"—a transplant to our state.

Sam reaches into his skiff, pulls out a worn canvas bag that looks more appropriate for a safari. He maneuvers the bag's strap over his shoulder in a way that tells me the satchel's contents are heavy.

I take a quick glance at the forest's edge and form an absurd question, choosing the words carefully. Or not. It's hard to know what will sound mad. "Do you have a baby?"

His seal-dark eyes pop wide. "A baby." It is not a question.

"I heard—" What did I hear? And what will I sound like if I admit it out loud? "I thought that was a baby's seat." I gesture to the inside of his University of Southern Maine boat, which even Gram's failing eyes could see holds no gear for an infant.

He looks to his anchored craft, then back to me. "It's just me." He offers a half smile. "Sorry to disappoint."

I wave him off. "No, that's fine. None of my business anyway." I take a step closer to the waterline. Now all I want is to comb through the water, return home.

"Going for another swim?" Sam scans my wet hair.

"Not today." Maybe never.

He gestures toward my lobster boat. "Is that you? Rilla Brae?" I nod.

"It's a good name for a boat."

"Thanks." My father thought so. I cast my eyes to my boat, the ocean, all the things I never thought would bring me sadness. "I should be getting home."

"Will you be out here again?"

I don't know. "No." And then, "You?"

"For the next few months. I'm researching the island for my summer internship."

"This island?" I'm not sure it would be possible for me to sound any denser.

"This very island." His gaze lifts toward the highest ridge of trees. "A lot of history here."

I think he must be mistaken, that his professor gave him an errant assignment, but it's not for me to say. I take two quick steps toward the shore before turning. I squint against the glare of the sun. "Is it just you out here?"

He laughs then. "I told you, I have come to the island sans baby."

I'm surprised by the hint of a smile that plays on my lips. "I mean do you have a research assistant or something? Or does your professor ever come with you?"

"Nah. Just me. There's no money in the budget for anyone else. Hell, they're not even paying me." His smile is so quick and easy it jumps like it's a living thing.

"So you haven't been here with a girl?"

His eyes narrow as his wide smile broadens. "No girl. No baby. Are you asking me if I'm single?"

Oh God. That's the last thing I'm asking. "No, it's just . . . I thought I saw a girl out here the other day." And only moments ago.

He pats his satchel. "Just me and my tools."

"Yeah. Okay . . . well, I should be getting home."

"I don't blame you. It can get pretty boring out here." He gives me a short salute and sets off toward the center of the island.

I watch him put distance between us and know that "boring" is no longer a word I would use to describe Malaga Island.

I row out to the *Rilla Brae*, scanning the waves, waiting still for the keeper of the song to rise.

CHAPTER FOUR

"Rill?" Reed's warm breath sweeps across the back of my neck, and I open my eyes to the settled dark of the pre-morning. "You awake?"

Reed is behind me, his torso snug against my back, his knees tucked into the bend of mine. His toes press against my underfoot, wordlessly reassuring me that everything is the way it used to be. In this early slip of time before dawn colors the sky, all I know is the softness of our shared sleep. But it is only a moment. Maybe not even a full minute before my grief awakens, ripping through me with its gale-force reminder that my father won't be in this day. Or any other.

"I'm awake."

"You okay?"

"I am." Lie. Lie. Lie.

He rounds one hand over my hip, pulls my body tighter

against his. His fingers play at my neck. They trail along the path to my shoulder. A familiar warmth spreads under and along my skin. I want to lose myself in Reed's touch.

Except.

"Don't. Please." I pull the sheets around me as I turn to him. His eyes drop with sadness or confusion. Maybe both. The sharpness of his cheekbones will never stop amazing me; they are too beautiful to sit on a boy. I stroke his face, first one side, then the other.

"Don't kiss you?"

"No, I like the kisses. It just can't be . . . more."

His body hardens, pulls away. It's a fraction of movement that cuts a ravine between us.

"I'm sorry." I'm not sure that's the truth. "My head's too messed up." Full truth.

Reed props himself against my headboard made of forgotten picket fence. When he stuffs a pillow behind his back, a draft creeps into the space between our bodies. He stares out at the water, even though there's nothing but blackness. "Whatever you need," he tells me. Like always.

"I'm not sure what I need." Full, full truth.

He gathers me to his chest, my ear coming to rest over the steady thump of his heart.

He whispers "It's all good" into the tangle of my hair, kisses me through the curls. "You're my moon, Rill." My heart hitches, reminding me that there is still space in my chest for something other than grief and doubt.

The first time Reed told me that I was his moon, we were only months into hooking up. It was sophomore year, and a part of me was still convinced we were doing what we were doing as a kind of taunt against our families. Asserting our independence and all. We'd been watching the stars from the deck of his boat and he told me, "The way the moon pulls the tide, you know. I feel like that when I'm with you. And even when I'm not . . . it's like I'm forever getting pulled to you." It was the closest Reed ever came to poetry, and that was okay. Better than okay, if I'm being honest.

But sometimes the moon and her tides can fool you. When the sun and moon sit at right angles to each other, they bring a neap tide that will soothe the ocean, making it hard to tell the difference between high tide and low tide.

Like me now, having a hard time telling the difference between what's real and what's imagined.

I sit up, throw my legs over the side of the bed to stand. "You need to get going." This is our deal. Reed sneaks out before sunrise, before Gram and Dad wake up—just Gram now.

He rises from my bed, slides his jeans onto his long leanness. How is it possible that his sun-blond hair can be so bright even when the day is still dark? Reed comes to me, nestles his lips against my neck. "Countin' the minutes," he says. His signature send-off.

"Love you," I whisper.

"Love you more." Then Reed is out the window, dropping spiderlike along the steps of the trellis. He disappears into the yard as morning pours across the sky in the distance, making Malaga's trees look like a shadowy mountain and a mirage all at once.

I slip on leggings and a tee and tiptoe down the hall. I want Gram to get the rest she needs, but it's zero surprise to see her bedroom door already open; we're a family used to waiting on the sun. My stomach rumbles, asking me if I think Gram might be making French toast with sliced hothouse tomatoes, but then I see the pool of electric light seeping from underneath the attic door where she paints. I leave Gram to her *place of repair*—her words—knowing that the attic door will be locked. It's always locked. That was Gram's request after I was born and my parents came to live in the house where my mother was raised. My family could call Fairtide home, but Gram needed the attic as her private place. I respect her privacy always, the way Dad taught me.

In the kitchen, I brew tea and test the powers of the lemon, still dubious about their mood-lifting capabilities. I fix two sandwiches while I eat an apple. I don't see Gram's note until I reach for my boat's keys. She's left me a spray of white heather. And a note:

> For protection.
> For making wishes come true.
> Love, G

I lift the dried heather to my nose, breathe in the echo of its confident earthiness. I grab my keys and head to my boat, sputter past sleeping Malaga Island to my traps and wonder what my wishes are. Because the one, the big one—having my dad back, my family—is impossible. And it's hard to want anything else. Except I do. A part of me hopes Gram's heather will give me protection from that dark place that stole my mother. Because I can't help fear that these visions make me too much like her.

The docks at Yankee Fishermen's Co-op sway with activity by the time I arrive, my tanks filled with today's catch. It's the start of the busy season, when tourists cram around lighthouses and feast on lobsters. I wait on the *Rilla Brae* as lobstermen haul their catch to the scales, one by one in the order we arrive, fishermen forever loyal to fishing's egalitarian principles.

When it's my turn, I put the *Rilla Brae* in gear and coast her starboard side to the edge of the wharf.

Hoopah—Neal Hooper in any other part of the country—ties the dock lines to pull my boat in snug. "Ya got some bugs in there, Rilla?"

I open the hatch. "One or two."

"Ayuh. Mind if an old man takes a look?"

"Have at it."

Hoopah boards the *Rilla Brae* like the good co-op owner he is and unloads my catch onto the scale. He rips me a receipt for the two hundred and sixteen pounds I deliver. He doesn't ask after how I'm doing, because he knows the answer. I'm surviving.

When I head out of the harbor, Reed's boat is approaching the wharf, but I don't wait for it to dock. Instead, I meet Reed on the water and we quiet our engines.

"Good catch?" he calls over the waves.

I nod. I don't tell him how the sea felt different today, a stranger.

"Just bringing mine in now. Pick you up for the quarry later?" Reed asks. It'll never not amaze me how his face is so often filled with hope, like everything is possible in any moment. I want to be the girl who swims away the afternoon with him, but it's already hard to remember the version of me that had the freedom to do anything so indulgent.

"Don't you have class? For your GED?"

"I'll head over there tomorrow. Gotta help my granddad, and then I need to chill. Come with?"

"Meet you there." I know this is a lie—I'll never go to the quarry again. But he's lying too. It's always *tomorrow* when it comes to school.

"Countin' the minutes." Reed throws me two fingers, a peace sign.

"Love you." I tell him. The truth.

I start toward home, but I just can't.

Instead, I drop anchor off the shores of Malaga. There's no University of Southern Maine boat today, so I climb into my skiff and untie it from the *Rilla Brae*. I row to the rocky beach with my suspicions trained on the water, my ears perked open. But the water merely curls over itself, fixing its focus on the business of slapping waves. At the beach, I drag my skiff onto land and grab my pack. My eyes are alert, searching for that girl, her baby.

I return to the highest part of the island and spot the USM research boat. It bobs off the south shore—if you can call the granite ledge a shore. My instinct leaps to protect the craft from the tangle of fierce currents.

"Hey." The voice comes from behind me, recognizable already.

I turn and Sam's hiking toward me, his face all smile. "Hey."

"Looking for me?"

Not quite. "I came for lunch. I didn't see your boat until just now. I can head home if I'm disturbing you. Or, you know, your work."

"Not at all. It gets lonely out here." He jams his hands into his pockets. "It's good to see you again, *Rilla Brae*."

His inflection tells me he's referring to my boat, but the way he says my full name trips something in my gut. Like he knows a secret about me without knowing me at all. It makes me more than uncomfortable, so I focus on what I do know.

The water around us.

The pull of the currents.

"So this may be none of my business, but you're pretty new to the sea, huh?"

"Is it that obvious?"

Yep. "A little."

"It's okay to be totally embarrassed for me."

Sam reminds me of my father in this instance, the way he invites me to my own opinion, encourages it.

"I basically got a crash course in operating USM's salty dog." He nods toward the boat. "Wait. That's the right word for a boat, right? Because I'm trying to act all cool, but I think I just blew it."

I smile at his rookie mistake. "Technically, a salty dog is a *person* who spends a lot of time on the ocean. I've never heard anyone refer to a boat that way."

"Figures." He laughs, runs his fingers through his fine black hair, which is loose today and hangs to his shoulders like silk. This is a boy comfortable with laughing off his mistakes, like it means nothing for him to be wrong. Like he isn't built to assert his manliness, his rightness. Honestly? After years of working with men who don't know any other way but to be right, it throws me.

"Would you be open to some advice from a salty dog?" I ask.

"Advice me. I'm all ears."

"So." I point to where his boat is. "You're boat's anchored on the south side of the island."

"Yep. South side." He says it like cardinal directions are the easiest thing to know at sea.

"The thing is, there's a rip in those waters, and when the tide changes, it'll be too dangerous to row back to your boat. The riptides are strong enough to drag an anchor across the sea bottom. You could lose your . . . salty dog."

"Jeez-us!" Sam's face pales. "Like an undertow?"

"Basically."

"Why didn't you open with that? That's a fairly important piece of nautical information."

"You're okay. You've got another hour or so before the tide changes."

"Yeah?"

"Yeah."

Relief softens his shoulders. "Yes. Right, good." His hand floats through his hair again. "That boat probably cost more than four years of tuition."

Much more. But it feels better not to disclose this fact. "If it were my boat, I'd move it now."

"I thought you said I had another hour?"

"Never trust a tide." The words are my father's.

"Okay, now I'm panicked." He points to the underside of his chin. "This face here? This is the face of panic. The real kind. The my-panic-could-kick-your-panic's-ass kind of panic."

I let out a short laugh. "You'll be fine. Just take caution is all."

"Okay." He stop-signs one hand. "Let's talk real here. I am now full-on scared shitless to get into a basically weightless row-boat to fix this situation. I read *The World According to Garp*. I know all about the Under Toad."

My heart flames with memory. "Did you just say 'Under Toad'?" How old was I the first time my dad warned me about the dangers of the Under Toad, the creature that lived in the strongest of currents? The giant toad that lurked below the deep, always hungry for children, ready to pull them down.

"Yeah, you know. From John Irving's classic."

"'Course." I didn't know, but my brain clamps around this fact, a shell hoarding a pearl.

"Look, at this point I think we can both agree that my best option is to build a meager shelter and live on the island permanently. Because now you've got me all kinds of freaked out, and I don't want to move that boat and risk crashing it, because if I crash it I can't return to school or home and I'll have to live here permanently anyway."

I only half hear him. I'm too consumed with the fact that he's given me the gift of a new detail about my father—how he learned of the Under Toad from a book. I'm so grateful to Sam in this moment, this stranger who will never meet Jonathan Brae.

"Do you want some help?" My father taught me to repay a favor with two.

"Yes. That is exactly what I want. No, need. Thank you."

"Happy to do it."

Sam and I climb into his skiff, and I row it to the larger boat. "The leeward side of any island is the protected side." I talk to drown out the song if it returns. I can't give anyone a front-row seat to the fallout of my hallucinations, even a stranger.

"Leeward. Got it."

I pull back on the oars, cut through the top layer of water.

"The sheltered side of any island sits out of the winds, away from the fierce currents."

"Keep away from fierce currents." He draws a phantom check mark in the air. "Got it." His grip returns to the side of the boat, the knuckles on his other hand already bone white as I guide us through the choppy waves.

"I'm sure everything would have been fine."

"You weren't so sure ten minutes ago."

"Well, worst case, your boat would have eventually washed up on the shore there." I elbow toward Fairtide.

"Why?"

"That's the way the current pushes here. Flotsam always ends up along that shore."

"I'd like to be very clear that I don't want my boat to become flotsam."

"Duly noted." I don't do a great job of hiding my smile as I turn to approach the research boat.

We board, and I guide the larger vessel out of the way of danger. Sam is watching me too closely. I know he's noting my speed, the way I navigate, but still. It feels like he's seeing all the things in me that feel too messed up. When I anchor his boat next to the *Rilla Brae*, I nod toward home. "I should be heading out."

"What about lunch? Isn't that why you're here?"

It is. And isn't.

"I could eat now that I know I won't be shipwrecked. Join me?" He sweeps his arm in a wave.

There's a flicker of hope that Sam will give me another piece of my father, however small. "Okay." I grab my bag for the second time today and hike up the island.

"My site's just over the ridge there." Sam points toward the trees, and I follow. He talks as we make our way, but I don't hear every word. As the trees come closer, they loom bigger than a stand of spruce. They form a forest box that holds secrets. They gather as a shelter for a disappearing girl. A screaming baby. Who knows what else?

I sit facing the forest, not willing to make my back vulnerable. It's not until I have my pack pulled off my shoulders and the front pocket unzipped that I see the dig site, just down the hill. He's roped off a twenty-foot section of earth, metal indicators and twine marking the area. The enclosed dirt sits lower, a few inches of topsoil meticulously swept away. To its side is a raised table, a screen stretched across the large, flat top.

Sam follows my gaze to the excavated earth. "The old school grounds." He sits next to me, but not too close. I'd be lying if I said I didn't appreciate how he gives me my space.

"Like a *school* school?"

His smile curls. "That's a lot of doubt for not a lot of words."

I unwrap my peanut butter and jelly sandwich. "It just

doesn't make sense. Why would there be a school here? It's too remote. Who could get to it?" Here is the moment when I should relate my suspicions that his professor likely wants him to excavate another island. Maine has more than three thousand miles of coastline. It's an honest mistake.

Sam rifles in his bag, growing distracted.

I take a bite of lunch, and the jelly is cold from being in my cooler. It wakes my mouth, and my hunger. Above me, a gull circles for scraps.

Sam empties the contents of his bag onto a patch of grass. "Oh, come on." His words are a huff.

"Something wrong?"

"I forgot my lunch." He swats his forehead with his palm. "Must have left it on the counter this morning. I'm kind of spacy about stuff like that. You should know that about me."

"Um . . . okay." I don't tell him that this isn't the first step in us getting to know each other, that I don't need to be familiar with his idiosyncrasies. This is me looking for a girl. Not a boy. Still, I pull out my second sandwich, offer it to him.

He waves me off. "No. That's super nice, but you made that for you."

I didn't. I made it for Dad. But Sam is the only person in the area who doesn't know about my father's death and I'm not about to change that. "My dad taught me that it's rude to eat alone."

"Yeah?"

I shake the sandwich. "Yeah."

He takes the offering and smiles. "I like your dad."

And just like that, Sam makes my father alive, right here in the present tense. I turn my head away, hide the choke in my voice. "So, this school . . ."

"Oh, the school's long gone," Sam says, bread tucked into his cheek. "The state took that away in thirty-two. No, thirty-one. Technically. It was December, so, yeah, 1931."

"What do you mean 'took it away'?" I turn to Sam. He has my full attention now.

"Why does anyone take anything? It had value."

"That sounds like something my dad would say." The minute the words are out of my mouth, I want to reel them back.

"So your dad's a smart man, huh? Genius-level IQ, no doubt." Sam smiles a smile that can only be described as triumphant.

"The smartest."

Sam's eyes gather the island spread out around us. "So he probably knows all about the school . . . Malaga's history. You should ask him about it. Locals always know more than researchers."

But I'm not so sure. Because it seems like this boy from away might know so much more than I do.

CHAPTER FIVE

Lunch lasts longer than I realized. I board the *Rilla Brae* and pull up her anchor. I wave to Sam as he stands on the shore, and I can't help but wonder if he really is camping on the island.

Doesn't matter. None of my business.

I grab the key from the console and my eye catches orange. Sitting on the top of my GPS screen is a perfect bloom. A flower. Fat as an open rose. My fingers rub its citrus petals and feel how they are thick, bold. "How did you get here?" A smile spreads on my face, knowing Reed must have boarded my anchored boat, gifted this gorgeous flower. I raise it to my nose and it smells of spice. Pepper? I know this blossom. "Flame" something, a plant from a warmer climate. One of the plants Gram pulls up every autumn, tucks into storage in the cellar each winter. Did Gram give this flower to Reed? Was he reckless enough to pick it from her garden? I look for a note on the dash, but there's only a small stone circle to hold the roundness of the bloom. I exchange the flower for one of the stones, rub the rock between my thumb and finger. It is deeply grooved where the water has spent centuries cascading over it, carving it. The rock brings the memory of my mother, plucking larger stones from the sea, weighing her skirt down.

I return the stone to its circle and shake off the fear that still haunts me after my mother's last night at the shores of Fairtide.

I head home to find Gram coaxing her trumpet vines around the pergola posts on our deck. Their eager green stems are long and healthy. Soon they will bloom with sun-bright yellow flowers that will look exactly like mini trumpets, heralding the official arrival of summer. Gram wears long sleeves when she's training these vines, because for all their beauty, they set a rash across her skin that she considers traitorous. I look around her feet, expecting to see a carpet of the flower I hold in my hand, but there's no orange in the garden this time of year.

"Rilla! I expected ya back hours ago." Gram plucks off her dirt-soaked gardening gloves, flattens them against each other before placing them onto her gardening stool. She walks to me, her eyes trained on the flower I'm carrying. "Where did ya get that?"

"Reed."

She lifts the stemless bloom from my hand, twists it slowly

to spin a look at its edges. "Where would Reed get a Flame Freesia?"

"You didn't give it to him?"

Gram eyes the flower with a suspicious stare, as if she wants to ask it questions directly. "It's not from my garden. Flames don't bloom until August."

"Maybe a florist shop, then?"

Grams *harrumph*s. "Reed at a florist?"

She's right. I can't picture Reed in a small store crammed with cut flowers. Reed's too wild, and he likely picked the flower from the wild. "Want tea?"

"A cup would be great." A bee lands on the Flame Freesia. Then another. Their buzz is electric as they disappear into the bloom's orange heart.

In the kitchen, I set the kettle to heat and walk my fingers along the shallow shelves of bottled herbs. I choose skullcap and shimmy the cork from the tiny bottle's neck. Its earthy fragrance wakes my senses.

Gram has her face turned to the high sun when I meet her on the back deck. The lone Flame Freesia sits on the table between our chairs. I don't even have the tea set in front of her before she turns to me, gives me an approving look. "Interesting choice." She reaches for her mug. Skullcap is named for its ability to put a cap on the mind that thinks too much. Also known to calm a person who is facing intense life changes. It's possible I should have brewed an ocean of this stuff.

"Was it a good day buggin'?"

I nod. "Not my best, not my worst."

"Can't be ungrateful for a normal day."

"Nope." Except we both know today's normal isn't our normal.

We sit with our tea warming our hands, even though the day is already warm. But this ritual has always been my favorite, staring out at the sea for a few quiet minutes with Gram before the day bends into night.

"That flower. When did Reed give it to ya?"

The bees are gone now, the air a soft wind. "He left it in my boat."

"*Mmm-hmm.* Today?"

I laugh. "Yes, today." It's zero surprise to see Gram obsess over a flower, but usually not one she already has growing in her garden.

"You'll ask him where he got it, won't ya?"

"Of course." And then it dawns on me that maybe Gram is feeling pushed aside. Is it possible she could doubt how much I need her, appreciate her? "Thank you for the heather you left for me. I hung it in the wheelhouse so it can stay with me all season."

"I'd give ya all the heather in the world if I could, Rilla."

To keep me protected. To help my wishes come true.

"I'd do the same for you." Maybe it's superstition to think

a flower can protect you, but I could have hung sprigs in Dad's wheelhouse every day. Something. Why didn't I ever think to do more to keep him safe?

"Can't say it didn't worry me when ya didn't come home earlier."

"I'm so sorry." The words race out of my mouth because I know what it's like to wait on the return of the boat. And wait. How could I do that to Gram? How could I be so selfish? "Gram, I wasn't thinking. I should have radioed to tell you that I was safe, that I was on the island."

"Island?" She turns to face me now.

"Malaga."

She nods the slightest nod, something clicking into place. "I thought that might have been your boat out there, but ya know these eyes of mine are as dependable as a storm."

"It was stupid not to radio in. I'm sorry. It won't happen again."

Gram pats my knee. "Ya just focus on being a kid, Rilla. Don't worry about the rest."

"But—"

"Ya know I hate that word." She nods toward my cup. "Drink up."

Drink the skullcap. Cap my skull. Gram's way of telling me I need calm. I take a sip, let the hot liquid warm my insides.

"Are ya storing your traps on the island?" It's a fair question.

A few local fishermen stack traps there for the off-season.

"No. There's a guy out there. Doing an archeological dig of some sort."

"The English language is so limited that 'a guy' is the only way ya can explain this person to me?" She *tsk*s in her way.

"Sam. His name is Sam. He's a USM student working on a summer internship."

"What's he looking to find?"

"Beats me."

She gives me that look that tells me to use my language with more respect. "He didn't give ya any idea?"

"He mentioned a schoolhouse."

This makes Gram's eyebrows rise. "On Malaga?"

"My reaction exactly."

"Sounds like that boy's digging in the wrong island dirt."

I laugh. "I wanted to tell him that same thing. He's not so great with boat navigation, so it's plausible."

"He'll figure out his mistake soon enough."

"Sam said locals would know more about the island's history than the researchers. Told me I should ask Dad about it."

A crease in her brow, a question low in her eyes. "He doesn't know about your father?"

"He's from away. I didn't exactly feel like telling him anything about our private lives."

"Saying a thing can be hard."

The hardest.

"So this school?" Gram's raises her tea to her lips, her question telling me that the subject will be changed.

"Sam says the state took it away in 1931."

"Impossible."

"I know."

"Ya know what else is impossible?"

"What's that?"

"That flower there." Gram nods to the petals sitting primly on the table, like it's offended her, like it's here just to make her uncomfortable. "It's native to Africa and has no earthly business blooming in Maine in June."

This again? It's just a flower. I know Gram's a master gardener, but even experts can make mistakes, right? "I double promise I'll ask Reed where he got it." And how he was quiet enough to sneak onto my boat. I look out at the *Rilla Brae*—the circle of rocks still on her dash—and another memory catches, flashing quick as bee wings. My mother, walking the shore in the sunlight. Me next to her. My small feet, her larger ones. Making footprints in the wet sand and then running when the tide lapped high enough to erase our steps, drag them out to sea.

"Rilla?"

"Yeah, Gram?" I shake my mind free.

"Ya okay?"

"I'm fine."

"Where did ya drift off to?"

I'm not sure. I can't say if it's an actual memory or something my brain pieced together from the stories Gram used to tell about my mother. "I remembered . . ."

Gram watches me, doesn't press.

"Running in the surf with my mother." *Your daughter.* The first person we both lost.

Gram straightens, clearly not expecting me to bring up my mother, which is zero surprise. For my eleventh birthday, I told Gram my wish—that she'd stop telling happy stories about Marin Brae. I know Gram thinks my mother's problems aren't my mother's fault, and she wanted to keep her daughter alive for me in some positive way. But it wasn't my mother's struggles that made me sad—it was the fact that she chose to stay away. I couldn't have those stories in my life if my mother didn't want to be in my life.

I rub my thumb and forefinger together, feel the ghost grooves of the rough stone's surface. That stone from the boat, the way it felt too familiar. I mean, of course it did. I've picked up a million rocks. But sitting here now, watching the sea with Gram, something more falls into place.

"We'd try to outrun the tide, see how long our footprints

would last before being washed away." And how my mother would pick up tiny stones even then, tell me how they were once giant rocks before the sea made them small.

Gram looks anxious, likely because this subject has been dangerous territory since I turned eleven. *When things were good*, Gram used to say about my early, early days. But I rarely remembered when things were good. I couldn't stop remembering that last night, when my mother tried to walk into the water and away from me. How she left in an ambulance. Gram's stories reminded me how my mother has chosen to be somewhere else ever since her last night here. That fact seemed the most important thing to know. Then.

"Ya two were always playing at the shore." Gram doesn't say more, and I realize for the first time that she hasn't been able to talk about her daughter for years. All because of my selfishness.

"And you'd watch us from the deck." We searched for the smoothest rocks, the ones that had been rolling in the ocean so long they had lost all their sharp edges. We used them as money, pirate booty. My mother made smiley faces in the sand, long sweeping smiles made of quarter-sized stones. It's a strange thing to remember safe moments with my mother by the shore. Like opening a book and being reminded that it was your favorite from forever ago.

"I can't remember a time when I didn't watch ya, Rilla." Gram stares at the lapping waterline. "They are some of my best memories. The two of ya walking the shore, how ya were always in step. She taught ya how to skip rocks, and you'd spend hours hunting for the perfect flat stones. You'd jump with excitement every time she made one of those slivers jump off a wave."

Do I remember that, or is it another story I heard so many times when I was little? The real and imagined are blurred together from those years. I feel sick at the thought of losing even one memory of my dad.

I bring the mug to my lips.

"Your mom and ya were so happy each time your dad returned from fishing. You'd run into the water as deep as ya could to meet hi—" Something steals the rest of Gram's story, the last memory of my mother at the shore, probably. The night that's etched deep into my story, carving out a Before and After. The night my mother chose the Water People over me. Over Gram. Over Dad. Gram watches the ocean, and her face flattens gray.

I was wrong to bring up my mother. I don't have room for any more darkness.

"I should head up, take a shower." I pluck the Flame Freesia and cup it in my palm. I breathe in its scent of pepper, and it jolts something deep inside of me, deeper and farther

away than my mother's memory. For a moment I am underwater again, the sounds of the everyday world drowned out,
a song rising too clear through the seaweed, the black ocean.
Come here, come here . . . The bloom turns hot as fire in my hand
and I drop it to the table.

"I think Reed would want you to have this."

I head to the kitchen, away from the ocean and its songs.
Away from any reminder of the night my mother filled my heart
with fear.

In my room, I set a fresh cup of orange-leaf tea on my nightstand, chosen for its ability to boost awareness. I balance my laptop across the bridge of my thighs and Google "Malaga Island."
There are only a few hits, some from USM's research. I click on
the first image and it pulls at me. The picture is yellowed in the
way of ancient photos.

An elderly woman sits in a high-back rocking chair in
front of a home—a shack, really. Her long white hair is coiled
in a thick braid pulled to rest over her heart. She has more
years on her than Gram—maybe decades more—and yet
there's a matchstick straightness in her shoulders, the black
sheen of the woman's eyes trapping knowledge. I try to quiet
the bumps that rise along the back of my neck as I study the
cracks in her skin, each deep and weather-beaten line a year

at least. She is Passamaquoddy maybe, or Abenaki? This area has shell middens heaped along stretches of coast by indigenous people—giant piles of carefully layered oyster shells, dirt and animal bones that date back to Maine's first fishing families.

I can't know if the old woman is Abenaki, but I'm certain her stare is untrusting. I squint at the white scrawl in the bottom corner of the photo: *1931.* Did she dare the cameraman to steal her soul with his flash? Did she challenge his thievery?

A knock rattles the window. I jump as Reed pokes his head into my room, laughing. "Nervous, much?"

I ease my laptop shut.

"Watching porn?" Reed asks, his smile playful.

"Yes. Tons of porn. I've been up here for hours, trolling the web for porn."

Reed plops on my bed, his weight heavier than usual. No, dense. It's drunk weight. His wasted fingers play at the corner of my computer, teasing the cover open.

I slide my laptop to the nightstand.

He nestles his head against my neck. His hand falls flat to my stomach. "You didn't come to the quarry today."

"I didn't."

"Why not?" His warm skin smells of sun and sweat and hard liquor.

"I wasn't feeling it."

"I missed you." Reed burrows deeper against me, his fingers twisting the longest of my curls.

I let the quiet shape us into one. Then, "You really threw Gram today, with that flower you left me this morning."

Reed laughs. "Your Gram? *Thrown* . . . as in confused?"

"Yep. She wanted to know where you got it. Like you have some connection to the seedy underworld of foreign plants." I nudge him. "Get it? *Seedy*?"

"Funny." Reed sits up. "What plant, now?"

"That flower you left. Gram says it's from Africa, doesn't grow here."

"I'm lost. I didn't leave any flower."

"You didn't?" I watch something like anger grow in Reed's features, tiny embers turning orange. "What? You're the jealous type now?"

"I am if someone's giving you flowers."

"I don't think you have anything to worry about."

"How's that exactly?"

"Someone must have left it because"—there's a choke in my throat, but I push past it—"my dad. Paying their respects, or whatever."

Reed settles, his face softening. "Oh."

I don't tell him about the rocks placed in a circle,

ceremoniously. Reverently. The way a child would mark the grave of a dead animal.

"Was your boat docked here?"

"What?"

"At Fairtide. Were you home? When you found that flower thing?"

"No." Reed's fishing for who boarded my boat without permission. "I was out at Malaga."

His eyebrows squint. "Malaga? Why?"

"I needed to think."

"That's why you blew off the quarry?"

I shrug, the only energy I'm willing to commit to the subject of the quarry. "Hey, have you ever heard of anyone living on that island?"

Reed laughs. "Ah, no."

"I know, right? But the thing is"—Sam, the Google images. They can't be wrong, can they?—"someone from the University of Southern Maine is out there on an archeological dig, looking for artifacts from when people lived out there."

"A billion years ago?"

"Eighty, but so close." I twist at a stray thread on my comforter. "There's this guy, Sam—"

"Sam?" He tries his best to look suspicious, but I can tell he's losing steam. "Maybe he gave you the flower."

"Not even."

"Let me guess. Sam's from away."

"Think so."

Reed settles his head onto the pillow, hangs his leg over mine. "'Course he is. People are always coming to Maine looking to change something around here. Now they're digging up our past? Lives are too boring where they're from."

"Maybe, but this is the university."

"Groan."

I roll my eyes and elbow his side. "You cannot possibly be so close-minded to all educational institutions."

"Oh, but I can." He laughs, like all of this is so easy to dismiss.

"He's just an intern, so maybe that says something, like they don't take the dig all that seriously. Who knows." I don't. I don't have a clue how research works, who's in charge, who foots the bill. "But there must be something to it. I Googled the name of the island. I think he might be right." I tell him about the elderly woman with the wise shoulders, the daring look in her eye. I tell him about the schoolhouse, how Sam says the state took it away.

I don't realize Reed's been asleep until his foot kicks out violently.

I throw off his leg and his breathing stutters, churning to a low snore. I grab my computer and find the woman once again, her skeptical eyes almost waiting for me. "Aren't we a pair?" I whisper. "You skeptical of me. Me skeptical of life on Malaga."

In the distance of the photograph, a rock ridge bulges from the earth. The ridge is too smooth against all the hard jagged rocks on the coast. The stone rounds like the back of a surfacing whale. I know this granite ledge. I rub my thumb over the outcropping on my screen. Whaleback Ridge. Its name is on every nautical map of these waters. Since I was a kid, I've thrown this whale a nod as I pass in the *Rilla Brae*. Because, why not?

I turn off the light, slip out of bed, and move to the window, where Whaleback Ridge swells in the moonlight. The rock whale juts from the earth, the sea below her.

Out on the island, the moon rakes its yellow over the tips of the trees, throws its shine to the edge of the water. I wonder as to the exact spot where this old woman sat in her long dark skirt and high-neck white blouse. I want to know where her house was, with its small roof and the tiny window that looked out over vegetable gardens vining out of crude raised boxes.

The small shingled home looked too frail to withstand another winter, but the woman—the woman appeared as strong as the Whaleback.

I grow hungry for her story.

Was she an island resident? Did she send her grandchildren

to the school? Did she help build the school, tell the men where to position the structure so the most light could cascade in through the windows?

My room beats with the push and pull of my standing fan as it gathers and twists the air. I press my eyes closed, conjuring this woman in the sunlight, rocking in her chair. Little ones from the island scrambling around her feet.

What stories would she tell? Did she see lantern light at Fairtide after Gram's grandfather built this home? Did our families know one another, fish the seas together?

The sway of her rocking chair mixes with the air moving in my room, back and forth, back and forth. Then her soft breath travels against the base of my neck, the heat of it sending my pulse racing.

My skin warms. My heart darts.

I open my eyes and turn around, but there's only Reed and his rumble of a snore.

Shadows shift in the far corner of my room.

My own rocking chair sways.

The steady *tick-tack-tick* sound of wooden rails slaps the floor. *Ticktacktick. Ticktacktick.* Back and forth. A slowing metronome. The chair glows gold in the moonlight as it creeps to a rhythmic stop. I rub at the skin on my neck, trying to quiet my fear. I dare to kneel before the rocker, even as I'm afraid it will move again. Afraid that there really is more than air in this room with Reed and me.

My heart thumps against my chest as I hover my palm over the seat, terrified that I'll feel something other than the frame of the chair. But there's only wood when I press my hand flat against the surface.

Wood, and the unearthly cold that's trapped there.

I pull my hand back, my nerves thundering.

CHAPTER SIX

It's pre-morning dark when Reed leaves, sleepy and hungover, the smell of liquor clinging to him still. "See you out buggin'," he tells me.

I nod, give him a kiss. It's all he needs before slipping down the trellis.

I dress for a day on the water: leggings, T-shirt. I scan the room for moving furniture even as I tell myself that the icy cold of the wooden seat was stirred up from the fan cooling my room, the rocking of the chair pushed by an electric wind. Still, my brain won't let go of some other possibility. Something not so easily explained away.

I don't visit the old woman's photo before heading downstairs. I don't go to the window to see Whaleback Ridge or Malaga Island to the north. I don't dare press my hand to the rocker. I focus on my day. The ocean. The things I know.

I open my door and trip over the body lying in the hall.

Her brown hair with its purple tips tumble over the rug in the hall, brightened by the glow of the stairwell light. "Hattie?"

Hattie sits up, rubs at her eyes. "'Morning." Her voice is throaty, scratched.

"What're you doing out here?" I sit against the opposite wall and gather my legs against my chest. I feel the anger rising in that mixed tumultuous place where my love for Hattie has twisted recently.

"I came to see you last night, but Reed was here."

"You slept in the hall?"

She nods, licks at her dry lips.

"Did you . . . ?" *Come in my room? Sit in the rocking chair?* It's impossible to ask the question out loud. Because I know who I will sound like if she says no.

Hattie looks at me with so much suspicion, like she can see all the wrong in me.

"Why didn't you knock, come in?"

"Honestly? I didn't know if you'd want to see me. You haven't answered my texts or voice mails." Hattie looks tired. And thin. Like my absence has made physical pounds shed from her frame. I wonder if I look as worn to her.

"I let you have your space, Rills. But I miss you. Too much." I hear the crack in her voice, the chasm of hurt that creeps around the curves of her syllables.

I miss Hattie too, if I'm being honest. Do I tell her how many times my thumb hovered over her name to respond to one of her texts? How much I wanted to reach out but couldn't?

"I figured the only way to talk to you was to literally stand in your way. Or, lie down." She gestures at the hall, sits up straighter. "I'll sleep here every night if I have to. I'll hold one-sided conversations. I'll just sit out here being all stalkery. I'll yammer on until you have to talk to me. And if that doesn't work, I'll talk only using quotes from *The Princess Bride*."

A laugh rises in me, but I pull it back.

"It's okay to laugh, you know."

But is it?

"I've been really worried about you, Rills."

"Why? What specifically?" Because she doesn't know the depths of what's happening.

"What aren't I worried about? You're out fishing all alone, and that shouldn't be all on you. I know you're freaking out about leaving for college, leaving your gram. But I know staying scares you worse."

My chest stutters over a hard breath, the kind that rises from the relief and fear of someone knowing you so well.

"And I know you miss your dad more than I could ever

understand. But I want to help, Rills. I'll do anything. I could work with you on the boat, do whatever."

I laugh. It's a beyond absurd offer. "You hate fishing."

"I do."

"So why would you off—"

"Because I'd do it, Rills. I'd get on that smelly boat with you at the crack of every day's ass. I'd drag those nasty creatures up from the bottom of the sea. I'd smile while I filled bait bags with rotting fish. I'd do all of that because I love you. And I'm here for you." Her voice hushes with the weight of her promise. "I'd do anything for you, Rills. Anything."

"You'd smile while filling bait bags with rotten herring?"

"If that's what you need."

"I don't know what I need."

"That's fair." She moves to my side. "I'm sorry, Rills. I'm sorry you weren't with your dad that day."

"I should have been."

"I know." She puts her arm around my shoulder. I'm grateful for the way her warmth spreads over me. "But maybe it wouldn't have made a difference."

"It might have."

"Maybe. But you have to forgive yourself, Rills. What happened to your dad wasn't your fault."

Grief rises in me. "It feels like it was all my fault."

"Your dad wouldn't want you to feel that way."

"I know." But still.

"You need to find a way to forgive yourself."

That seems like the hardest thing in the world. "I'm not sure how to."

"We'll figure it out." Hattie pulls me closer, and I let her hold me for the time it takes the sun to rise. She lets me cry. Doesn't tell me to hush or that everything will be okay. She just lets me be me.

When I'm out on the water, the VHF squawks with static. Then Reed's voice. "All in, *Rilla Brae*?"

I grab the mouthpiece. "All in." I'm at sea. I love him. I'm all right. And I feel some normal fall around me. Hattie is back and the rocking chair doesn't matter. Nothing matters beyond what's real. Gram. Hattie. Reed. The waves under my boat.

I haul fifty traps by midday, load them with bait and set them back into the deep. It's a mere fraction of the hauling Dad and I would do together in peak season, and even though I'm proud of my catch, I'm aware that it isn't enough. That I'm not enough. Maybe I do need Hattie out here.

At the wharf, I hop off the *Rilla Brae* as Hoopah weighs my haul. One hundred and four pounds.

"Not bad," he says, tearing my slip from his receipt pad. But it's not great, either. Hoopah knows I need a hundred pounds per trip just to cover gas and bait. Never mind the costs for maintaining the boat. If he sees the calculations race through my head, he doesn't say.

I'm about to step back onto the boat when Old Man Benner elbows past Hoopah to crowd my face. He reeks of dank cigar and bitterness.

Old Man Benner condescends a nod at my boat. "Whatcha got there, girlie?"

Girlie. I straighten my shoulders and pull up my sarcasm. "You've been fishing all your life and can't recognize a day's catch?"

Behind me, Hoopah snickers. I stand taller, fully aware that my father wouldn't have tolerated me talking to any elder this way. But I know he wouldn't have tolerated Benner's assholery either.

Benner rips the slip from my hand, scoffs. "A hundred pounds ain't come close to a day's catch. Didn't ya fathah teach ya nothin'?"

My teeth grind in hate, barely letting words move past their gate. How can this man possibly be related to Reed? "You don't know a thing about my father."

"I know he's gone now and Little Miss Fancy's gonna need money for that uppity school ya so keen on running off ta."

"Easy now, Benner," Hoopah says.

I stare Benner down. "My work has exactly nothing to do

with you, Benner." But I hate that he's right. I do need money, better hauls. Dad averaged close to five hundred pounds a day. Few families could survive on less.

Benner flicks the receipt at my chest, and my reflexes snag it before it sails away in the air current.

"Ya've got ya business done here today, Benner," Hoopah says. He steps between me and Old Man Asshole so that their two chests almost touch. "Seems to me it's time ya move it along."

Benner looks Hoopah dead in the eye. "Only one doesn't have business being he-ah is that girl, and there ain't a fisherman who doesn't know it ta be true." He lets his emphasis hold tight on the *man* part of fisher*man*. Benner spits his tobacco onto the dock and plunges his finger into Hoopah's sternum. "Ya let girls fish and this whole industry'll be ruined." Benner clips his thumbs into the bib of his rubber overalls and slinks off. I try to breathe.

Hoopah squeezes at the ball of my elbow. "Don't ya mind him. He went and got a fishing hook caught up his arse years ago."

I force a laugh, like Benner's words can't penetrate my skin. "I should be getting home."

"Don't ya be takin' anything he says with ya, now. Ya leave his words he-ah on the dock where the gulls can shit on them, ya he-ah?"

"I hear."

"Ya dad was a good man, Rilla. Ya come from good stock."

Do I? Everyone knows my mother left me and Dad, and now Benner makes me want to retreat, the same way she did. I can already hear the gossip I'd leave in my wake if I took my packed bags and headed due south for Rhode Island.

Brae girl leaving her family behind, just like her mama.

Brae women ain't built for the sea.

Always knew she'd run. Jonathan probably knew it too. Probably what made his heart give up right there in his chest.

It's that last bit of speculation that breaks me. I nod to Hoopah. It's all the good-bye I can manage. Because if I open my mouth, I don't know what will bubble up. A cry. A scream. Or some monstrous combination of both.

As I navigate away from the dock, I don't turn around. I can't bear to see Hoopah staring at me. What if his eyes can't hide the fact that he doubts me as much as I do?

I turn toward home even though I know I'm not going home. I knew it hours ago when I stuffed my pack full of biscuits. Even then I knew I was headed to the island.

This time, I'm not looking for the girl.

I need an escape.

I need to see Sam.

I need to drown in the island's story. The old woman's story. Any story that's not my own.

CHAPTER SEVEN

The USM research boat is anchored on the lee side of the island, which sends up a small flicker of pride in me as I throw anchor and toss my pack aboard my skiff. By the time I've rowed to shore, Sam is on the craggy beach waiting for me.

"Hey." He throws his greeting casually, like he expected me, which is unexpected. Sam extends his hands, nods toward my pack. I pitch it to him, and he catches it easily.

I tuck the oars inside my skiff and drag the open boat across the stretch of beach. The fiberglass scrapes over the sharp edges of the mussel shells and jagged rocks, sending up a dull roar that drowns out all other sound. I take a quick glance toward Fairtide Cottage. Home. Where I should want to be. Then Sam hands me my pack and I strap it across the span of my back. "You hungry?"

His face turns up in a smile. "How'd you know?"

"Forgot your lunch again?"

"Judge me not by my culinary incompetence." He smiles in a way that tempts mine, pulls it into being. "Wanna eat up at the dig site?"

I do. So much. "Sure."

We hike the island's granite face. I see the photo again, so clear—the old woman in her rocking chair in front of her meager home. I try to orient the past in the present, but all traces of her and her house are gone. There's only untamed nature on the island now, sea grass sprouting between cracks of the granite, an island growing wild over its secrets.

"I'm in the middle of a discovery." Sam's voice is high and happy, so much like a young child playing at the shore.

"What sort?" A physical ache of hunger tightens my stomach, so intent on knowing what Sam's discovered.

"Come see." He takes my wrist and tugs me closer to his worksite. My step quickens to match his gait, his excitement. I don't even think Sam realizes he's pulling me, so singular is his eagerness. He stops when we reach the excavated layers of earth. He lets go of my wrist, points to the far corner of the exposed dirt with its low, twine rope fence. "There." A slice of wrought-iron metal peeks above ground. There's a pattern etched deep into the metal. The detailed ironwork flows like the vine of a thick, creeping flower, scrolling and lifting in circles and sways. It is beautiful, even as its grooves are caked with the clinging clay soil.

"Is this not the coolest?"

"What is it?" It takes all my restraint not to jump inside the excavation site and claw away the earth with my bare hands. There's so much urgency to discover the truth about the people who lived here, and I'm not surprised when the whispered song rises from my memory like a low-clinging fog: *Come here, come here. My dear, my dear.*

"Dunno." Sam shrugs. "That's the best part. It could be anything. Anything at all."

It's an elaborately flourished piece of metal. It was special to someone. Someone rowed it all the way out here, hauled it to the island's peak.

Someone.

Someones.

A gust of wind rakes through the trees, bending the spruce boughs at their tips. It hits me all at once that Malaga really was inhabited, and not that long ago. Its residents left pieces of their lives behind, echoes of their existence. "You must have some theory, though? Maybe it was a gate"—but then I remember the crude structure the old woman called home—"though maybe too ornate for that?"

Sam watches the exposed black metal as if his stare can protect it. "I'm not a fan of speculating until I'm sure of a thing. I'm the same way with people." He turns to me, lifts his eyes quickly to meet mine. "What I do know at this stage is that this object is a window to the past, Rilla. It's remarkable because it's here and we found it and it doesn't need to be lost again. It has a singular story, a language, a poetry all its own."

The iron grate poking from the earth is similar to the six-burner cast-iron stove Gram uses to cook our meals and heat our home. That stove is heavier than a steamship, and no one from Gram's side of the family has dared moved it in more than a hundred years. I used to think our antiques made us look like we were poor, like we couldn't afford a trip to the Home Depot appliances section. Now I like that I can find my great-great-grandfather's woodworking expertise in the curves of our nineteenth-century dry-sink-turned-bookshelves. And my great-grandmother's embroidery in our home-sewn flag from 1944, which hangs in our living room, wide as the wall. She sewed it the same year Sinclair and Thomas Murphy—Gram's uncles—gave their lives on the beaches of Normandy. The red stripes are faded now, the blue square of stars almost purple from time bleeding its color. Still, the blue reminds me of that ocean in France when my great-uncles arrived with their guns and their bravery. And the red reminds me never to forget the color of the sea after too many lives had been lost in the surf. Sam's words revisit: *It has a singular story, a language, a poetry all its own.* "You sound more like a poet than a scientist."

"Can't I be both? There's so much beauty in our buried history. Pain, too. If you ask me, that's the stuff of poets."

I think of my dad, buried now but not forgotten. Grief grabs at my chest.

"It seems too simple"—Sam extends his hands, palms up, then down—"that our mere hands can unearth this small part of our collective past." He squats before the site, turns his ear to the ground as if he can hear it whisper the story he seeks. As if excavation isn't done with his tools, but with his every sense. I wonder if he hears the same pull of the girl's lullaby: *Come here, come here.*

"That's what all this is about. Bringing the forgotten back to life." He stands now, traps his hair back with the snap of a band. "The people . . . you know. Their stories."

I want to tell him about my father's story, how I'm one of only two people who can keep it alive now, but I don't. The way Sam honors his discovery makes me know this moment is for something bigger than us and our individual stories.

He gestures to a flat rock nearby. "I've got a long way to go here yet. This dig will go on for years and probably without me. But first, sustenance. Yes?" His energy is welcoming and safe, a world apart from Benner and his unapologetic sexism.

"Sustenance it is. You're not the first person to make Gram's biscuits a priority."

"Biscuits? Ah, come on. You never said anything about biscuits. You really do need to work on your openers, Rilla Brae." Sam takes a few loping strides and drops onto the ledge, settling into an easy cross-legged position. He pats the granite next to him, inviting me down. I sit and see Whaleback Ridge in the exact position of the old woman's photo. This is near the spot where she gardened from her small porch, rocked in her tall chair. My curiosity burns. Did that ornate metal piece belong to her? What story does it hold?

I pull off my pack and sit opposite Sam. "I asked my gram about Malaga." I unload the plastic containers, spread them out between us.

His eyes fire. "Should I get my notebook? She must know a ton."

"Just the opposite." I pop the top from the biscuit bowl, hand it to Sam.

Sam raises a biscuit to his nose, draws in its butter scent. "Heaven." It is a murmur, as if he's talking to himself.

I take a biscuit and it's dense with cold, almost heavy in my hand. I set out the jar of jelly, place a spoon into its thick boysenberry center. "My gram didn't know anything about the island."

"Bummer, but not too much of a surprise, I guess."

"How so?"

Sam looks out at the distant sea. "There's a lot of shame surrounding what happened out here, Rilla. People aren't in a hurry to claim the shameful things."

I think of the old woman, the suspicion in her eyes. What happened to her?

"When I first arrived in town, I had to get my mail forwarded. The postmaster was making small talk, asking me what my summer would look like. When I told him about the university's dig, he was very clear that I had no right dredging up the story of Malaga."

Allen Hilton, the postmaster with his grizzled gray beard. He's old but not old enough to know about Malaga firsthand. Eighty years is a long time. Anyone who might remember was only a kid then.

"When I told him I had a job to do, he warned me that the island was haunted."

"Haunted?" A shiver crawls up the ladder of my spine. Haunted? I think of my vision of the tidal wave. The rocking chair. Is a ghost trying to make its secrets known?

He shrugs. "I think it was an attempt to scare me off. Or maybe it's a way for him to make sense of the senseless—name it something impossible."

Impossible.

"But I think this island holds more history than the

university could ever uncover. And there are endless ways for secrets to slip out into the world."

"You mean ghosts? You're talking about ghosts now, right?" The girl singing at the shore. Her disappearing boat, the way her dress vaporized into the trees.

"I will say that I am by nature an unflinching optimist. This world has never once stopped reminding me that it holds infinite possibilities." He takes a bite of biscuit, chews it down. "But ghosts? No. I'm a pragmatist and a scientist, if they are even separate things. I believe secrets can be recovered from the ground." His gaze returns to the crisp blue field of ocean. "And people. I think secrets find their way out of people when the time is right."

Did a ghost make the water rise in a tidal wave that claimed our lawn one second and was gone the next? Could a ghost have been in my room, rocking in the chair behind me? Is the girl singing to make her secrets known?

I wish I had the nerve—or the trust—to tell Sam about the girl I've seen on the island, her song that reached me under the weight of water. But my dad is gone and I don't want to admit out loud that my loss has made my mind bend, possibly enough to resemble my mother's. "You've never seen anything out here . . . you know, suspicious?"

Sam laughs a laugh that is so quick and full, it almost scares me. "Well, there was some questionable behavior displayed by a couple of mating harbor seals on the beach last week. Other than that, nothing I'd classify as otherworldly. I haven't exactly had a hand reach out from the earth and grab me or anything."

Chilled bumps blanket my skin. "Creepy much?"

He shrugs. "A hand from the ground is like Creepy 101. The universally worst ghost fear. Like, when you were a kid, did you look under your bed before going to sleep? Afraid something would grab at your ankles?"

I shake off the memory of the rocking chair, the ice cold trapped in the seat. Me, searching for a girl who may be haunting me on land, calling to me in the sea. "Most nights I was too scared to look under my bed, so I'd leap from my desk chair to my mattress."

"Ha! Exactly. The brain is a powerful tool, Rilla Brae. And mine is weak. It's pretty easy for me to project my worst fears onto a place, and I'd like to not do that while I'm out here, please and thank you." He takes a bite of Gram's biscuit and his face softens.

I pretend like my head isn't crammed with questions and slather jam onto a biscuit half. I offer Sam the jelly when I'm finished.

Sam waves off the jar. "I've never been a big fan of condiments. I take my berries round and my bread plain."

"My gram made it. Boysenberry. It's wicked good."

"Wicked good, huh?" I nod, and he laughs.

"What?"

"Nothing, it's just that using the words 'wicked' and 'good' next to each other like that is a contradiction in any other part of the world. You realize that, don't you?"

"We're not in another part of the world. We're Downeast with some wicked good biscuits."

He smiles and smooths the jelly onto the soft doughy middle of his roll. When he takes a bite, he chews slowly, almost intimately. Some part of me thinks I should look away, but I don't.

He winks open one eye. "This, Rilla"—he holds up his jellied bit—"is a testament to embracing the unexpected. I had no idea I was starved for biscuits and homemade boysenberry jam, but I think it's all I'll ever want to eat for the rest of my life." He takes another bite, and a slow, deep smile relaxes his features, closes his eyes. "Damn. This is amazing."

"Even with the jelly?"

"I was talking about the jelly."

"Gram's specialty."

"Is it weird that I'm in love with your grandmother?"

I smile. "There is literally nothing weirder." Okay, not true lately. But still.

"I would like to marry her, please."

"I don't know about that. No man's been good enough for her yet." Gram never married my grandfather or even lived with him. She wanted to be a mother but never a wife, as scandalous as that notion was when she was pregnant with my mother. "I'm not sure she'd have you."

He feigns being offended. "What? I'm a great catch. I mean, I'm riddled with baggage—same as anyone—but still, great catch."

"I'll be sure to let her know."

"Please do. Put in a good word for me. And maybe ask her to bake up another batch of these rad biscuits."

"Rad, huh?"

"So rad."

"Are you trying to outdo my regional linguistic flair?"

He laughs. "Maybe add to it. Like, these biscuits are wicked rad."

My smile deepens. "Work the sea and she'll make them for you every day." I look out toward home, hope Gram isn't worried about me. I should have radioed in when I got to the island.

Sam reaches for another biscuit, and I pull a leaf of young goldenrod from its stalk. I bring it to my nose, trying to coax out the smell of honey the plant will produce weeks from now. Today it smells only of green. I slip the leaf between my palms, rub back and forth. The grinding is said to make good fortune rise. My father taught me how Maine's indigenous people used the goldenrod seed for food, but I don't know if this species is edible. But could it be a descendant of the old woman's garden? A seed that has set roots with each spring? "I found some photos online. Of the island."

"Yeah?"

"There was this one woman, an older woman by herself in a—"

"Rocking chair."

"You know her?"

"I know the photo. There aren't many photos that exist of the islanders. Believe me, I've studied them all." He waves his hand. "You were going to say something about it and I interrupted you. I'm sorry."

His apology surprises me. A boy who apologizes for interrupting a girl might be as rare as photos of the island. "She had a vegetable garden in front of her house, some raised beds." I pluck another early goldenrod from its stem. "I was just thinking that if she grew herbs, this plant could be part of a kind of floral footprint she left behind." It's impossible not to think of Gram's floral footprint at Fairtide, all her gardens, each with their own purpose. Each flower and vegetable telling its own story, thanks to the bees.

"Floral footprint, I like that." Sam smiles wide. "The university has mapped out where each resident lived, where they kept their livestock, but we don't know a lot about the gardens and I don't know anything about plants. You?"

"Some." If she grew herbs, maybe she was a healer. Something about this feels right. "Sam? Why did the islanders leave? What happened out here?"

Sam reaches in his backpack, pulls out a moleskin journal, its elastic straining from all the added pages. "What happened was the end." He passes me the book. "This is the beginning, or as much as we know."

I flip open the neat pages. Taped to the first page is a printed photo—a group of children, their youth nearly a hundred years old now. Some faces black, some white, some brown. The children are thin in the way of children then. I search the faces for my girl, but the kids are years younger than she appeared. The little ones wear the same wary look, shared across the squint of their eyes. None wear shoes. Their shirts are thin and worn and ill-fitting, slouching around the neck or rising too high at the arms. These children stand so close to one another in a line of seven, shoulder pressed against neighboring shoulder as if for protection.

Their faces are drawn in the way a hard life can wear at the softest of edges. Even childhood edges.

"These kids lived out here?"

"They did."

Sam moves to my side as I read the names etched in eerie white ink against the aged black-and-white photo. I recognize some last names, families who still work this sea.

"The state sent census workers out here in the summer of 1931. That's when most of these photos are from. That official visit is why we have a list of the residents' names, ages, races."

I tap my thumb against the grainy photo. "This doesn't make sense."

"What in particular?"

"How could there be so much diversity on this tiny island? Saying it's an anomaly is an understatement."

"Because Maine is ninety-five percent white?"

"Exactly." I can't take my eyes from the photo, the children with their backs to the sea.

"The island was an anomaly. It was settled by the descendants of Benjamin Darling, a black man who purchased Harbor Island in the late seventeen hundreds."

Harbor Island sits just beyond Malaga, a sister in the sea. So many Maine maps name it Horse Island.

"Darling's descendants moved to Malaga around 1860. Eventually some Abenaki people came to live here. Some Irish and Scottish fishermen too."

"Ahead of its time."

"At the wrong time." Sam nudges his pencil at the corner

of the moleskin. "It's all in there. I've included copies of some newspaper articles written around the time the census workers arrived. Real yellow journalism stuff. Be prepared. And I've made notes about the island's history in the margins." He leans in, flips to a random page, nods at his scribbling. "See? There."

> Oral history has been lost due to enduring feelings of shame, embarrassment. Malaga remains a racially and culturally charged subject. Former governor publicly apologized to the Malaga descendants who've begun to come forward in recent years.

Then, a headline from the *Bath Enterprise*: NOT FIT FOR DOGS—POVERTY, IMMORTALITY AND DISEASE . . . IGNORANCE, SHIFTLESSNESS, FILTH AND HEATHENISM . . . A SHAMEFUL DISGRACE THAT SHOULD BE LOOKED AFTER AT ONCE.[1]

In the margin, Sam has scribbled: *eugenics used to sway public sentiment.*

My grip on the journal tightens. I want to accept this loan. "You're sure? You don't need it for your work?"

"I have every photo, every word memorized." He taps his pencil to his temple. "I keep them with me every day."

"Only if you're sure."

"I'm more than sure."

"Thank you."

"It's no trouble."

I wish my dad were here more than ever. So we could talk about Malaga with this person from away who knows so much more than I do about our own backyard.

I flip the page and there's the old woman, sitting in her rocker, daring the camera to steal her soul. Her gardens are tall with tomatoes, sprawling with running squash vines. And flowers, too. I see the small dark heads of marigolds companion-planted to keep the bugs off the tomatoes. And a blossom so familiar. A bloom no different from the Flame I found on my boat. The coincidence rakes my spine. "This one." I point to the full hem of the woman's dark skirt. "This is the photo I saw."

Sam leans over my shoulder. "The matriarch." It's eerie how my skin flames with cool bumps. "I like to think the islanders came to her for everything: advice, comfort, wisdom."

"But you don't know for sure?"

He shakes his head. "It was only eighty years ago. You'd think we'd have records for everyone on Malaga, but the islanders where solitary people, living off the grid for a reason. Census records tell us a lot, but no one's been able to identify that woman. And the shame of what happened here has kept descendants from coming forward. Even now."

What shame did this woman suffer?

"We might not know her name, but we know she was strong. All the islanders were."

"Had to be."

Sam nods. "Exactly. Think about how difficult it must have been to live out here then. Everything was harder. Fishing was harder; the winters were harder. Medicine, money, all harder to come by."

"Maybe that stuff wasn't important. At least not as important as their freedom—to live life on their own terms."

"That's the most fascinating part, Rilla. The islanders were strong-willed, enduring. Even if they looked poor to mainlanders, they *chose* to live their secluded life over anything the mainland could offer. Their poverty was nothing compared to their wealth of spirit. I've got mad respect for them."

"So why did they leave?"

"They were forced off the island. The only reason we even have photos or any documentation at all is because of that census visit. Governor Plaisted wanted to assess the size of Malaga for development. When the newspapers started writing articles about the poverty of the Malaga community, well, that's when things got bad. Poverty was considered a disease then, the poor afflicted with feeble brains. They were thought inferior, and the governor claimed they had no right to live on land that held so many developmental prospects."

"So, what? Like eminent domain?"

"The state didn't need it. Three weeks after his visit, the governor posted a notice of eviction. In the end, the islanders didn't own the island, even though they'd been living in the area since the Civil War. None of the nearby towns wanted to be associated with Malaga after the press began a hate campaign against the so-called squatters. When no town claimed the island, the state took it."

This all sounds impossible. The old woman must have known this hate was rising around her. Did she read the papers? Did the network of fishermen keep islanders informed of mainland news? "How did you learn about Malaga? I mean, how are you even here? How do you know all this stuff?"

There's a short silence that's filled only with the lapping tide, the shouting gulls. Then, "I was twelve and living in Arizona's southern desert when I found this old book in my parents' shed." Sam laughs, in a way that's more sad than funny. "Kind of a survey on the states. I had to hold the spine just right so it wouldn't crack and fall apart when I opened the book. It had a section on Maine and its fishermen—way back in the day, like the 1850s—and something about this coast felt like the last frontier to me. When I found that section about Maine's islands . . . well, it kind of . . ." He trails off, lets the sea fill the quiet between us. "I guess you could say it showed me how big the world could be—you know, for me. If I let it be that big. That book's the reason why I came to Maine for school, applied for this internship."

"A book you read when you were twelve?"

He laughs. "Twelve-year-old boys are very impressionable." He looks out toward the horizon though it's clear he's seeing something bigger than the sea. "I was . . . well, optimally impressionable at that age. I never stopped researching Maine's maritime history, and when I came across Malaga's story, I wanted to meet the people who never got a chance to be heard."

I want that too. In this moment, it's all I want. "It seems like a good thing to want."

"Maybe, but there's a reason why no one talks about this place." He nods to the portfolio. "Read what's in there and you'll see. Sometimes it's easier to keep secrets buried than to live with our truth."

I don't even realize my knuckles have drained white from gripping the moleskin until I look down. "I'll read every word."

"That reminds me." Sam pops open the front pocket of his pack and pulls out a book. For a second I think it might be his old, cracked encyclopedia from the desert, but he passes me *The World According to Garp*. "For you. In case you want to revisit the Under Toad." Sam's smile is soft, like he knew full well I had no idea the Under Toad was born in a novel but he doesn't want me to feel bad about it either.

I swallow down something that feels bigger than gratitude. "Thank you."

"Don't thank me. Thank John Irving. The man's a master."

"I feel bad I didn't bring you anything." Dad and Gram raised me to return kindness with multiplied kindness, and gift giving is no exception.

"You're a funny one, Rilla Brae."

"Funny how?"

"Funny because you can't see that you've brought me biscuits *and* saved my very borrowed boat from utter destruction."

These things are nothing. Dad called them "expected and necessary gestures of polite society." He'd say it in a bad British accent and pretend at a pipe at his mouth.

"And you came here with your curiosity and conversation. Those are gifts I don't even know how to pay you back for."

Huh. I pull the books to my heart because I can't find words to thank him for the Under Toad, for allowing my father to reach across death to find me in this way.

"I saw it at the used bookstore in town and thought of you.

I would've bought you a fresh and clean and new copy, but . . . well, there's zero pay in internship work."

"Come work for me." My offer surprises me, and doesn't.

Sam lets out a quick laugh. "Work for you? You have treasure that needs excavating?"

"Sort of. Well, okay, no. I need a sternman for the summer. Someone to help me haul lobsters off the bottom." I need someone to be me in the way that I helped my dad.

He laughs fully now. "I know nothing about lobstering. I almost lost my boat to the perils of the granite shore, if you recall."

"I never said you could drive my boat." I throw him a quick wink. "And it's okay if you're a newbie. I'll teach you what you need to know. You bring a strong back and we'll figure out the rest. We go out before the sun rises, so you'd have your afternoons free to come out here."

"Done."

"Done? Just like that?"

"Just like that. Hell, if I don't jump at everything life offers me, what's the point?"

His enthusiasm. I think that might be his real gift.

"Can you be here at six o'clock tomorrow morning?"

"Will you have biscuits?"

"Warm ones."

"Then, Rilla Brae, you've got yourself a sternman. An incompetent one that hails from the dusty desert of Arizona, but a sternman nonetheless." Sam stands and extends his hand. I stand across from him, and we shake on our promise, even if it feels like more.

CHAPTER EIGHT

After dinner, Gram disappears to her attic to paint and I head to bed. The sun sinks down the sky, trailing its pinks and oranges as I text Hattie:

Me: Found a sternman so you don't need to bag chum ☺

Hatt: Thank GOD!

Me: Hang tomorrow?

Hatt: Rodents of Unusual Size couldn't keep me away

I smile, throw on Reed's old Red Sox T-shirt, which is soft with age and wear. As I climb into bed, I grab the moleskin and pull at a piece of paper sticking out of the top. An inventory list written on a piece of University of Southern Maine stationery. My fingers trace the blue-and-gold seal at the top, how it's proudly embossed on the page. I envy Sam, the way he carries his university with him. I imagined it would be that way for me at the University of Rhode Island. That the moment I was on campus, I would be home, my identity linked to my education, my future. But now I think that's the Rilla Brae who may never get a chance to exist.

I focus on the simple list, written in Sam's steady, neat hand. There are check boxes next to the names of tools, some having eleven marks next to their names. Eleven days. It seems like nothing, a hiccup of time, yet the last eleven days have filled with the unexpected and morphed into eleven lifetimes.

I'm careful with the pages of the binder as I turn to the photo of the two-room schoolhouse with its fresh white trim paint and sturdy lines. All of its windows straight, their panes unbroken. On the school's front porch, thirteen children pose: small boys in smart vests, a young girl with a doll. No one looks like my girl from the shore, as if it's even possible for her to live then and now. Under the photo is a notation about the missionaries from Massachusetts who made the school a reality. My heart buckles.

The school. The children. All gone now.

There's another photo of the same children standing on a ridge, the open sky behind them. The features of the children on the right blur under the shade of a tree just beyond the photo's frame. The children pose dutifully in their finest tiny sweaters, overalls, and dresses. The youngest girl still clings to her doll.

Were the islanders fearful of the photographer? Untrusting?

Even now Mainers are a guarded lot. What must it have felt like to have a stranger bring the camera to the island? A person from the mainland carrying a huge and strange device that ignited a loud, smoky flash?

The next page is an official notice. That same photo of the children on the ridge is centered within the poster. Below the group, a declaration: IMMEDIATE ACTION TO REMOVE MALAGA ISLAND PEOPLE.

And there it is, their fate.

The eviction notice from the state of Maine.

Island residents forced from their homes.

My room begins to warm as if the heat is too high even as the window is open to an easterly wind that pushes the cool smell of salt and sea into my room. The heat fires on my neck and I can feel the redness rise from anger, from disbelief . . . but also, something more.

Breath.

Breath on my neck.

Then Reed is scrambling up the trellis, and I slip the binder under my pillow. I consider telling Reed I'm not feeling well, that I need a good night's sleep, that I'm beat. But it's Hattie who crawls through the window, and I jump up, meet her in the middle of my room.

"Hatt? Everything okay?"

"Totally. Just didn't want to wait for tomorrow."

I let out a huge sigh, for what, I don't know. Maybe just relief that it's Hattie and she is good and kind and I need good and kind.

I move to my bed. No, more like collapse onto it.

"Tough day at the office?" Hattie lies down next to me.

"Long day."

"Tell me about your sternman. But only if he's hot."

I elbow her. "Dork."

"Okay, I'll settle for dependable."

"I'll know tomorrow. He's from the desert, never fished. Can you imagine? I hired a total landlubber."

"Careful, Rills. I've seen *Deadliest Catch*. I know how a crappy greenhorn can take down a crew."

"Liar." I elbow her again. "There's zero chance you've watched *Deadliest*."

"Not true. My uncle made me suffer through one episode and I wanted to stick needles in my eyes. And I'm telling you, there was a greenhorn who sucked. Everyone hated him. He was trouble."

"I don't think Sam will be trouble."

Hattie twists to face me, props her head onto her elbow. "Sam, huh? What does this Sam look like?"

"He looks like a boy."

"Ugh. Booooring. I want deets."

"I have zero deets."

"See? That's the problem with you married ladies; you've forgotten how to ogle."

"I'm not sure I was ever much of an ogler."

"Then let me be your guide. Is he tall?"

"Yes."

"Broad shoulders?"

"Yes."

"Sexy, smoldering stare?"

"No clue."

"Thin or bulky?"

"Medium."

"Oh, I like medium. What's his hair sitch? Blond, brown, black, red?"

"Black. Really black." Like a waterfall. That's what I'd thought of Sam's hair when I first saw it loose. "And long. Like, to his shoulders long . . . not like eighties metal rocker long. It's super silky and straight—"

Hattie barks a loud laugh.

"What?"

"Um, pay attention to this dude's hair much?"

I groan. "You're ridiculous."

"Maybe so, but is he single?"

"No. He has eleven wives."

"Only eleven?"

"So far."

"Har-har."

"I know what I know and that is"—I count on my fingers—"he's from the desert, a fact that *may* make him useless on the ocean, but we'll see; he's a student at USM; he likes my gram's biscuits; and he's researching Malaga Island for his archeology department."

Hattie goes to my bureau, pulls out a T-shirt, and strips down.

"You staying the night?"

"Of course." Her head pops through the bright blue tee with a whale on the front, a souvenir from a tacky shell-filled gift shop on Cape Cod. "I told Reed tonight was my night."

She must have really wanted to be here; talking to Reed has never been high on her list of favorite—or even tolerable—things to do. "Glad you two are managing my evening social calendar with such flair."

Hattie climbs under the covers. I prop my pillow behind my head and knock the journal free.

"What's this?" Hattie says, tapping at its edges. I've always liked that about Hattie. How she never grabs for anything, never assumes she has the right to share in a thing unless it's offered.

"It's a bunch of Sam's research."

"And you have Sam's notes tucked under your pillow because you looooooove him?" She smiles her deliciously brilliant off-kilter smile.

"You are so hilarious! How did I not notice this until now?" She waves me off. "Whatevs. Show me the goods."

"It's nothing. Just Sam's notes."

She squints. "Does Sam have a last name?"

"Probably."

"Okay, you've hired a dude whose last name you don't know to go out into the middle-of-nowhere ocean with you where there is exactly zero cell service and no one around to witness if he chops you up into little bits and tosses you overboard. Do I have this right?"

"Um, gruesome."

"Gruesome or truesome?"

"Not truesome. He's good people."

"I need to know exactly how you know about him being good people."

So I tell her. I tell her about my three visits to Malaga. I tell her about Sam and his archeological dig, our lunches on the island, Sam's instalove for Gram's biscuits.

I don't tell her about the other reasons I'm drawn to Malaga. Or my random visions. Hattie doesn't need to worry more. Or maybe I don't tell her because saying the words would make my hallucinations too real.

"So this book is his research and he just gave it to you?"

"I'm only borrowing it. To learn more about the island."

Hattie plops back on her pillow, stares at my ceiling. "Why?"

"Because it's interesting."

"Why would you want to dig any of that stuff up, Rills?"

"No pun intended?"

"It was punintentional." She turns to face me. "But, Rills. That shit needs to stay in the past where it belongs. It was awful then, and it's awful now. No amount of you knowing about it is going to change what happened."

I sit straighter. "Wait. You know about Malaga?"

"'Course."

"How do I not know this?"

"It's not like I'd just go around chatting about it. It's horrible what happened to the people out there. They were evicted from their homes, some locked up in an insane asylum." Hattie stops, looks at me, her eyes searching for forgiveness. "Rills, I'm sorry. I wasn't thinking."

Hattie—like nearly everyone on Maine's Mid Coast—knows my mother spent years in an asylum in Upstate New York. I would often picture her with scalp-short hair. So short that even lice didn't want to live in it. Because that's what they do in institutions, right? Cut off all your hair and put you in a white room where the only person who talks to you wears only white and hands you a tiny white paper cup with a tiny, bright red pill in its center. The dressed-in-all-white nurse removes the all-white cup and tells my mother to swallow the all-red pill and she does. And sometimes the pill makes her rock back and forth in a corner and sometimes it makes her stare out a window without being able to see anything at all.

This is, of course, pure fabrication by my runaway brain.

Gram and my dad both tried to convince me of her reality, how my mother went to the hospital after that particularly bad night when she walked into the water. Then voluntarily checked herself into a facility where she could take walks on sun-fed grass and talk to professionals that helped her quiet her demons. The rational side of me knows the woman who gave me to the world is in a good place, but it's the small pushed-away part of me that thinks she must be in an ancient asylum, caught in restraints and medicated hazes. Because if she's trapped in a place where she can't think straight or talk out loud, then I forgive her for not coming back for me. But if her feet are free enough to feel the warm green grass push up between her toes each spring, how can I forgive her for all the seasons she stayed away?

"It's okay." My heart races. No, throbs. "You weren't talking about my mom."

"No." Hattie's voice is soft. "I'm talking about the islanders who were locked away so the state could take their land."

I see the old woman, the worn lace high around her neck, the sun at her shoulders, the small bunches of herbs drying on the rafters of her crude porch. The children on the steps of the schoolhouse, the same kids on the ridge with only the wide, fresh sky behind them. I can't see the islanders in an institution with its bleached, dying air.

"What do you mean locked away?"

"Come on, Rills. Why are we even talking about this? It's awful."

"I need to know." I think of the girl, her baby. Are they connected to the island's past? And how? "Please, Hattie. I'll love you forever if you tell me what you know."

"That's a weak trade, Rills. You're supposed to love me anyway, regardless."

"I do. You know I do."

"For reals?"

"Forever reals."

Hattie slides up, sits with her back against the headboard, eats at the corner of her thumbnail. "You remember when my nana got sick?"

I do. It was only a few years ago. Hattie's nan eventually died from the Alzheimer's that had plagued her for years. Her nan had forgotten to turn off the stove one morning. Hattie lost her grandmother in that trailer fire, and her funeral was one of the hardest this peninsula has endured. Until recently.

Alice Barter was a lot of years older than Gram, but they were close. Her death hit Gram hard enough that she let weeds grow in her gardens. Gram disappeared into her attic studio for weeks then, Dad and I leaving tea and food outside her door that would mostly go untouched.

"Well, she wasn't fully lucid in the end."

"I remember."

"Nan would talk about things from her past. Confuse me for my mom. All the normal horrifying confusion that comes with Alzheimer's."

I squeeze a small prayer to the universe that Gram will never suffer that fate.

"This one day I was helping her with chores around the house like I'd done a million times since she started getting sick, and then she told me how island graves were dug up and trucked to Maine's School for the Feeble-Minded. At first I thought she was mixing up her story with a TV show—the way she would sometimes confuse an episode for reality."

"She wasn't?"

Hattie sighs. "Nope. She said, 'No, Hattie. Malaga. You could throw a stone to that island from Rilla's window.' She sounded annoyed with me, like I should have made the connection. She said the people there were inbred and insane."

"And that's why they were institutionalized?"

"No. I mean, yes. That's pretty much the official reason—even if it wasn't true."

"What was the truth?"

"The islanders were poor and biracial and the state wanted their land."

"You're sure this was Malaga?"

Hattie nods. "The next day I drove up to Pineland—that's what they renamed the old state . . . 'school'"—Hattie uses air quotes—"even though it was a mental institution and people were basically jailed there."

"And?" I'm breathless.

"I saw the graves. Seventeen people from Malaga buried under five headstones, all marked with the same date: November, 1932. But, Rills, that was the date the state reburied the bodies, not when they actually died."

"Hattie, you're talking about mass graves."

"I'm aware. Those gray stones were tucked in the back of that cemetery like the deceased were supposed to be forgotten."

"What you're saying is literally unbelievable."

"I couldn't believe it either. That's why I made my mom go with me. She wouldn't admit it, but I think she needed to know my nan was still lucid when she was talking about Malaga's history, you know? That she still had her mind somewhere under all that sickness."

"And she did?"

"She knew those bodies were buried together like they weren't individual people. She knew they were from Malaga."

"Jesus, Hattie."

"A few days later, she told me she regretted it."

"Regretted what?"

"Her exact words"—Hattie takes a deep breath, lets it free—"I'll never forget them. She said she regretted 'not having enough love in my heart.' I think she was trying to tell me to live my life differently, without discrimination."

Not having enough love in my heart. The words are heavy with a hurt that weighs me down even now. "I can't believe you never told me."

"How could I tell you that my nan had been part of all that hate? Maybe even someone who *wanted* an entire island community to be erased?"

"Of course." My words, barely a whisper. It's the same way I would go quiet when my teachers prepared for Mother's Day Tea in elementary school, or when kids would come to my house and see my gram where a mom should be. Some things are just too hard to talk about.

"Like I said, Rills, who wants to dig that up? It happened and it was awful. Nothing we do can ever undo what happened."

"But this is our *home*, Hattie. Our *history*."

"That's exactly why it should stay in the past." She turns her head to face me. "Ever since we were kids, you've had one foot in another place, Rills. Your future, your college away, traveling. I always knew that would happen for you. Just like I knew it would never happen for me."

"Hatt—"

"Let me finish." She holds up her hand. "I have to live here, Rills. I'll never live anywhere else. So I need to see the good and only the good."

I get it. Hattie's always joked about being a statistic, even though I know it kills her to think of herself that way. She's got a barely present mom who had her when she was fourteen. Hattie's mom lives off aid from the state, if you could call the life Hattie's mom provides living. And Hattie's so bound to her dependent mother, no matter how many times she forgets to buy food or pay the heating bill. No matter how many of Hattie's dreams her mom has shattered.

"I'm here too, Hatt. Maybe even for good now."

Her eyes go steely. "Don't you ever let me hear you say that, Rilla Brae. If I have to boot you hard enough to get your too-smart-to-stay-here ass to Rhode Island, I will. I'm not above it and you know it."

Hattie's belief in me has never faltered. I wish she could have a future with more choices, but for all her wanting to leave our small peninsula, I know Hattie could never abandon her mom. And Hattie is the strongest person I know. "I'm so sorry you couldn't tell me and that I wasn't there for you. But I get it."

"You do?"

"Of course." Families. Love. Truth. All so complicated. "Would you go with me? To see the graves?"

Hattie's face pales. "Aw, come on, Rills. Don't ask me to do that."

"I can go alone."

"No. I'll go if that's what you really want. I just don't see what good it will do."

"It probably won't do any good, but I have to see for myself."

"Then I'll be the Thelma to your Louise."

I squeeze her hand. "I've missed you," I tell her. I've missed my sister.

"Same." She drops her head to the pillow, stares at my ceiling. "But you need to remember that all that matters is you, Rills. You and your future. Getting to college. Getting out of here."

She's right. And wrong, too. Because the truth of Malaga

matters. The fate of Malaga residents isn't just something that happened to innocent people. It was a tragedy inflicted on innocent people *by other people*—the families that still populate these shores. Maybe even my family.

"Sometimes I think hell isn't a consequence, Rills. It's not a place you go to if you mess up bad enough on earth. I think hell might be here. In our every day."

She's talking about her own life now, how she's rarely seen her mother smile. And I know she's ashamed that her mother has never worked a job. Hattie doesn't know what it's like to have pride in her family, and I think she's never been able to conjure that pride in herself. Not after years of being told that she's the reason their home life is crap. Hattie says it's the alcohol that makes her mother say things like that, but I hear the fear that sits behind Hattie's words. Like maybe she knows that's how her mom really feels and cheap beer only loosens her tongue enough to say the truth.

"But tomorrow's another day, right, Rills?"

"My dad always said tomorrows arrive lighter."

"You're lucky you got a dad like that."

I pull her hand to my side. "I know, Hatt. You deserve better than what you got."

"I got you, Rills. That's enough." She slinks down into the covers. "I need sleep. See you in the morning?"

"You getting up at five?"

"Um, that would be a hell no."

I give a small laugh. "Figured. I'll be quiet when I leave." I place the moleskin on my shelf and turn out the light. "Thanks for coming over."

"Thanks for being kickass."

"Thanks for showing me how."

Hattie's body is warm next to mine, so close, but I can't help how her story distances us in a new way. There's a hunger in me to know what Alice Barter regretted in the last days of her life. I want to know the whole story of Malaga Island, everybody's version. Even the version that's the horrible truth.

"Good night, Hatt."

"'Night, Rills." Hattie rolls tighter against me, like we did when we were little. Back when Dad would slip us candy to eat in bed and we'd wake with Junior Mints and gummy worms stuck in our hair, Gram always there to wash and comb out the sugar.

I wait until Hattie's breath rises and falls with sleep before I open Sam's notebook again, read every article he's collected. Hattie and her grandmother's failing mind were right.

Eight of the forty Malaga residents were abducted and forcibly committed to the state institution. One, a healthy infant. Three of them children. One because he couldn't identify a telephone, something he wouldn't have seen in his seven years of island life. For that this young boy was labeled "feeble-minded" and ripped from Malaga and the sea and his family and taken to an isolated place, where he died forty-three years later. Six of the eight people who were committed died at the institution.

There's a *Harper's Magazine* article from the time: THE QUEER FOLK OF THE MAINE COAST[2]—and recently, a website named for the island, its header: MALAGA ISLAND: A STORY BEST LEFT UNTOLD.[3]

But I can't imagine any story being better for being silenced.

Researchers claim that a few islanders built simple rafts after the notice of eviction was served. They floated their homes to more hospitable shores. But the islanders' biracialism and extreme poverty made them different, and difference is all anyone would've been able to see then.

I doubt there were more tolerant shores to find.

My community is no longer a peninsula with a proud fishing history; we are a peninsula whose fishermen rose up against other fishermen. And our discrimination was not quiet.

In newspapers, local grange halls, and places of worship, men shouted for the removal of other men, women, children. Their hatred shouted all the way to the statehouse, landing in the governor's office. The governor wanted to build a hotel on the island, and so the scourge campaign began.

It's the words in a recent article from the *Portland Press*

Herald that break me: "The governor ordered the eviction of the community, and officials institutionalized eight residents, some for failing to identify a telephone. . . . Noobody has lived on the island since."[4]

All that.

And nothing.

Nothing but loss.

I search the photos and articles for the girl with the brown skin and the white dress. The one who sang at the shore. The one who might know more about me than I know about myself.

But she is nowhere in these pages. A ghost.

CHAPTER NINE

The silver slice of moon cuts through the darkness. I'm on the solid deck of the *Rilla Brae*, the midnight sea surrounding me.

I hear my father in my head, his words reaching me from a great distance as an echo inside of an echo. "Bugs move at night, Rilla. Leave them be." Fishermen know to let the stocks replenish.

Still, I'm fishing at night.

I know it's wrong, and I head from the wheelhouse just as another voice soothes me, tells me that this is right. *Come here, come here.* Warmth spreads through my body, thickening. I look for the girl. My girl. The girl that holds more secrets than a midnight sea.

Is the song in my head, or is she here, singing?

I feel the buoy line in my hand, stretched across my palm. I tug at the rope, test its tautness. A trap pulls from the opposite end. I lean toward the water, drawing up the rope foot by foot. One hand over the other. Tendrils of seaweed cling to the braided twine, slicking through my fingers. The rope drags up the salt of the sea, the hard smell of fish and buried layers.

And then the line goes slack.

The frayed end of the rope is all that's left in my grip. I stumble back, unsteady now on the deck of the *Rilla Brae*. I lean against the wheelhouse and stare at the shimmering black of the deep. My gear is gone. Lost to the sea, a ghost trap.

Until there's a flicker of movement and a small splash as the trap's metal corner cuts through the ocean's surface. I peer over the side of the *Rilla Brae*. The trap is carried on the waves, impossibly floating—swimming—toward me. Crawling toward my boat.

Moonlight flickers at its wire edges. The trap bobs on a wave.

Under a wave.

On a wave.

Behind a wave.

Coming for me.

Then the sweet song of a voice that sings louder now: *Come here, come here.*

I stay.

Seaweed crowns the wire cage. It inches nearer. I flatten my hands against the boat's fiberglass edge, lean over to greet this determined trap the way I have pulled thousands of traps before.

When it reaches me, the trap stops still, mere inches from my boat. My hands on the rail are heavy useless things. I can't lift them.

The trap bobs, holding its place despite the push of the waves. It doesn't bang against my boat. The cage hovers close but not too close. I will my arm to move, and my hand is set free of an unknown weight. I reach for the trap. The seaweed shifts. Its tangled tresses swim in the moonlight. Slither to the side. The seaweed is twisted with something darker, finer.

Hair.

My fingers rake at the long, swimming hair just as the mass of tangles slip.

Off of a girl's round face.

My girl.

Her face green with the sea now.

Washed with time.

Her body is slack, forever heaped over my trap. Her lifeless arms drag at the sides, fingertips brushed by the lifting ocean. Something like air gets lodged in my lungs, but it's colder. Unwelcome. I scream, but the sound never comes. It is just me and a floating dead girl and the night and the cold and the sea and the moon.

I tell myself to fall back, fall away from the edge of the boat. Into my boat. Away from her. But I know the dead girl senses my retreat, my beat of cowardice, and she will not let me leave her.

The dead girl's eyes dart open.

Her hand rises from the deep, a serpent. Dark. Scaly. Forgotten. Her cold fingers lock onto the skin of my wrist.

Fire burns under her touch.

She pulls me to her, her dark cracked lips preparing to croak a whisper into my ear. I scream so that I can't hear her words. I scream to drown out her message. I scream as she pulls me down to the cold black sea that forces the weight of its water and salt into my lungs.

I dart upright in bed, my sheets soaked with a panicked sweat.

Hattie sleeps next to me.

I pull air into my chest and let my lungs fill. My fingers search the stillness of the mattress below me. I peel my mind from the dream, layers of fear still binding me in their thick wrap.

That is when I feel it, the burn at my wrist.

Raw and angry and on fire.

I'm careful not to wake Hattie as I switch on my light, rub the handcuff of skin that's red, angry, screeching. The deep heat rages all the way through to my wrist bones, makes me curl into its pain. I tuck my arm into my stomach and try to still my mind. Try to erase the dead girl with the seaweed hair. She is not real.

My eyes catalog the things that are: my books, my dresser, my bed. Me, in this room. My friend next to me. The girl from the sea was a dream, nothing more. Still, I can't help think of the Water People, those mysterious people who called to my mother from the deep.

Maybe they were as real as the band of burn on my wrist.

Maybe they are coming for me, too.

I dress and tiptoe to the kitchen, where I rummage for the tin of Gram's homemade calendula flower ointment. I smooth the salve over the charred skin, carefully dabbing, letting the thick balm sink its coolness into my skin. Gram enters the room cat-quiet. She grabs my hand, inspects my wrist.

"Where'd ya go and get a burn like that?"

I slide my hand from her grasp and lie. "The engine." It's the only lie I can remember telling my grandmother, but how can I tell her the truth? I'm distinctly aware that burns don't manifest themselves from the dream world. And was it a dream? Its details cling to me even now, more like a vision. And when did I wake up? Before or after the vision? I shake my head quickly, still unable to make sense of time and place.

Gram's *harrumph* tells me she suspects I'm hiding something. She knows the engine wouldn't make a collar of a burn. "Best wrap that wound."

She shuffles past me, setting a few jars of her jams onto the table, their glass lids *tink*ing as I inhale the heavy yeast smell of rising bread. I tuck down my questions, my fears about the swell of my wrist, the girl from the deep. Or Malaga. Or both.

Are my dreams—my visions—where the dead and the living meet?

I conjure my best everyday voice, let it lift over the throbbing of the burn. "Smells amazing."

"I should hope so, seeing as they are your favorite." Gram piles biscuits into a wicker bowl lined with a red cloth napkin. "Reed not staying for breakfast?"

My heart stutters. "Reed?"

Gram fusses with the jams, sticking a small jelly spoon inside each clear jar. "You're eighteen, Rilla. No sense having that boy sneak out any longer." She mumbles something about him breaking his neck on the trellis, but I can barely register what she's saying.

"You know Reed stays over?" How long has she known?

She turns, hand on her hip. "You're old enough to know I've got my eyes open, Rilla. Now sit." She pushes a plate in front of me. "Ya tell Reed to use the front door when he leaves in the mornings. My roses shouldn't have to bear the brutality of his clodhoppers after today."

I reach for a too-hot biscuit.

"Don't ya look so shocked. I might be old, but I still see things." Gram splits her flaky roll with the push of her thumb, pours honey along the exposed insides.

"D-did Dad know?"

She knits her brows in my direction. "Ya know I'd never be that careless with his heart."

Her words freeze me. There were times I was careless with my dad's heart, when I yelled at him, throwing blame for the most insignificants bits of living. My curfew. Getting up so early.

I massage the skin above my wrist, the burn stinging deeper now, almost familiar, comforting. "Hattie stayed last night, not Reed."

Gram looks pleased. "I'm glad to hear it. Ya two girls are the opposite sides of a clamshell, made to be stuck together. And has Hattie had the pleasure of meeting your sternman?"

"Not yet."

"You'll bring Sam by tonight, yes?"

"Yes."

Gram packs biscuits in a warmer, part of the deal we made before I went to my room last night. Gram promised to make extra biscuits if I brought Sam to Fairtide to meet her. "I'm packing enough for the both of ya."

She means Sam, but I hear the familiar words: *The both*

of ya. Me and Dad. He is everywhere with us still. His life is woven into this kitchen, into our habits. And I can't ignore the way my heart thunders with the suspicion that my mother is here too, her madness visiting me with a power all its own.

CHAPTER TEN

When I step aboard the *Rilla Brae*, my legs remember how they steadied against the rolling waves as the dead girl crept toward me. The girl bringing death the same way the universe brought Dad's. Dark. Horrible. Unexpected. The sea spreads its secrets around me, its depths another world.

Today is the first time I hesitate at the *Rilla Brae's* ignition. I can't remember ever pausing before bringing the engine to life, but now I fear what I'll pull from the sea, as if the dream were a premonition. And it's the second time in as many weeks that I've feared the water.

But I hear Gram's advice about never setting a place for fear at your table. I turn the key and calm with the familiar vibration of the boat. I slip into my rubber coveralls and focus only on fishing. The ocean refuses to accommodate doubt. "All it takes is one wave, Rilla. One wave and one moment when you aren't paying attention. Survival on the ocean is fragile." Even then Dad warned me of the slip of time between life and death. In those days I never imagined we'd exist on opposite sides of the divide.

I throw the engine in gear and head to sea. I channel between Whaleback Ridge on my port side, Malaga at starboard. The island is a mere mound of rock, unprotected from the violent sea, its former residents unprotected from violent judgment. Alone in the wash of water. I slow my speed, raise my gaze to the shadow of the island's crest. I picture the old woman in her rocking chair, rising to tend her gardens. The men at sea in their open boats, vulnerable in ways they may not have known. And was the girl there too? With her song?

"Did you know people lived on Malaga?" I ask Dad, and maybe my mother too. Because maybe they are here. With me and the sea.

I'm relieved when I don't get an answer. I was only six when the ambulance took my mother away. I remember the sirens that screamed at the end of my mother's last night at Fairtide, how they were loud and screeching and frightened my heartbeat. It took a lot of years for me to understand what a psychiatric hospital was, and how the Water People sent her there. Now I want to know how the hallucinations started for her, the slipping of her mind. Because maybe I am more like her than I thought.

I press against the throttle, gaining speed. I give the sea my full attention.

Sam's on his boat when I arrive, anchored off the lee side of Malaga. Even in the predawn dark, I can see his eager wave as I approach. I cut my engine when I'm close enough to yell to him: "You wanna jump in your skiff, row to me?"

"Nah. Come closer. I can make the leap."

My money's on him going in the drink. But Gram says that bravado is the only thing a man can master without a woman's help, so I let Sam have his.

"You got it." The current is choppy and carries my boat closer to the USM craft. I worry about marking up the sides of his pristine boat. The *Rilla Brae* is an old, working boat and bears her share of scars. A new scratch would have plenty of company. I throw the fenders out along the side, let their Styrofoam cushion keep a few inches of distance between the crafts. "Grab the rail, but don't bend too far. One wave can pull away your balance."

"Aye, aye, Captain."

Captain. It's the word I used for my dad when we were out on the water. A word used everywhere on the sea. But today it feels wholly mine.

Sam leaps onto the *Rilla Brae*, and I'm impressed.

"I didn't think you were gonna make it." I train the floodlight ahead of us. "Gravity and balance are entirely different animals out on the sea."

"Lesson one, huh?" Sam joins me in the wheelhouse.

"Nope." I thrust the *Rilla Brae* in gear. "Lesson one"—I give his bare legs the side eye—"is never wear shorts for lobstering."

"What's wrong with shorts?"

"You'll see."

"I didn't bring anything else."

I nod toward the back corner of the wheelhouse, where my dad's rubber overalls hang. "Put those on. You're gonna need them."

Sam reaches for my father's Grundens, and in this small space, Sam's body feels too close to me. I press my pelvis into the wheel, trying to create distance between us. I'm grateful when he steps to the back deck to slide the coveralls on. But when he returns, wearing my father's uniform, my heart flattens in my chest.

I drive hard to the first buoy and then slow. I hand Sam my extra pair of gloves and the grapple hook. I nod toward the buoy. "That one's ours. The green stripe intersected by orange. They're all painted the same. That exact combination lets the other fishermen know that this is the Brae line. Each one bears our license number. Never try to pull a pot that doesn't have a buoy with our colors, our license."

"Why not?"

"That's the way wars start out here. Men shoot men for that treachery."

"For real?"

"It's about as real as it gets."

Sam gives me a short salute. "Got it. No wars."

"The line sits under the buoy so you have to snag it, pull it up."

Sam follows the halogen light as it reaches over the frothing waves. He throws the hook, submerging it before he pulls back nothing but seawater. He tries again. And again. "There is a rope, right?" He's smiling. I've seen other newbies begin to look nervous by now, try to convince me of their manliness. But Sam's humble, and humble is a good passenger to have on a boat.

"There's a line." I wait through six more attempts before he snags its length. The morning sun drags its color into the sky.

He pulls the swollen rope up from the water, but as he turns to me in his excitement, the line slips from the hook. His smile only grows. "Let me guess, that's *not* supposed to happen."

"Not."

He thrusts up his hand like a stop sign. "Okay, okay. I got this now. Hook the line, but *don't* let it slip from the hook."

"You catch on fast." We should have hauled at least two strings, three pots each, in the time it takes Sam to drag up one, but my father was patient with me whenever I was learning anything new and I extend the same courtesy to Sam. "All we need is one good pot for supper, so let's try for that." They're the words I tell Sam, exactly as my father said them to me when he first let me use the grapple hook. I was eight and my arm hurt from thrusting that long wooden stick into the water. I slept with a bag of frozen peas on my swollen shoulder that night, but I never told my dad how much pain my first day on the hook had caused. The pride I felt for doing the work on my own was the closest thing I'd ever felt to flying.

"Where'd you go?" Sam asks.

I shake the memory from my head. "I'm here."

"Check it." Sam shows me the hook, the thick rope tucked into its steel claw.

"Well done." I tie the rope to a metal cleat at the rail. "Normally, we'd set the line into the pulley, but your first pot is a special one. All first pots are pulled by hand on this boat."

"Like this?" He works the line through his gloves, hand over hand.

"Just like that."

His back struggles against the weight as the trap nears the surface. His stance widens with the strain of the task. Then the surface of the water changes, pops.

"Holy crap. Is that it?"

"It is." My breathing waits on its contents, like always.

The corner of the trap peeks out from under the waves, sloughing off water as it rises. Sam pulls the line closer to the boat, and the way the wire cage creeps through the swells reminds me of the one that crawled to me in my dream. My vision. I squint my eyes to the sun, reminding my brain that this trap is real. Being out here is real. "Pull it all the way to the boat," I instruct.

He does. The metal pot bangs against *Rilla*'s side, and Sam looks guilty.

"It's all good. Now bring it up. But don't bend too far. Remember that balance isn't the same on a boat." I stand behind him, ready to yank the back straps of his overalls if he loses his footing on the wet deck.

But he lifts the cage flawlessly. He holds it above his head like a prize. His smile beams as water cascades down his arms. "Christ, this is heavy!"

"You don't actually have to hoist it over your head."

"Sure I do. A kid from the desert gets to pull his first lobster trap exactly once."

I grab at the opposite side, help him carry the cage to the top of the cooler. "Desert's a long way away."

"That is kind of the point."

Something in his response startles me, makes me wonder what he's running from. Or to.

I want to ask Sam more—know more—but how can I ask that of anyone when I'm not ready to share pieces of my own story? I return to instruction, the concrete and fixed language of hauling. Something I can control. Something that I've mastered. "Normally, we'd unload this on the rail. Saves time. But since it's your first trap, we can do it here." I tap the cooler. "I'll walk you through the steps."

"I appreciate that." Then he bends to see eye level into the trap. "Holy shit. There are lobsters in there."

I smile. "That's a good thing."

"No, I mean. Real. Lobsters. And they're all brown and creepy."

"They are."

"I've only seen them on a"—he looks around and lowers his voice—"a plate before, ya know?"

I laugh. "I do."

He stares into the trap again, like he's at an exotic zoo. "Do we take them out?"

"They won't venture out on their own."

Sam takes a step back, gestures toward the trap. "Ladies first."

I unhook the corner ties and throw up the hatch door. I pull out the first lobster and she's small. I nod to the gauge hanging outside the wheelhouse. "Grab the ruler there." He does. I turn the lobster so that her hard shell steadies on my palm. Her front claws search for anything to grab hold of. "A legal lobster has to be larger than three and a quarter inches but smaller than five. You measure from the top of the head here"—I point to the beginning of her shell, the part that actually starts just below her head—"to here." I move my thumb along the bottom of her shell, that place just above her tail. I tuck the metal gauge against her side. "This girl's too small, so we throw her back."

"In the trap?"

"No. She goes overboard."

"Her lucky day."

"You wanna do the honors?"

Sam reaches for her belly.

"That's a great way to get your thumb chomped."

His hand retreats.

I turn my free palm. "Like this. Hold her upside down; it'll put her to sleep. So her pincher claws can't reach your fingers."

I respect Sam's confidence, how he slides his gloved hand under mine, grabs hold of this creature that must feel so foreign to him. He holds the lobster at arm's distance, but his smile broadens across every inch of his face. "I am holding a lobster, Rilla Brae."

"You are."

"Like, a lobster. Straight from the sea."

"Not *like* a lobster, a real live, living lobster." At this rate it will take us a hundred times longer to haul. "You need to set her back to the deep."

"Right. So, like face-first? Tail-first?"

"Any way is fine. Just chuck her overboard."

"Rilla!"

"What?"

"I will not 'just chuck her overboard'"—he makes awkward air quotes that pulls the lobster too close to his face. He thrust her out to arm's length again. "I didn't take you for being so callous."

"It's actually callous to keep her out of the water this long."

"Oh. Right. Of course." Sam leans over the edge of the boat and suspends the lobster above the surface. The dawn sky is still too dark to see her descent, but I've seen enough lobsters returned to the sea to know that she dives skillfully, reunited with a world she can understand. I pretend I don't hear him say, "So long, little lobstery."

I try to hide my smile. "Six more." Sam watches as I measure the remaining bugs, all legal length. We band their claws and place them in the cooler that circulates fresh seawater. "Now we rebait the trap." I pull the small bag of netting from the trap's kitchen and hand it to him.

He looks around the boat. "What do I fill it with?"

I kick at a five-gallon bucket. "Throw in a scoop of bait and hang it in the front of the trap. Then we set it back with its buoy and do it all over again."

"Sounds easy enough."

Sam pops the plastic lid off the bait bucket, and the whiff of rotten fish pushes him back so hard he falls on his ass. I extend a hand, which he takes.

"Always gotta watch your step."

"Good God, woman. What is in there?"

"Chum."

"Chum actually sounds a thousand times better than the way that smells."

"Chum is dead, chopped-up fish."

"That would be a precisely accurate description for the aroma emanating from this tub." He scoops the fish and aims it toward the bait bag, but a wave heaves us and the chum slams into his thigh, blood and fish bits dripping down his leg.

"Chum is also one of the many reasons we don't wear shorts when fishing."

Bloody fish parts slither down his overalls. "That is a brilliant rule." He nods. "No shorts. Never shorts." He takes another scoop, fills the bag. "I might never wear shorts again."

"Maaaaybe a bit extreme," I say as I show him how to hang

the bait bag within the trap's kitchen. "Okay. Now just close and latch the door and you're all set."

He hoists the empty cage to the side of the boat. "Do I just throw it back?"

"Make sure the buoy line is free first."

"So it doesn't snag my foot?"

"You're a fast learner."

"You're a good teacher." He steps outside the coil of rope and drops the pot overboard. The line runs to follow the trap, slithering out over the boat's edge. Then, finally, it snaps the buoy over the edge. The painted buoy bobs at the water's surface, waiting. "Can I ask you something?"

I write the coordinates of the trap into my logbook. It would be easier, faster maybe, to set them into the GPS system. But Dad was old-school, so I am too. "About fishing?"

"Yes."

"Ask away."

"How do you know if a lobster is female?"

I put down the pencil, turn to him. "It's illegal to harvest egg-bearing females. That's why you check their bellies. If you see eggs, you need to notch their tail with a *V* and throw them back. Sometimes you won't see eggs, just the notched tail. It means she's a breeder. We throw them back to help sustain the lobster population."

"But that one's tail wasn't notched."

"Nope."

"And she didn't have eggs?"

"She didn't." I head toward the next buoy in our string.

"But you called the lobster a *her*. Why?"

I know the reason, but I've never told anyone, not even Dad. Sam sees me hesitate.

"You don't have to tell me if you don't want to."

And maybe that's why I tell him. Because I don't have to. Because he gives me the space in which to make my choice about what I share and what I don't. "I've been fishing for lobster all my life."

"I kinda got that."

"I was taught at a really young age that lobsters take care of us out here. They feed us. Nurture our stomachs and our economy. I guess that always seemed like a maternal thing to me. As if lobsters were like really good mothers and grandmothers. Taking care of their own, taking care of others."

"Damn."

I pull my eyes from my water course. "What?"

Sam rights the grapple hook so it stands next to him like a staff. "You sound more like a poet than a fisherman."

I like the way he gives my words back to me. I return his gift with a smile.

At the final string, my buoys are entangled. I see the blue-and-white markings of the crowding buoys long before I reach the string. Old Man Benner's colors.

I take the gaff hook and pull the last string to untangle my line from his. My anger grows with every second lost to this task.

"Does this happen a lot?" Sam asks.

"Buoy lines can get tangled in the currents, but this is a whole line." Three traps in a row. "Old Man Benner set over my traps."

"On purpose?"

"Yep. It's a way for fishermen to send a message." Benner wants me gone. And he's telling me that he's willing to crowd me out.

"What kind of message?"

"That this particular fisherman is an asshole." I pull Benner's pot, a complete violation under any circumstances. I open the hatch, take the keepers.

"I thought you weren't supposed to fish another person's line?"

"You aren't." I stack his three traps on my deck and hide his blue-and-white buoys under a tarp so no one will see my treachery.

We head to the co-op to offload at the wharf. I introduce Sam to Hoopah, who shakes his hand. "Glad to meet you," Sam says.

Hoopah eyes him. "Not from these parts, are ya?" Hoopah's "parts" is distinctly missing an *R* and sounds like "pahts." Dad used to joke that a hard *R* was as endangered as some of the fisheries in this part of the country.

"Southern Arizona," Sam tells him. Most of our tourists come from Massachusetts, New Jersey, and New York. Arizona is exotic in comparison.

"Ya far from home."

"Farthest I've ever been," Sam says. I almost expect him to tell Hoopah about the dusty book that started his journey to Maine.

"Rill!" I recognize Reed's voice, and I cringe.

I'm aware of how exhausted I look after staying up too late to study Malaga's past and how sleep didn't come easily after learning of the island's fate. The stress of my dream can't be helping my overall look of wellness. And I don't want Reed to sense my rage at his grandfather's bullshit antics. We never talk about our hauls; it's a pact we made when we started dating. Lobstering is competitive enough without having to keep score against your boyfriend.

Reed comes to me with his long strides, his smile that pushes everything else off his face. He plucks at one of the black elastic straps of my orange overalls as he approaches, gives me a kiss on the cheek. My hand drops to find his, like always.

I link my fingers through his and whisper, "Hey, good-lookin'."

"Get a room!" a deep voice calls from over near the huge container of bait. Stanley Wyatt is a likely suspect. The bait shack is where the retired fishermen sit and smoke and gossip.

"And a condom!" another fisherman calls. Probably Holm Stegner, Stanley's sidekick.

All the men crack right up, most stroking their thick beards while they laugh.

I turn to Sam with an apology in my eyes. "The wharf's a little . . . rough."

Sam shoots me an it-doesn't-bother-me look, and I realize I know Sam's expressions—only a few, but still. "It's all good."

Reed nods toward Sam but asks me, "Who's this?"

"Ah." I throw a short wave between the two of them. "Sam, Reed. Reed, Sam."

Sam extends his hand. "Sam Taylor, *Rilla Brae*'s resident sternman."

"Reed Benner, Rilla Brae's resident boyfriend." Reed drops my hand, shakes Sam's.

Sam throws me a look that says *Benner?*

I nod. "Sam's in town for the summer."

Reed looks him up and down. "Summer jerk, huh?" Except he says "summah jerk."

"Summah not," Hoopah answers automatically from where he weighs my catch behind Sam.

Sam looks between Reed and Hoopah. "I'm lost."

"Don't listen to them," I say. "It's a local thing."

Reed moves closer to him, too close to Sam's face. He waves his hand in the general direction of the village. "Summah people flood this place every year." His "year" sounds like "yee-ah." He's laying his accent on thick. "Summah jerks."

"And summah not," I say.

A smile pops across Sam's face. "Summah jerks and summah not. Ha! That's good stuff." His smile broadens.

Hoopah slaps Sam on the back, like he's just passed some brotherhood test. He pulls Sam over to his station, starts schooling him on the mechanized belt that hauls each catch to the lobster pound.

"Can't get fresher seafood than that," Hoopah's saying as Reed invites me to the side.

"What happened to your wrist?" Reed grabs at the space above my bandage.

"Burned it on the engine."

Reed leans in but doesn't drop his voice. "Jesus, Rilla. Was it because of him?" He nods in Sam's direction. "Does he even know what he's doing out there?" Fishing the deep is the last place people from away are welcome.

"He's fine."

I can tell Reed doesn't like my answer, but he doesn't push.

Instead, he tucks a stray curl behind my ear and I tilt my face to his tender touch.

"Just ask her to marry you already!" Jimmy McKnight taunts from across the wharf. I know it's him because he's lapping up a round of high fives from the equally ridiculous men surrounding him.

"Did Hattie stop by last night?"

"She did."

"Things cool between you two?"

"Totally."

"Good. She's seemed miserable lately without you."

I wait for him to acknowledge my misery, my loss, but he only asks if I can go to the quarry with him tonight. Ugh, that quarry.

"I can't. We're having company for dinner. I'm actually running really late. Long day on the water." I thumb toward Sam. "Training . . . you know."

"After dinner? Come by then."

"I'm beat. I really need sleep."

He takes my hand, rubs the skin along my knuckles, conjures up his best puppy-dog face. "That's not a no."

"It's not a yes. How about tomorrow?"

"Okay. Tomorrow." He kisses me on the forehead, which gets a construction-site whistle from the Wharf of Immaturity.

I turn toward my boat, but Reed pulls at my good wrist. He's looking at Sam as he asks, "Who's your company?"

"What?"

"For supper. Who's coming over?"

"Garden Club ladies." I don't know why I lie to Reed now. I never used to lie to Reed, and the guilt it brings makes me never want to do it again. I've been lying too much. Small ones, but they still feel wrong. Like me trying to protect myself—or hiding the way my mind is slipping—is hurting others.

"Have fun." Reed kisses me good-bye with a little too much pressure. The cackling calls rise from the peanut gallery as soon as his lips reach mine. Still, I like it. His lips, his taste. It's familiar and safe at a time when I need familiar and safe. A not-so-small part of me wants to cancel plans with Sam and Gram and be with Reed instead. I want to be the girl who can go to the quarry, watch the bonfire flames shoot long, spitting embers into the sky, laugh with my friends because laughter is good. But Gram won't allow me to fish with Sam again until I bring him home to meet her, and fishing has to come first.

I pull away, with effort. "See you tomorrow."

"Counting the minutes."

After we make our way out of the harbor, I toss open the doors to Benner's traps and drag them onto a nearby shore. I throw a scoop of dead herring into a plastic bag and leave it inside the top trap to rot in the sun. I cut his buoys from their rope, plant their shafts into the soil so that they stand upright, like soldiers.

"A warning?" Sam asks when I return to the boat.

"Just telling him to back off. He'll know what it means." Every lobsterman knows what it means.

CHAPTER ELEVEN

When we dock at Fairtide Cottage, we hose down the deck and our rubber overalls. I unlatch the small cooler from the boat and hoist it onto the dock. "Supper," I tell Sam, and he nods. When my feet touch the grass of Fairtide's lawn, the weight of the cooler changes as Sam grabs the other side, shares my load. I toss him a look of thanks.

"This is home?" he asks as we walk up the rise of the back lawn.

"The only one I've ever known."

"So it's you and your grandmother and your parents?"

I keep my eyes fixed on the steps before me, how my legs adjust to moving against solid earth. I choose my words carefully to protect my privacy. "Just my gram and my dad. No mother."

"Dads and grandmothers are great," Sam says. I'm grateful that he doesn't ask why my mother's not around, or where she is.

I like the way he knows her story isn't my story. Or it never used to be, though now I'm not so sure.

Gram stands on the porch with her hands on her hips, the only mother I've ever really known. She looks expectant and satisfied all at once.

"I can't imagine a better place to live," I tell him.

"I'm a little jealous, if I'm being honest." Sam takes the whole cooler from me then, balances it across his hips.

I'm curious about his jealousy, if I'm being honest.

"Good catch?" Gram asks when we join her on the porch.

"Great for a first day." Gram knows exactly what that means and gives me a short nod. I don't tell her about Old Man Benner's trespass. Instead, I make introductions. "Sam, this is my grandmother, Eleanor Murphy. Gram, this is Sam."

"Sam Taylor," he says, nodding.

She waves Sam through the doors and into the kitchen as if they were old friends and introductions are a bother. "The suppah sides are all prepared and the water's waiting. Just set them in there, Sam, and I'll do the rest."

"Smells delicious in here." Sam's chest expands with his deep breath. "I might never want to leave." It's possible Sam will ask Gram to marry him because the air really is thick with culinary temptations.

"We should go wash up and change."

Sam tugs at the side of his dirty T-shirt. "Good idea, but I'm seriously underprepared."

I point toward the bathroom door behind the kitchen. "There's soap, and you can grab a fresh hand towel from under the sink. I'll find you a shirt."

"Perfect, thanks."

I head to my room and strip off my work clothes. I pull on an identical uniform of a T-shirt and leggings, the clean version. I go to the upstairs bathroom to splash fresh water on my face and scrub the salt from my hands and forearms. My stomach rumbles with a deep hunger now that it senses Gram's cooking is near. I grab an ancient, oversize black Ramones concert shirt from my drawer and hand it to Sam when I reach the base of the stairs.

He pinches the shoulders of the shirt between his thumbs and forefingers, lets the fabric hang. "Respect."

My dad would have liked Sam.

I join Gram in the kitchen as Sam changes. I pour milk for Sam, set out Gram's mug and mine and take a quick inventory of the table. I add a large open bowl for the broken shells, lobster crackers for all of us, and pour the melted butter into three individual warmers. I can't help but wonder if Gram felt the same strangeness as she set out three plates tonight, but I don't ask. Instead, I run my hand along the length of her back as I pass her at the stove, letting her know I'm here, that I am close and I'm not going anywhere. Maybe the gesture is more for me than her.

Gram removes the bread from the oven and nods toward the boiling water on the stove. "Bugs are ready."

I grab two potholders and sidle up to the large soup pot just as Sam joins us in the kitchen. "I'd love to help with that if you'll let me."

It's not a *Here, let me get that* or an *I've got this*. It's an offer of assistance, but not because he's a man asserting his strength. He asks because he's a guest and wants to help. I don't miss how Gram's eyebrows raise at this same realization. I pull the pot holders from my hands and pass them to Sam.

"Great. Just drain the water in the sink."

"Slowly," Gram warns as she slices through the tender top crust of fresh-baked oatmeal bread. "It's boiling."

"Trust me, I'm all about the slow." Sam carries the pot to the sink and empties the water in a smooth, steady flow.

I pull out the steaming lobsters left at the bottom, their shells bright red now, their claws still bound by the thick blue elastic band we applied after pulling them from the sea.

Sam brings the platter of lobsters to the table, places them in front of Gram. "Can I get anything else?"

"Nonsense." Gram waves him to his seat. "The food's getting

cold waiting on all your politeness." I love the hint of a smile that seeps out with Gram's words.

Sam takes his seat, Dad's seat. Sam is smaller than Dad, with slimmer shoulders and a quieter voice. My dad filled a room with his laughter and his bulk.

Sam spreads his napkin across his lap and scoops roasted potatoes and garden snap peas onto his plate. When he adds an ear of corn, he inhales the steam. "Is that sage?"

Gram nudges my hand, clearly approving. "Nothing better to season early corn than sage butter."

"Couldn't agree more, Mrs. Murphy."

"Don't ya 'Mrs. Murphy' me, young man. I'm Gram in this house, and if you're in this house, then I'm Gram to ya, too."

Sam smiles a grateful grin. "That just might be the best thing anyone has ever said to me."

"Well, then, son, you've lived a boring life and ya need to get out more."

"Gram!"

"No." Sam laughs. "She's right. I do need to get out more. Don't we all?"

Gram gives him an admiring nod. "Tell that to Rilla here."

"Something tells me Rilla makes her own choices."

I feel a blush rise in me, the way its heat is stirred by his compliment.

"Eat up," Gram orders. We do. As Sam and I eat to calm the hunger born from a long day at sea, Gram exercises her expert interrogation. She asks the questions behind the questions. She never asks outright if Sam can handle himself on a boat, if she can trust him with my life. Instead she asks if he has siblings (a brother), if he's close with him (very). How he feels about being so far from the desert and the friends he's known all his life. Gram is unearthing his morality. His core. Because all the boat stuff can be learned. Gram is trying to determine if Sam is someone who will have my back if there's danger. Someone to trust, rely on, in good and bad weather. Sam answers every question with grace, and to Gram's credit, she makes it all seem like good, wholesome conversation instead of her intent fact-finding mission.

"Can I ask you something now?" Sam says to Gram as he sets a bright red lobster onto his plate, removes the blue claw bands with his fork after watching me do the same. "How do I do this?" He taps his fork against the shell.

"Do what, now? Eat a lobster?"

"Yes. Exactly that. Fresh seafood isn't exactly a staple in the desert."

Gram lets out a laugh so loud and quick that her head jolts back. "Rilla, we've got ourselves an honest-to-goodness land-lubber at our table."

"Maybe so," Sam says, his smile as bright as Gram's. "But I'm a big fan of the lobster, and I'd be a bigger fan of it being in my stomach. The question is, how does one make that happen?"

Gram leans forward, squints her eyes at Sam. "You're a funny one, Sam Taylor." She sits back, stares at him. "I like funny."

Sam's smile has actual wattage.

"Want some help?" I ask.

"I would be very grateful for some help."

"Follow my lead." I grab my second lobster from the serving dish and crack the body from the tail, letting the hot water drip into the bowl, over my fingers. Sam copies me. He mimics every move I make as I extract the meat from the lobster, and it feels oddly intimate. Gram watches my wrist, the bright white bandage there.

After dinner, Sam gives Gram a hug and Gram gives Sam a heaping plate of leftovers and a whole loaf of fresh oat bread. Sam and I walk down to the *Rilla Brae*. The light is leaving the sky, but a deep blue still clings to the horizon, even as it's determined to turn black.

When we reach the dock, Sam says, "I didn't realize you could see Malaga from your house." His expression tells me there's something he's not saying.

"I've got a bird's-eye view from my bedroom window."

"Is that your clever way of saying that you're spying on me?"

I push at his shoulder with mine and he laughs.

"I know. Hopeful thinking. I get the very clear sense that you have more important things to do than spy on me." He gestures toward the lip of the dock, asking if we can sit. I do. Sam joins me. He takes off his sneakers and socks and tosses them behind him onto the grass. "I should wear boots tomorrow."

"You should."

"My sneakers smell like chum."

"They do." I smile, find the rising paper moon. "I hate to tell you, but those sneakers will never not smell like chum now."

"That's unfortunate. A tragic end to a trusted pair of Chucks." He dips his feet into the cold ocean water, and the waves bounce against his shins. "How do you not spend every second of your life out here?"

"I basically do." I remember thinking how much I'd miss this shore when I was set to go to Rhode Island. I pull my knees to my chest and concentrate on the waves lapping against the pillars of the dock, the way their white foam sprays up, reaching. There's no fog tonight. Only a fair wind.

"This is how I pictured it would be, you know. Maine. The shore. But it's actually more beautiful than I imagined, and it's just your backyard, like it's no big deal, like it's not the most magical place on earth."

His words make the familiar new.

"Your grandmother is great too. Good family is important."

"You miss yours, huh?" A fact Gram unearthed.

"Sure. They're the best." He liberates a small pebble from between the aluminum wharf boards and rolls it along the cup of his palm. "I'm adopted."

"Lucky." Just as I say this word, I want to pull it back. Who am I to say he's lucky when I know exactly zero about what lucky would look like for him?

"Huh." He looks at me, his eyes wide. "Not the usual response when I tell people I'm adopted."

"There's a usual response?"

"Unfortunately, the follow-up question rarely varies. People ask where my *real* parents are." I feel his weight shift beside me, how uncomfortable it is for him to say those words. "So I'm kind of fascinated to know why you think I'm lucky."

I stare out at Malaga, the mound of earth darkened by night. "Your parents chose you. Out of all the kids, they chose you. Maybe you weren't old enough to choose them, but—"

"I was twelve when I was adopted. Three when I met my mother, but twelve when it all became official and legal and forever."

I smile. "Twelve was quite a year for you."

"You have no idea." He tosses the pebble across the waves, where it disappears.

"So you got to choose your mom and dad?"

"I did."

"See? Lucky."

A low grin spreads on his face. "Can't disagree." He throws another pebble and it *kerplunk*s before disappearing into the waves. "Even after everything I wouldn't want it any other way."

I want to ask after his "everything," but I'm not ready to share my own.

"Your grandmother would get along great with my mom. She's a little"—he searches for the word—"nontraditional. An eccentric-artist type. But she's superwarm. Like your gram."

"My gram's a painter."

"Yeah?" He turns to me, crooks one leg between us. "What does she paint?"

I shrug. "I have no idea. It's kind of her private thing."

Sam nods, full of knowing. "Everybody's got one, right?"

"One what?"

"Their private thing."

I think of my "private things": Dad's death. My mother's struggle with sanity. My hallucinations, which might make me too much like her. Then there's the guilt over wanting to leave the only home I've ever known. And the desire to know if my family forced Malaga residents off their island.

Sam throws another stone. "My dad's a sculptor, makes things with recycled junk."

"Your parents sound cool."

"They are. Tucson is kind of a mecca for cool. Musicians, artists, sunshine. It's a mix that makes some parts feel more like a commune than a municipality."

"I can't imagine. Most Mainers can trace their family back ten generations on the same land. Mainers aren't big on leaving Maine."

"What about you?"

"I'd planned to go away for school, but I always knew I'd come back." Even as much as I tire of gruff men barking over property lines and fishing grounds, this place is in my blood. "Hard to leave what's in your blood."

"Hence no one leaving."

I laugh. "Exactly."

Sam pulls his other foot from the water, sits cross-legged. "You still plan to leave for college?"

"I don't know. The answer is kind of wrapped up in my private thing. It's one of my private things anyway."

"Fair enough." He turns back to the sea, dangles his feet. "You know how I told you that ancient book was the reason I came to Maine, to Malaga?"

"Of course."

"Well, that wasn't exactly truthful, or at least not the whole truth."

I find I want to know Sam's whole truth. I want to know if he holds back parts of the truth because he's protecting pieces of him, no different than me.

"My family is the real reason I'm here."

"Are they from Maine?"

He laughs. "No, no. Nothing like that. It's complicated and kind of wrapped up in my one private thing, so . . ."

"So . . ."

We let the ocean stretch and pool and breathe around us while we kick our feet in the cold tide. We let the starlight watch us. We guard all our private things under the moon's steady gaze. Something about the quiet night brings me peace. I don't need to think about Dad or Malaga or school or the wound at my wrist. Right here, right now is all that matters. Tomorrow can cram its worry into me. But tonight I allow calm to reach inside of me.

My eyes open to the dark just before my alarm clock has a chance to bleat its five a.m. call. I feel Reed behind me, his limbs tucked against all my curves. I bask in his heat. I'm sorry for lying to him, and I press my weight into his frame, enough to feel his warmth spread against mine but not enough to wake him. Not yet. No part of me wants to separate from his rest just yet. In a few minutes we'll both need to get up, get out on the water.

I close my eyes to his breathing, its steady rise and fall. In and out. The warmth of his lungs expelling and falling into my hair. In and out. Push and pull. I focus on it so singularly that his breathing is the only sound that fills my ears until his breathing becomes louder. Deeper. It's not a snore, but something fuller, greater. As if the very room expands with his breath, retreats with his inhale. I dart open my eyes. The white noise of his breathing crams my ears. Reed's snoring is never this loud. No one's breathing can be this loud. I reach my hand down to his arm slung over my waist and want to shake him awake. Stop the noise. Quiet the room, my head. But my hand slips over his skin and feels the cold of him. The shocking, blinding cold. Cold in the way no living skin has the right. I turn in my bed to face him, shake him, wake him. But it's not Reed who lies against me.

Her eyes dart open as if I've woken her, as if I'm the one who startled her. The girl is next to me. The one from the shore, the one from the deep. Her black eyes stare at me, asking a question I can't answer. She smells of the sea, this girl. Her coarse black braids hold the sweet scent of the wind, the salt of the ocean. My heart thuds in my chest and my brain struggles to make sense of my room, my bed, this girl here with me. My fingers rake at the sheets, trying to find the edges, trying to free me from the bed.

My legs kick. My frantic arms push distance between us. Then she speaks.

"I'm here," she tells me. Her voice is gravel and water. It holds a slippery hoarseness that shakes the words she pushes over her full pink lips. In her breath is something more, the dank earth, the smell of rooted plants. She opens her mouth wide and on her tongue sits the perfect blinding orange cup of a Flame Freesia.

I scramble out of bed, throwing my covers over her as I rip free from my sheets. The scream in my chest won't rise or gather sound. Because something about me trusts her. Wants to know why she's here. Wants to know: why me? I press my back to the corner of my room, the windows and the sea behind me, the lump of this strange girl in my bed. Her body and face are hidden by the mess of my blankets, but her dark braids swim over the stark white of my pillowcase. They are seaweed and earth and hair, plaited together.

"Who are you?" I whisper, daring her to speak again. Daring my brain to make this real. I press a hand to my head, try to keep my mind from slipping. As if it is that easy.

Questions race as I wait in the silence for her response. Nothing comes. I fill the quiet with a mantra, the repeated *youarenotreal, youarenotreal, youarenotreal*. Is this how it happened for my mother? Uninvited, persistent hallucinations that grew into something bigger, harder to push away?

I shove the heels of my palms into my eyes, pushing away the vision of the girl in my bed, pushing away any connection to my mother's lost grip on reality. This has to be a dream. I just need to wake up. I stand, force my dream self to press harder against the wall, my fingers clawing at the plaster, as if I can escape this room and this nightmare by sheer force. The room quiets. The house quiets. The only breath is my own, so I squeeze closed my eyes. I open them. Slowly, carefully.

The girl is gone. I force a small step toward the bed and hover my hand over the impression her body made. My heartbeat thunders under every inch of my skin. I slip my hand along the comforter, the places where her outline still shows. The quilt is cold. Winter cold, and I shiver. I rip the cover off my bed, let it collapse into a heap on the floor.

I step back. My hands reach behind me, feel for the lip of the window seat, and I lean against its dependable wood. I force my breathing to calm, try to pull myself back to reality. It was another dream. It had to be a dream. I grab harder to the seat's sill, trying to ground myself in the now, wake myself from a nightmare.

I pull in my breath, force it out. Pull it in, out. I listen to the waves, the tide rolling and receding, rolling and receding. I match my breath to that of the sea. I pull the wet air into my lungs, remind myself that this is home and I am okay.

Behind me the sea calls, its force beating at the shore.

It was nothing but a dream.

Light begins to stream into my room from the rising sun. Just a soft wink of pale yellow at first. The waves grow louder, churning harder. I turn to see the whitecaps pounding into the shore and then I tumble back.

The girl is here.

In my window.

Perched on the trellis the way Reed has done so many times. She is all head and shoulders, her legs unseeable on the rungs of the ladder. My heart thumps loud as the exploding waves, but I don't move.

"Who are you?" My words are a desperate plea.

The girl—this *real* girl who is no dream—puts a finger to her lips. The skin around her nail is rough red from the abrasive sea, the battering cold. Dirt clings under her nails. "Shhh." She whispers now, this soft command floating out from behind her raw finger.

I don't scream. I can't scream.

I want to run from my room.

But I want something more.

Something bigger than my fear.

I want her to tell me who she is, what she wants from me.

I memorize her every feature. Her braids long and black, as shiny as deep-water seaweed. They fall around her shoulders as if she were underwater. Except in one place. One side of her hair is matted, like she spent the night sleeping on that side. No, not matted. Flattened, smashed. One side of her skull is sunken. There's a scrape along the flesh of her bottom lip, a deep cut that will take a long time to heal. Her mouth opens. I hold my breath, waiting for her words. Waiting for this girl to speak. Waiting for madness to take me. My body tightens with the need to yell at her, tell her to go away, but the word that forms is "Please."

She turns and drops down the trellis. I bend through the window, my eyes tracing her every step as she disappears under the still dark space under the maple tree, tendrils of her dress fading, vanishing.

Even though I feel her here still. Panic sends me to my bedside, searching the pillowcase where she'd lain her head. I'm careful with my movements, precise not to disturb the blankets. I scan the pillow. See a tangle of the girl's few long hairs. The clump is thin and wavy but with something stuck to its end. Dirt? It flakes off when I touch it, caking apart like dried blood.

She is real.

The girl.

Or, she *was* real.

I return to the window. Slam it closed. I shut my room tight so it's only me and my memory of the girl.

And that's when I see the orange bloom she's left behind.

But it's not the flower that chills my nerves. It's the words scratched into the wood of my windowsill.

FIND ME

CHAPTER TWELVE

I take to the sea, knowing I can't keep my private things quiet any longer. I need Sam's help, and I need to figure out how to ask for it.

"You look sore," I tell Sam when he climbs slowly aboard the *Rilla Brae*. The sky has let go of the dark, the sun carving out the line of the horizon. I'm late getting on the water. It took too long to recover from the girl's visit, the flower she left behind.

Sam leans back, one hand crooked against his hip, like a man four times his age. "I've never ached so much in my life."

"First days on the water are tough."

"You Mainers and your understatements."

I offer him my thermos. "It's meadowsweet and marshmallow root. It'll help soothe your joints and muscles."

"Do you have a vat of it, then?"

"There's always more if you need it."

He takes the hot tea as I put the *Rilla Brae* in gear, head out toward the first string. I watch Malaga until it slips behind us. Its shores are empty today, but I think the girl is here. In the sea below us? Watching me from somewhere I can't see? A chill rakes my spine, and somewhere in my exhaustion I feel an unprecedented surge of pride for my mother. For her realizing that she needed help, and for seeking help. For dealing with her slippery thoughts the only way she knew how. Maybe she needed help to protect what was real: me, Dad, her mother. In this flutter of pride I think maybe she walked away to spare us, save us. In this moment I'm grateful to her. In this moment I begin to understand how walking away could have equaled love. Protection.

"So I woke up with the profound desire not to slow you down today," Sam says.

"You didn't slow us."

"Again. Mainers and their understatements."

"Okay, maybe yesterday was a little slow. But that only makes us even."

"How do you figure?"

"I didn't get you back to the island like I promised. You missed a whole day of scientisting."

He gives a deep, full laugh. "Scientisting, huh? Real serious stuff." He blows at his thermos cup. "I didn't feel like I was missing out on anything yesterday. It's important to me that your gram knows she can trust me out here, even if I don't know what I'm doing."

"You'll know more in eight hours. We've got a hundred traps to haul and rebait."

"Then what are you waiting for?" Sam sets his mug onto the console and pulls on Dad's rubber overalls. I'm oddly comforted by the enthusiasm in his voice, and the rubber boots on his feet.

I navigate around the buoys in this swath of water, careful not to catch a line in my propeller. Settled by the fact that Old Man Benner's buoys aren't anywhere near my strings today. There are a few boats already pulling pots. I don't miss the way each lobsterman's chin raises at Sam, trying to get a better look at this stranger from away.

We haul and reset most of my traps by late afternoon, and though I'd love to get another dozen in the water, I head to the wharf.

"Calling it a day?" Sam says.

I maneuver my boat against the wharf. I throw her into neutral, cut the engine. "I don't want to be the captain that doesn't keep her promises. I need to get you out to Malaga." But it's my need that draws me to Malaga.

"Aye, aye." Sam hops off the boat, gives Hoopah a high five as if he's been doing it for years.

I let Sam do the off-loading. He's a fast learner, and that's everything I need right now.

"Good ta see ya, Rilla." Hoopah climbs aboard, leans his back against the wheelhouse.

"It's good to be seen." I toss the remnants of the chum buckets overboard. The gulls screech, their long wings and fierce beaks fighting each other for the bloody fish that coat the water. I spray the bait containers semi-clean, tuck them back into place.

"Good day on the water?"

"Getting there."

"Looks like ya help's working out." He throws a nod in Sam's direction. "I remember the first day ya helped ya dad at sea. Never seen a man with more pride."

I was barely four and remember it only from pictures. "A long time ago."

"Time's a tricky thing, Rilla. Feels like yesterday ta me."

Time is the trickiest of things. The way the girl reaches me across time, across death. The way it feels like maybe I've known her before.

"Ya need to stay on the water."

"How's that?"

"Old Man Benner's got his eyes on ya fishing grounds."

I clean the chum knife with a rag, hang it next to the ruler. "I'm aware."

"Then ya know ta be careful."

"I will, Hoopah. I appreciate you looking out for me."

"I owe your fathah a hundred favors or more, Rilla."

And I see the loyalty in his eyes, that spark of remembering, of never forgetting. I want to know if the girl had someone looking out for her too. Or is she asking me to remember? Because no one else has?

"He'd appreciate it, Hoopah. You know he would."

"Hope so, Rilla. Hope so."

Sam reboards the boat, hands me today's weigh-in slip. Four hundred and eight pounds. "Not bad."

Hoopah lets out a laugh that soars up from his middle. "Ya right about that, Sam Taylah." He wags his finger at Sam but says to me: "Ya got yourself a good sternman there, Rilla, and I'm glad ta see it." He shakes his head like he's letting the last bit of laughter break free. Then he sucks his lip between his teeth, lets out a whistle that calls his dog to his side. "See ya tomorrow, Rilla."

"Tomorrow."

"See ya." Sam waves, still enthusiastic, even though every inch of him must ache.

I navigate away from the dock, and Sam moves to the back of the boat, readies our lines for tomorrow's run. When I near the shores of Malaga, I put the engine in neutral, let the tide slide us toward the University of Southern Maine boat. My mouth plays with the question that's been on my mind since reading the girl's plea. "Sam?"

Sam's rinsing his hands overboard, wringing the day's work from his fingers. "Rilla?"

"How would it be if I helped you on the island?" This is the easiest way to ask for help that I know—by offering it.

"Malaga?"

"Are you digging on another island?"

He laughs. "No." He slips off his coveralls, hangs them in the wheelhouse. "It's just that . . . I don't know . . . You always seem like you're kinda in a rush to get off the island."

"Maybe." Definitely. "But not anymore. Not since I read your research."

Sam reaches overboard to grab his skiff, drops over the edge and into his boat. He waves me aboard. "I'd dig it if you worked in the dirt with me, Rilla Brae." He gives me a soft wink and I laugh.

I wish I were brave enough to tell Sam about the girl, her request. And how I think she was from here. That I think the island might have more than artifacts buried. That secrets are restless on the island. I drop anchor, strip off my Grundens, and join Sam in his boat.

At the site, Sam hands me a trowel no different from

the kind Dad used for masonry work around our property. He shows me how to carve out small sections of earth with a gentle hand, then screen the dirt for remnants of buttons, glass, tobacco pipes, anything that wouldn't come by the dirt naturally.

Maybe to find the answers, I need to know everything Sam knows, the truths that might exist outside of photographs and articles and the eviction notice. Then maybe I'll be able to tell him about the girl's visits, her song. I want the whole puzzle of the story, so I start with one piece as I sift a small dollop of earth against the thin metal lines of a screen.

"My best friend, Hattie . . . her grandmother remembered what happened out here."

Sam leans back from the edge of the site, rests his forearms on his thighs. "Tell me." His eyes are hungry.

"Hattie's nan told Hattie about the islanders being taken to Pineland."

"'Taken' is a nice way to put it; 'forcibly committed' is more accurate."

"Yes, right." The faces of the children crowd my head. Which one didn't know what a telephone was? Who was that boy who spent four decades locked in an institution because he couldn't identify an object that had no function in his island life? The girl would have known that boy, all the children. They would've been family, in the way of island living. "Hattie's nan told her she regretted it, what was done to the people here."

Sam's eyes narrow. "Regretted it how?"

My screen empties of dirt and I let it hang from my grasp. "She told Hattie she was sorry she didn't have more love in her heart. I can't let that go, you know? That she was sorry, like it was a personal regret."

"What are you thinking?"

I sculpt out another small chunk of earth, easy with my blade as I slice. "I'm thinking Hattie's nan knew what was happening on these shores and was complicit, or her family was complicit. I think she was basically telling Hattie that maybe if she had had more love in her heart, she might have tried to stop what happened out here. At least, that's what I want to believe." I see Hattie's nan hovering over me, straightening my uniform, always making triple certain I looked proper for Brownies— even though she knew Gram already did the same for me before I left the house. "She would've been really young then, though. Maybe ten or twelve years old." I want her youth to exonerate her from the crimes that were committed.

"The population here was pretty small then, and word would have traveled by gossip. She likely heard about it at a community gathering."

"Or over supper."

He nods.

Everyone on the mainland would have known what was happening eighty years ago. The news articles didn't print themselves, and they were too salacious to have gone unread. And what about Gram's parents? Did they want the islanders gone? Dad always taught me to judge a person by their capacity for kindness and nothing else, but this was an entirely different generation of men.

Men who evicted other men. And their families.

"I think most mainlanders wanted the island cleared by the time the order of eviction was served. Malaga became a local embarrassment after Boston papers started running articles and photos. But I don't think it was always that way."

"It couldn't have been. Malaga residents were left in peace for decades, no different from other island communities around here." I sift the dirt clear of the excavation site, watch small bits drop through the fine screen.

"And the people probably would have been left alone if the island itself wasn't so desirable. It seems like all the research agrees on that one point in the end—that the racial and economic tensions regarding Malaga really boiled down to the fact that the mainland saw a chance for developing tourism to the island."

"*That's* the shameful part of this whole story. That an entire culture could be erased so someone could build a hotel. It feels like the shame should sit with the state, the developers, the mainlanders—not the people of Malaga or their descendants."

"Power of the press, right?" Sam uses a brush to smooth away dirt from the exposed wrought iron.

The grate looks so familiar to me now. I recognize it. My adrenaline rushes, bringing satisfaction for connecting one small piece of this island's history.

"Sam." I'm not sure why I didn't make the connection before. I grab his moleskin from my pack, open it to the photo of the empty schoolhouse decorated for Christmas. I point to the child's desk in the foreground, its ironwork legs identical to the ornate metal Sam excavates.

"I know. Pretty cool, right?"

"You're not surprised?"

He shakes his head.

"But you said you didn't know what it was."

"I don't. I won't know for absolute certain until it's above the earth."

A not-so-small part of me deflates. The part that was hoping I could discover some long-forgotten piece of this island's story. "I hope that's what it is. I want some part of the school to survive out here."

"Hope is an important thing, Rilla. I think the missionaries who raised money for the school had a lot of hope. The school probably represented hope to the residents."

"Until it was taken away."

"Yes, well, I'm not sure the school or the islanders could have suffered a different fate."

I feel cold breath on my neck, the same biting cold that joined me in bed this morning. I turn to see the girl, but there's no one. Still, the shiver climbs inside of my bones. "Why do you say that?"

"Discrimination is discrimination. Racism is racism. There's no getting it right when one group thinks they're inherently superior to another."

"But the islanders were institutionalized. That's the part I can't get my mind around. Why take their freedom away? Why lock up innocent people?" Why lock them in a place where people were sent to be forgotten, and worse?

"Malaga Island residents weren't innocent, Rilla. They were immoral, living out of traditional wedlock. Shiftless. You read the articles."

"You can't possibly believe that propaganda."

"Of course not, but it's important to contextualize our findings in this field. And back then, difference was unacceptable. Mainstream society didn't know how to look at the poor or disabled any other way. So they built warehouses—institutions—to store people away. They believed they were removing a danger to middle-class values."

"But the middle class was the danger. The islanders probably knew that on some level, don't you think? That's why they lived off the grid."

"Probably."

"So how could no one from the mainland dissent? Your research doesn't include even one document that defended the rights of islanders to stay on Malaga." It was their home, where generations buried their dead.

"I'm certain many people objected, but their voices didn't make headlines. The summer residents—the people so invested in clearing the island—had more money and power than all the families on the peninsula put together." He pulls back his brush, looks to me. "And think about it. If you're sold a picture of what progress looks like—a shiny new hotel on the private Malaga shores, and this hotel will bring jobs for furniture builders, housekeepers, maintenance workers—well, that all sounds appealing. The hotel would be crammed with foreign visitors hungry for the freshest seafood. It would have been a pretty easy sell to get most people on the mainland to support that iteration of progress."

"They just had to clear the obstacles in their way." People. Families. Generations.

"Exactly. And what better way to dehumanize people than science? Eugenics boasted scientific evidence that proved poverty and degeneracy were heredity. We're talking about a time when the government legally sanctioned sterilization to stave off the spread of birth defects, immorality, poverty. Consider the particular racial makeup of Malaga residents during a time when interracial marriages were illegal by state law—these were all signs of depravity to many people back then. People who had more political and economic power than the islanders."

"People who had all the power." My strainer catches something. A shard. "Sam. I think I found something."

He sets down his brush, comes to my side. "Pottery."

It's a sliver of brownish-red glaze, the kind of earthenware Gram uses for floral vases. One-gallon jugs that once held milk, rum, syrups. I shake free the loose bits of dirt around the finger-length shard. Sam pulls tweezers and a plastic Baggie from his messenger bag.

He plucks the chip with the tweezers, rubs the remaining clay away with his thumb and forefinger. One side is dull gray, the interior of the pottery. The other, red and shiny—the glazed exterior. "See there." He points to a blue printed curve, the remains of a circle.

"The maker's mark."

"What remains of it." Sam examines the pottery, bringing

it close to his eyes. "This could be an early piece, Rilla. As early as the Civil War. You can tell by the glazing." He drops the broken pottery into the small bag and seals it. He scrolls something across the bag's top edge.

As Sam documents, I remember my mother gathering up the fragments of stoneware that washed up on our shore. Those broken bits of pots from the Water People were so precious to her. She collected them. Are they still in the house somewhere? Has Gram kept them?

"This is a great find, Rilla. I'll send it to the university for analysis, but there might be more if we're lucky." He nods to the dirt, and I shape out another clump of earth, add it to my sifter. But my mind is elsewhere.

The Water People. I shake the dirt in my sifter until there are only small, jittery rocks popping across the screen. I sit back on my heels, my breath so shallow, my heart racing. My mother looked for them when we'd walked the shore. But now I wonder if it was the Water People at all, or if it was one person. A Water Girl.

"I'm not gonna lie. Things like eugenics make me ashamed of the field of science. But that's why it's important to tell this story. It's been buried too long."

The girl. My mother. The Water People. Have our stories always been connected?

"This find could tell us something about the economic practices of the islanders, depending on where it was made. How the residents traded, bartered. We know the islanders were fishermen, but they were craftsmen, too. There was one particularly talented carpenter who worked on the mainland; another was a master mason. One islander was a pastor, or a deacon—we're not sure which—and he would provide sermons off-island."

Did my mother hear that same song? *Come here, come here.*

Is that what drew her to the deep on her last night at Fairtide?

"The people here never asked for handouts from the state." Sam presses a long, plain wooden marker into the ground where I discovered the pottery. "The islanders were a self-sustaining fishing community and weren't dependent on taxpayer support, so while they weren't wealthy, they did have a system of economy."

My dear, my dear. What are the words my mother called to the Water People while Gram held her? Did she talk to the Water People, or sing to them?

Did she repeat their song over the waves?

"Rilla?"

"Yeah? I'm here."

"The only form of welfare they ever received was that school, and no one out here asked for it."

I press my mind into the now. "Isn't education a basic obligation of the state?" I sink my trowel into the earth, feel the way it slivers its path through dense clay and small pebbles. I pull back another scoop, add it to my strainer. Sam watches the excavated bit of earth as it sifts, excited to see what will spill free.

"Yes, well. The governor twisted the gift, called it charity and used it as a tool to show mainland taxpayers that their hard-earned money was supporting the 'shiftless'"—he uses air quotes—"life of the islanders. The Malaga Island people had lived on this island for nearly a hundred years. The shell heaps out here tell us that they dug for mussels and ate what they caught in the sea. We have writing samples of the children, showing they were literate." He scoffs. "Most of them had better penmanship than me." He watches my strainer come up empty and he can't hide his disappointment. "They were totally self-reliant. They'd survived almost everything. Slavery in the south, impossibly bitter winters."

"Disease. Childbirth."

"Exactly. Their community was strong enough, vibrant enough, to attract immigrants from Europe. People who wanted to live life with freedom in their bones, no matter how much hard work that entailed. They endured hardships that would be unimaginable to us." His gaze drops to the marker in the ground before me. "But they couldn't survive greed. That's what it came down to in the end."

A gull calls from the shore, her throaty screech rising over the waves. The sounds Sam and I hear are no different from what islanders would have heard, the timeless call of the sea.

"Would you mind if I dug here too?" Sam asks.

I shift a few inches, make room for him at my side. "Have at it. You're the only one who knows what they're doing here."

He elbows me, a soft push. "I'd say you're doing just fine."

"Rill?" The voice comes from behind us, and I turn.

"Reed?" It's hard to make sense of him in this place. "You're here?"

"Good to see you, too." Reed's eyes dart from mine to Sam's.

Sam stands, gives Reed a short wave and a "Hey, man."

"Can I talk to you, Rill?" Reed looks at Sam. "Alone."

"Of course. Sure." I brush dirt from my knees and follow him to the beach.

When we reach the shore, Reed faces me, the rush of the lapping ocean biting near his heels. There's a heat coming off Reed that reminds me too much of his grandfather. "So yeah, I'm here. Mind telling me what the hell you're doing out here?"

I take a step back, search his face. "What's with all the aggression?"

Reed runs his fingers through his sunlit hair, and I watch it shimmer back into place. Such a contrast to the tightness of his face, the hard lines that make his mouth sour. "How should I feel about crashing whatever this is?" He throws an annoyed gesture toward the dig site. "How much time are you spending with this guy, Rill?"

"Sam. His name is Sam and he's my sternman and we're spending an appropriate amount of time together."

"Appropriate? You two looked pretty tight."

I cross my arms over my chest. Everything about Reed's attitude feels too harsh, too angry. "Do you want to save us both time and get to whatever it is you're actually accusing me of doing?"

He turns to the sea, the rainbow tips of lobster buoys speaking such an easy language, one we can't conjure between us now. "I'm jealous, Rill. Is that what you want to hear?"

"No, of course not. You have exactly zero reason to be jealous. I just needed . . ."

"Someone else."

"No. You know it's not that."

"Then what is it?"

I see the sadness in his eyes now, the need. I see my Reed, the person I used to trust with all of my private things. I take a deep breath and then let most of the truth escape. "I feel like home and routine and expectations are crushing me. My dad is everywhere, but he's not here anymore and there isn't anything I can do about it and that crushes me too."

He reaches for my hand. "I know."

"Coming here is just different. Sam doesn't know about my dad, so . . . I don't know . . . I guess I get to step out of my grief for a little bit. I know it's selfish, but I also know I need a little selfish right now."

"I get it. It's just . . . It's messing with my head, Rill."

"I'm pretty sure that's the pot." I try a smile.

"No. Actually, it's you being here with another dude. A dude I don't even know."

"Then get to know him. He's nice. I need Sam's help since my dad—"

"Fuck. I know. I'm a shit." Reed rakes his hand through his hair again, lets out a shaky breath.

"You're not a shit. You're just jealous when there's no need to be. Coming here is an escape, that's all. It's temporary."

"Yeah?"

"Yeah."

"You still love me?" Reed's eyes plead.

"I still love you."

"You're my moon, Rill. I want to be the one to help you."

"You can. You are. I just need a little space. Things are . . . complicated. You know."

"With fishing?"

Fishing. School. Grams. The girl who wants me to find her, the one who may have reached out to my mother and plays with my sanity now. The girl who might have the deepest connection to Malaga. "Fishing's part of it."

"Then let me help you."

"You know you can't." Our pact. No talking politics or fishing between us. I move my finger back and forth between our chests. "What we have wouldn't survive if we mixed in business. We both know that."

"Maybe." He hugs me to him, kisses the top of my head, his lips warm. "I just miss you, Rill. We barely hang out anymore."

I realize for the first time that I haven't told Reed that I'm considering deferring college, maybe not leaving Gram at all. Why haven't I told him? There is so much I haven't told him. "I miss you too."

"Can I come by tonight?"

I almost say yes, but I don't want anyone visiting but the girl. I won't be afraid this time. I'll listen to her. Maybe ask her if she knew my mother, if she knows the Water People. If she is a Water Person. "Tomorrow would be better."

"Not for me."

I tickle him at his ribs. "This isn't all about you."

Reed separates us, but holds my waist at arm's length, a sly smile at his lips. "Why not? Why can't it all be about me?"

I smile.

"You're sure this"—he thumbs toward Sam's site—"isn't anything to worry about?"

"I promise there's nothing to worry about." I tell Reed this full truth. I don't want to hold Sam the way I'm holding Reed. Still, I'm hungry for the way Sam makes the world new for me, the way he's my only connection to the girl right now. And maybe, to my mother.

Reed sets another kiss to my forehead. "Your moon?"

"Always."

When I return to the dig site, Sam's working the area of soil that held the small piece of redware. "Everything okay with the boyfriend?"

"More than okay." But is this really true? Why have I been holding so much back from Reed?

"Is it me?" Sam's rolling the earth on his screen so that the loose pebbles circle the edges.

"No. And yes."

"Complicated?"

"What isn't?"

"Too right." Sam gives a short chuckle. He stands, comes to my side. He smells of the sun and the sea and the salted earth, so much that's familiar. "But us spending time together complicates things more for you? Because I kind of get the vibe that there's a lot that's complicated for you, and I don't want to be the person who adds to that."

"You're not." Reed is. I am. This island, it's history.

"You're sure?"

"I'm sure."

"That's good to hear, because I would *totally* lose in a fight with that dude."

A soft smile spreads across my face. "It won't come to that."

"My ego thanks you."

"Sam? I do need to get home. There's this . . . well, I need to talk to my gram." There's only six weeks until the start of school.

"About Malaga?"

"No. A private thing."

He takes a step back, nods me toward Fairtide. "Then what are you still doing here?"

CHAPTER THIRTEEN

When I return home, I shower and get a text from Hattie: Did any Coast Guard hotties board your boat today?

Me: sadly, no

Hattie: What a waste

Me: why do I even bother going out to sea?

Hattie: IKR? Unless you can lick the face of one of those GORGE boys, what's the point????

Me: ☺

It feels good to joke with Hattie. Do the normal things like everything is normal.

I brew St. John's Wort for mental clarity.

I ask Gram to the small front parlor so she's away from her kitchen, the chores that keep her busy in that space. I need her full concentration.

Our parlor was created when formal visits were customary.

I know the walls have heard their share of difficult conversations. Births, deaths, hardships, and celebrations. Maybe even discussions on the fate of Malaga Island residents. Did my ancestors support profit or humanity? I want to think the latter, but I know it's naive. Every early Maine settler fought hard against the harshness of the climate. I've always believed that the struggle against the elements was enough to unite us along the coast, even today. But Malaga's history tells the opposite truth.

Gram joins me, takes a seat in the wingback chair. I grew up knowing the story of each one of our well-used antiques, but that chair was different. I was young when it arrived from Portland, brought by an elderly man who drove it to our doorstep saying Gram's grandfather had saved his family from starvation when that old man was a small boy. I remember the story not making sense: How could the thin, wrinkled man with his missing tooth and heavy limp have ever been a young boy?

That man told me and Dad and Gram about the winter my great-grandfather stocked his family's shed with salted cod and crammed their cellar with potatoes. I want to believe my family helped the islanders in a similarly charitable way. Or maybe the islanders helped my family.

The old man said he could never repay the debt, but wanted to give us a chair he'd crafted with his own hands nearly sixty years ago. And his chair was beautiful. My small fingers traced the carvings on the dark wood arms, followed the lines of intricate fish forever swimming upstream within that wood. It was a year later when I found my great-grandfather's name carved into the inside of one of the legs. NATHANIEL IKABERTH MURPHY: SAVER OF MEN. I'd been under the chair looking for a rogue Lego but I'd found a piece of my family history. I never told Gram or Dad about his name being carved there. I liked thinking I had a secret tucked away in my very own house.

Now I think my family has always had secrets.

I pass Gram her mug, and she settles against the rise of the handcrafted chair. "Let's get to your business, Rilla. I'm not growing younger."

"I need you to tell me about our finances." Counting other people's money—making assumptions about what they can and can't afford—is something Dad raised me never to do. But now I'm asking after his money, what he left. "Can we even afford to send me to school?"

"You earned your scholarship. No one is going to take that away."

"But the other stuff? Paying the bills. Keeping the boat and the house."

She puts up her hand. "We've got enough to keep the boat and the house in good repair. We're not the richest folks, but we'll be all right."

"What does 'all right' mean?"

"It means ya need to remember that your scholarship is merit based, Rilla. The University of Rhode Island is offering to pay your tuition because they want you. Have ya ever known anyone in our family to steer off course once they set their mind to its particular coordinates?"

My mother. She steered way off course. "No, I haven't."

"Ya got a mind that's smarter than any I've come across yet. It seems to me ya already know the right thing to do." Her future is so tied to the choice I make. She'll have to survive more loss if I go.

"But how can it be that simple?"

"Nothing simple about it, Rilla. Ya leaving for Rhode Island will change everything." She stares at me with determination. "But we can handle change. Nothing we haven't done before."

"You'll be okay, like, we can afford the house? Hattie's mom can't keep the lights on most months."

Gram nods. "Well, Hattie's circumstances are . . . well, they are what they are. Our concerns are different."

"You can keep the lights on if I'm not fishing?"

She *tsk*s. "I can read by candlelight if it means the first person in our family going to college."

"Gram."

She waves me away. "Ya know what I'm saying, Rilla. I won't be around forever, and I'm not leaving this earth until I see ya with your next diploma. Ya hear me?" She shifts in her seat, leans forward. "My grandfather built this house before mortgages ever existed. I've got enough to pay my share of taxes to the government and keep the water flowing. I find I don't need much more than that. Your scholarship will cover your books and you'll have to earn your spending money same as always."

"I'll haul in the summers when I come home. Work during school breaks, even in the winter."

Gram sets down her mug, crossing her hands over her middle. "Seems like you've got it all worked out."

I don't have anything worked out. "Far from it."

"What is all this doubt ya have? Why are ya bringing this up now?"

"I miss him, Gram. I miss Dad. I know you do too, and I hate thinking of you here all alone."

"Being alone doesn't make a person lonely. You'll still be with me. No amount of distance can change that."

Gram's words make me think of my mother, gone for more than a decade. And me being too selfish to let Gram keep my mother with us by telling stories of when things were good. "Do you miss her? My mother?"

Gram gives me a startled look. "Every single day."

"Do you . . . talk to her?"

"She writes every now and then. I think it's hard for her, knowing that she's stayed away." Gram searches my eyes. "Can I ask why you're asking?"

So many reasons I never expected. "I was out on the island today, with Sam. I found a piece of pottery, the kind that washes up on our shore all the time." I pull in a deep breath, let it out. "It reminded me of her. The way she'd talk about the Water People. That's what she called them, right? The voices she heard."

Gram nods. "Yes."

"Did she ever tell you what the voices said?"

"No." Gram lowers her head. "I just know they were enough to drive her away."

"Did you ever hear the voices?"

Gram looks to me. "No, Rilla. That was a particular struggle only your mother had to deal with."

"Does she still hear them?"

"I think things are better for her now."

"Better now that she's not here?"

"Yes. Hard as that is, yes."

It's a hard thing to hear.

"Was it . . . ?" I search for the words. "Did she always talk of them? The Water People?"

Gram leans back, her whole body shifting into memory.

"No. She was a happy child, Rilla. I never had an ounce of worry beyond normal child-rearing concerns."

"So then . . . when did she start to hear voices?"

Gram's finger worries at her thumbnail. "Are ya sure ya want to know this, Rilla?"

"I'm sure."

Gram takes a deep breath, lets it out slow. "I started noticing her losing track of time, walking along the water when she was pregnant with ya. I'd heard her talking to the waves."

Pregnant with me? "What did she say?"

Gram shakes her head. "Different things. Nothing special. But it was her tone that always struck me. How she sounded like she was trying to soothe someone. At first I thought she was talking to ya while ya were growing inside her."

"Was she?"

"Maybe sometimes. But other times I'd listen to her and I knew I was only hearing half of the conversation. She talked like there was someone answering her. I could only hear silence, but your mother was hearing something else. I was real worried about her in those days. Your dad and I watched her near 'round the clock."

"Did she try to walk into the waves then? When I was inside her?"

A look of horror crowds Gram's features. "Oh, no, child.

Nothing like that. She loved ya, Rilla. She never would have hurt ya."

"But she did hurt me. She left and never came back."

Gram nods a quiet nod. "Yes, I'm sad to call that the truth. Things got worse for your mother in the years after ya were born. I saw her slipping away, and it was the hardest thing to watch."

After I was born. While she was pregnant with me. Was I the reason the Water People came to her? Am I to blame? "Sam's work out on the island, it makes me think how we're all connected in ways that we might not even know." In ways we don't even understand.

"I believe we are." Gram and her theory about bees pollinating our stories, our connectedness.

I'm about to tell Gram what I've learned about the history of Malaga, but how can I bring her any more sorrow? "You're sure you'll be okay if I go?"

"I'm an old woman, Rilla. I'll be fine knowing that you're living the life ya want to live." She comes to me and puts her hand to my shoulder, squeezing her love down into my bones.

"I think that means leaving." I place my hand on hers. "But not in the way she did. I'll be back, Gram. You know that, right?"

"I want ya to live the best version of your life, Rilla. Nothing could make me prouder."

I stand, hug my grandmother. We stay connected like that

for a long time, neither of us knowing exactly what the future will bring, but each of us willing to take a chance on it anyway.

When Gram disappears to the kitchen, the decision to leave feels too final, like there's no turning back. Dad used to joke about the loneliness of an empty nest, but he never could've expected that Gram would be left alone in our nest. Would he really still want me to go if he knew she'd have no one?

When I hear Reed's knock at the back door—three quick raps, like always—I jump. I try to see through the blur of time that fogs my days lately. Hadn't I told him I wanted to be alone tonight? That was only earlier today, wasn't it?

Then I fear something's wrong, the way a similar unexpected knock sounded at our front door the day Dad's boat was found at sea.

I dart to the kitchen, where Reed's handing Gram a bouquet of wildflowers.

"You staying for dinner?" she asks.

"If you'll have me."

"Always a plate for ya at our table, Reed Benner."

I go to him. "Everything okay?"

"'Course." He smiles a sleepy, lazy smile, his cheeks red. Same as his eyes.

Reed turns to Gram as she's perfecting tonight's chowder, adding the flaked haddock in last so it stays tender in the creamy broth. He suggests we eat outside, so we carry the place settings to the picnic table on the lawn, where we devour Gram's soup and watch the sun fade. The air is cool as it carries the breeze from the sea. Malaga sits in the distance, watching us. Sam's boat is still at its shores, and I can't help but wonder if she's there too, the lost girl. I remember the way my mother used to look out at the ocean, as if she wanted to be a part of it. But maybe she was staring at Malaga. Reed catches my gaze, follows it to Sam's boat, the island. I hate that I haven't told him everything.

When Gram slides her spoon to the bottom of her empty bowl, she wipes at the sides of her mouth and stands. She gathers up the salt and pepper, their tiny glass bottles *tink*ing as they marry in her grasp. "I'm going to paint and then retire."

"Good night, Gram," Reed says. "Dinner was delicious." He heads to the fire pit just off the deck.

I stand, give her a kiss good night. "Thank you. For everything."

"Being your gram is the most precious thing in the world, Rilla. Ya keep enough room in that head of yours to never forget that."

"I promise."

Gram goes inside and I clear our plates. When I return, Reed has already coaxed a quick, high flame from the dry pine kindling. I sit on the giant log placed fireside by my dad years ago.

"Everything okay?"

Maybe. I don't know. "Fine, why?"

He shrugs, pokes at the flames with a long branch. "You seem distant."

"You're stoned and *I'm* distant?"

He laughs. "Fair point." He adds a thick oak log to the flame, and the fire *whoosh*es under the weight of the new, dense wood. "You were quiet at dinner is all."

"I told you I was tired, that tonight wasn't a good night to come over."

"I missed you. Is that so horrible?"

"No. It's just . . . dinner was hard."

He sits next to me, his thigh pressing against mine. "How so?"

I lean my head on his sharp shoulder, feel the flame's heat trapped in his shirt, the smoke already burrowed into the fabric of his tee. Still, there's ice in the breeze, and I flatten my palms to the smoke of the fire pit, trying to warm my skin from the chill. "There's a lot I'm going to miss. My gram. Things like this, sitting here with you."

"Miss?"

"When I leave in August."

I feel his shoulder tighten, his back straighten. "That again?"

"What again?"

"College. Rhode Island. All of it. I just don't get why this place"—he gestures to the sea with his fire stick—"can't be good enough for you."

I sit up, meet his eyes. I don't want to have the conversation we've had a hundred times. Reed's never understood why I need to study business before applying my knowledge to the aquaculture industry here on Maine's coast. He wants me to train locally, get hands-on experience at the oyster farms and fisheries that line our coastline. And I know I could. It's just, I want to see more of the world, and is that such a bad thing? "Maine's my home, Reed. It'll always be the best place in the world."

He takes my hand. "So stay."

"You know I can't."

"You can, Rill."

I shake my head. "I can't. Not now."

"Especially now. With your dad gone." He swallows hard. "I want to see your gram looked after."

"And I don't?"

"'Course you do. It's just . . . I don't want you to go, Rill."

"I know." Leaving Reed will be hard.

The warmth of the fire spreads along my face. I reach my free hand to it, let the flames heat my palm, and there is a hint of something at Malaga's shores. A spit of fire.

"You don't *have* to leave."

"I have to leave." Gram's pride. Dad's pride. My college essays: one about what it means to be a first-generation college student, the other on the economy of sustainable fishing and balanced oceanic harvesting.

Another spark of flame rises on Malaga's shores. It multiplies, like tiny bursts popping up from the soil. I squeeze my eyes shut, knowing I'm tired, that the flames are warm and here and in front of me, not in the distance.

I hear Reed but don't hear him. I catch only a few words. "It's not the same, Rill."

I press my mind back into the moment. "What's not the same?"

"Look at you. You're here and you're not even here."

"I am." I use my elbow to pull his knee tighter against my leg.

"I don't know where your head is lately, Rill, but it's not with me. Ever since you started hanging out with that dude from away."

Flames grow larger on Malaga. Dancing upward and across. The small fires spread to reach one another, like children joining hands. I shake my head, shake the scene. The distant fire won't leave. The flames comb up the length of the shore, walk to the island's peak. The fire rages at the edges of the water, heat pushing against the cold, wet sea. I look to Reed, how his eyes are fixed on the same island and yet he says nothing.

He can't see what I see. The fire isn't real.

"I'm the idiot for thinking you'd stay here with me, with your gram."

"What?" It's not fair to Reed, the way I only half listen. I stand to see the rising blaze on Malaga.

"What is wrong with you, Rilla? You can't even listen to me for five minutes."

"I'm listening. I'm here." But I'm staring out at Malaga, Sam's boat still anchored offshore. Sam, still on the island. "I gotta go," I whisper. Check on Sam. Make sure the flames are only in my imagination.

"You said that. I just didn't think you'd ever be selfish enough to leave your gram."

"Wait, what?"

"You're gonna leave the same way your crazy mother did. Except you're worse because, if you leave, your gram will be all alone. Alone, Rilla. That's some cold shit. I didn't think you had it in you."

My brain pushes away all distractions. The flames, Sam on the island. I see only Reed. Hear only his words, their accusation. I know he just wants me to stay, but still . . . the anger that fuels his words feels deep. Brewing. "I think you need to go."

"Might as well. You're not even here. You can't stop fixating on that island for five fucking seconds." He stands, flicks his stick into the flames, and storms off. His words kick at me. I watch his shape disappear into the darkness, his silhouette fading beyond the swell of Gram's gardens.

I go to the dock, but there's no longer a reason to reach Sam. The fire has disappeared, if there was ever a fire at all. I hear the distant churn of Sam's engine, see his boat's safety lights pop green, red, white. I stand at the shore for a long time, wanting the fog to rise. I wait for the girl to sing to me. Or the Water People to talk to me. Wait for Sam to dock at Fairtide. Wait for the sting in my heart to settle. But none of these things happen. I grab a bucket from the dock and fill it with water to douse the flames in the fire pit.

Why did Reed really come tonight, after I told him I needed rest? Because it feels too much like he was checking up on me, making sure Sam wasn't here or something.

I wish he'd listened and stayed away. I wish he'd never gotten the chance to say his awful words, make me feel like I'm abandoning Gram instead of making her proud.

I go upstairs and press my hand to Gram's attic door as I head down the hallway, the light from her studio gathering around my feet as I stop and say my silent good night.

*　*　*

Later, a summer storm arrives. The wind feels confused, blowing from every angle, howling against its own groan. Waves batter the shore. I read through Sam's notes, looking still for my girl and maybe for anything that will help me make sense of what happened to my mother. What happened to the innocent fishing community of Malaga. I focus on Sam's notation about one of Malaga's residents:

> Eliza Griffin was by all accounts a fiercely independent woman who made her home from a detached sea captain's hull. She left behind many generations of wooden lobster traps, all in varying sizes and shapes. Archeologists use this as a map of lobster trap evolution.

There's no photo of Eliza Griffin, just a picture of the old ship's hull she'd made into a home. I think Gram and I would have liked to know Eliza Griffin.

I wonder if this fiercely independent woman is buried in a mass grave now.

I try to focus on more of Malaga's history, but I keep hearing Reed calling me selfish, accusing me of abandoning Gram. Being too consumed with the island just offshore and the flames

I clearly hallucinated. I Google "grief and hallucinations," "grief and schizophrenia." Anything that could give me a reason for my mind lately. But all I can hear is Reed criticizing me for being cold, his words repeating like a lash. And there's the ever-present fear that my brain is slipping. How can I even go to college if I'm losing my mind?

And then there is the tapping . . .

Tapping

Tapping

The maple tree's branch against the window. The glass is closed, doing its best to trap the whistling wind outside. Still the air in my room is swollen from tonight's rain. The light on my bedside table flickers on and off, on and off, before the generator's gas-fed engine rumbles to life on the lawn.

The limbs of the maple tree scratch against the panes as if asking—no, begging—to come in. I turn off the light to save power and read my screen until the scratching becomes relentless, thrashing against the glass so hard I think it will break the panes. I go to the window, and the moonlight shows me the gray bark of the wood, so thin and grizzled and yet thumping—slamming—against the window. I grip the sill, and my fingers crawl over the bumps in the grain, one groove leading into another. I know without a doubt what those cuts in the wooden windowsill say: FIND ME. But there's more. The grooves are too many. The markings in the wood call to me. *Come here, come here.* My fingers feel wet as they trace the indents. The sill gives off a warm heat, like steam from boiling water.

I gather my flashlight and train its light on the scratch marks.

There are new words scored into the wood.

DONT GO!

Fear rakes my spine, blanketing my bones with cold. Was the girl listening to me and Gram? Me and Reed? How is she everywhere and nowhere?

Is she here now? Watching me with her oil-dark eyes and seaweed braids? Or is she in her white dress, the way she appeared to me at the shore?

My heart races for this stranger being in my room. For the dragging lullaby that whines on the wind, for the thin, reaching tree limbs that tap at my window. *Tap. Tap. Tap.* The long gray branches extend to scratch the face of the window. But then, something more.

A branch at the bottom, one that doesn't rise or fall with the gusting wind.

Tap, tap, tap.

These wispy limbs are steady. Too steady. I take a step toward the window.

Tap. Tap. Tap.

And I see the fingers.

Five reaching fingers, drumming against the glass. Each nail caked with dirt, with cuts on the knuckles, the flesh.

It's impossible to pull breath into my lungs. My skin fires with the need to open the window. I take a step forward, my hand raised for the task. Something—or someone—is unsettled. Do I have the power to settle it? Make it right? But why me?

Tap. Tap. Tap.

I jump back, scramble to the opposite side of the room. I grab my phone, call Hattie. "Can you come over?" My voice is so loud, trying to drown out the tapping.

I pace the room as I wait, my eyes trained on the sill. I know Hattie won't judge me. She can tell me what's real, what's imagined. She can help me because I need help.

By the time Hattie arrives, the tapping has grown louder.

"Geez. Fierce storm." Her voice is so nonchalant.

I can't stop pacing. I watch Hattie's eyes, try to see if she can see the fingers, see if the tapping is overwhelming her, too. "I'm freaking out, Hatt."

"Over a storm?" She plops onto my bed.

Maybe. "Everything. This night. Staying. Leaving." Ending up like my mother. Now that Hattie's here, I can't make the words come. I can't admit my visions, my slipping mind.

"Tonight's nothing but wind. As for the other stuff, you're

smarter and stronger than a hundred fishermen. You'll figure it all out. Besides, you're psyched you're not at sea during this storm. You can hang with me and let it pass. You just need to chillax."

But I need so much more.

I need to show Hattie the carved words. I need to tell her who wrote them. But I can't see the look of doubt cover her face if I were to let the full truth slip.

"I've never know a storm to freak you out so bad," she tells me.

Even though I know this is so much more than a storm.

The fingers tap against the glass, reminding me.

CHAPTER FOURTEEN

The seas are rough today, as if the winds are still holding on to some of last night's storm. High swells batter at the sides of the boat and slosh water up over the rails.

I steady my stance as I throw open a pot and measure the catch. I band four lobsters and toss them in the tanks. Sam fills the bait bag, and I hook it to the top of the parlour within the cage, secure the trap shut. I'm surrounded by sea, but all I can think of are the words scratched in the wood of my windowsill. The words that were still there this morning.

FIND ME
DONT GO!

The words written by fingers that haunted at my windowpane. A girl who seeks me out across what? The veil of death? It's all too impossible to make sense of, and yet I try.

"That's disappointing," Sam says when he pulls up an empty trap.

"Can't think like that on a boat. We call it 'changing the water.'"

"Changing the water?"

"Sure, pulling up an empty trap drains it. Then we reset it with new water."

Sam laughs. "Fisherman's optimism."

"Something like that."

Sam goes to the back of the boat for a new bucket of bait.

My mind is too preoccupied when I take the lobster pot to the rail. I hold my fingers looped through the wire cage and stare out at the deep, its mysteries. I toss the cage to the waves and set the boat in gear.

The boat lurches forward.

The line catches my ankle.

Strangles.

I hop quick, trying to free my leg. The rope yanks at my foot. I squirm, reach my fingers for my ankle. I feel the rope there, the way it twists. I force my thumb underneath its coil, wrench at the twine. The rope only wraps tighter as the cage drags the line to the deep.

I reach for the throttle, but the rope pulls me hard. My tailbone slams against the slick deck. "Sam!"

The line chokes my boot. I fumble at the rope, try to separate my leg from the diving trap. My fingers slip on the wet. The rope jerks my leg straight over the edge.

Sam scurries to me. "Tell me what to do!"

"Throw the boat in neutral!" I twist, grab at the smooth wet floor. My gloves rake over the slippery deck. My leg hangs off the rail. The boat is too slick, so ready to give me over to the deep.

The motor calms. The boat stops.

"Rilla!" I see the black tips of Sam's boots. His steps are wild, panicked. "Rilla!"

My hips are wrenched to the edge of the boat. My hands scramble for anything, everything. The trap pulls me harder, my mind racing. There's no stopping a trap once it's set to the water.

"Sam! Help me!"

"Tell me how!" He pulls my arms. His legs slip out from under him. The trap tugs.

The boat flashes around me, the sea slamming, my panic rising. If I try to hold on to any part of the boat, I'll rip my arms from their sockets. I try anyway, but the cage is at home in the sea, and it pulls my hips over the edge. The buoy whips against my back, needing its dive into the water.

Sam reaches for my slipping, scratching hands.

"Knife!" I scream. My chest gets dragged over the edge.

The line chokes my boot. I fumble at the rope, try to sepa-rate my leg from the diving trap. My fingers slip on the wet. The rope jerks my leg straight over the edge.

Sam scurries to me. "Tell me what to do!"

"Throw the boat in neutral!" I twist, grab at the smooth wet floor. My gloves rake over the slippery deck. My leg hangs off the rail. The boat is too slick, so ready to give me over to the deep.

The motor calms. The boat stops.

"Rilla!" I see the black tips of Sam's boots. His steps are wild, panicked. "Rilla!"

My hips are wrenched to the edge of the boat. My hands scramble for anything, everything. The trap pulls me harder, my mind racing. There's no stopping a trap once it's set to the water.

"Sam! Help me!"

"Tell me how!" He pulls my arms. His legs slip out from under him. The trap tugs.

The boat flashes around me, the sea slamming, my panic rising. If I try to hold on to any part of the boat, I'll rip my arms from their sockets. I try anyway, but the cage is at home in the sea, and it pulls my hips over the edge. The buoy whips against my back, needing its dive into the water.

Sam reaches for my slipping, scratching hands.

"Knife!" I scream. My chest gets dragged over the edge.

smarter and stronger than a hundred fishermen. You'll figure it all out. Besides, you're psyched you're not at sea during this storm. You can hang with me and let it pass. You just need to chillax."

But I need so much more.

I need to show Hattie the carved words. I need to tell her who wrote them. But I can't see the look of doubt cover her face if I were to let the full truth slip.

"I've never know a storm to freak you out so bad," she tells me.

Even though I know this is so much more than a storm.

The fingers tap against the glass, reminding me.

CHAPTER FOURTEEN

The seas are rough today, as if the winds are still holding on to some of last night's storm. High swells batter at the sides of the boat and slosh water up over the rails.

I steady my stance as I throw open a pot and measure the catch. I band four lobsters and toss them in the tanks. Sam fills the bait bag, and I hook it to the top of the parlour within the cage, secure the trap shut. I'm surrounded by sea, but all I can think of are the words scratched in the wood of my windowsill. The words that were still there this morning.

FIND ME
DONT GO!

The words written by fingers that haunted at my window-pane. A girl who seeks me out across what? The veil of death? It's all too impossible to make sense of, and yet I try.

"That's disappointing," Sam says when he p[u] empty trap.

"Can't think like that on a boat. We call it 'changing

"Changing the water?"

"Sure, pulling up an empty trap drains it. Then with new water."

Sam laughs. "Fisherman's optimism."

"Something like that."

Sam goes to the back of the boat for a new buck

My mind is too preoccupied when I take the lo the rail. I hold my fingers looped through the wire ca out at the deep, its mysteries. I toss the cage to the w the boat in gear.

The boat lurches forward.

The line catches my ankle.

Strangles.

I hop quick, trying to free my leg. The rope foot. I squirm, reach my fingers for my ankle. I f there, the way it twists. I force my thumb undern wrench at the twine. The rope only wraps tighter drags the line to the deep.

I reach for the throttle, but the rope pulls me h bone slams against the slick deck. "Sam!"

Sam presses something into my palm. I latch on as I take a deep breath, my last before my body is pulled into the ocean.

The rope wrenches me toward the sea bottom. Salt water rushes up my nose, down my throat. Choking me. "Rilla!" Sam's muffled cry reaches me from another world.

Bubbles rise all around me, rushing over my arms, my head, my hands. *My hands.* There's something in my grip. My fingers move over its form. The sharp blade used for chopping chum. I grab rope at my ankle, twisting and fighting the sea. I slice hard and fast through the twine, over and over, but precision is slippery in the dark water and my lungs are too full. I'm out of oxygen. I need to breathe. The knife slips from my grasp. I can't see the light of the surface anymore. Can't hear Sam. There are no traces of the sun down here.

I'm floating now. Free from struggle.

This is the sea.

My home.

Peace visits me, as if the world has gone quiet for a full, beautiful moment and I can, too. If only I rest. Rest. The sea presses at me with her cold, swallowing me and my collapsed chest. I thrash one last time against the deep when I see the lobster trap rising below me. It's on its way back to the surface, and a voice tells me to hold on.

The voice starts yelling. Screaming. *Don't go!*

It's a high voice, a girl's voice.

My girl's voice.

Two words ripped through the water from some other place, some forgotten time.

Then another sound reaches me. Another sound that has no business rising in the deep. The sweet soft melody of the lullaby: *Come here, come here. My dear, my dear. If you come near you'll find me here.* She's here with me now. My girl. The lost girl. Under the water with her kelp braids and her song.

I call to her for help, my last push of stored breath. Bubbles explode around my mouth, my cry distorted, muted by the sea. And then I'm being hauled, my body rising through the layers of water pressing down on me, crushing my lungs, my head. My hair swirls around my face like twisting seaweed. I see myself from a great distance, from some faraway place. I see the girl and me, how we share the same eyes. And something more?

I'm propelled up through the water inch by inch. The dark ocean layers fade to sea-glass green. Then sun. Its light just above the surface. I reach for its warmth, kicking my legs against the drowning depths.

My body breaks through the top of the waves and my lungs pull in the beautiful light air. Air. All around me. In me. Someone's arm is on me, under me, dragging me aboard the boat. This person turns my head, forcing the water to spill out of my mouth. I cough it from my lungs. I purge the salt from my stomach. And everything goes black as the under ocean. In the darkness, I hear the girl singing. *If you come near you'll find me here. My dear, my dear.*

My voice cracks over the words: "Don't go."

And Sam's voice. "I'm here, Rilla. I'm not going anywhere."

By the time we reach Fairtide, I'm able to gather the strength to walk to the house. I won't let Gram see me sea-beaten and broken. Sam offers his arm as I climb off the boat. The arm that dragged me onto the deck, turned me on my side, saved my life. I softly dismiss his hand with the brush of mine. "I can't worry my gram."

"I think that might be an impossible request." Sam holds his fingers at my lower back, there to catch me if I slip. Again.

Gram meets us in the middle of the lawn. Worry distorts her face. "What has happened to ya, girl?"

I force normal into my voice, but the salt has charred my throat. "I had a little accident, but I'm fine now." My words are deep, scratched things.

Gram tucks her shoulder under my arm and walks me to the house. Sam follows. My grandmother's strength is as solid as the granite in the earth. Lasting, resilient. "Tell me where ya hurt. Your head? Do ya think ya have a concussion?"

"I didn't hit my head."

It feels as if my blood is leaving me, draining out through my feet. I lean on Gram and she lets me. My rock.

"Sam, tell me what happened." With every step that Gram takes, me at her side, I grow smaller, lighter, weaker. So weak that maybe if I close my eyes I'll disappear. Gram squeezes my waist, and I pull myself up, gather my strength for her.

"She got her foot caught in a line and was pulled overboard."

I hear Gram's heartache escape in a dull breath. And something like a mumbled prayer? "How could ya let that happen, Rilla?"

"It was an accident."

She holds me closer. "An accident or a sign? You're doing too much. Your head is in too many places."

She doesn't even know the truth of it. "I'm fine, Gram."

"You're as white as flour, and your eyes are swollen with bloodshot. I'd say you're the picture of not fine."

She and Sam walk me up the stairs. Gram at my side, Sam behind us both.

I fold onto my bed. Gram raises my feet, settles them onto my mattress. She waves Sam to work. "Get that pillow under her head, nice and easy." Sam does. He's gentle with my neck, lifting it softly before sliding my pillow to cradle my pounding head. My brain spikes with pain, the sharp stabs of a million headaches. I raise my hand to my forehead, pressing against the ache at my temples, around the back of my skull. "That'll be the salt water in her system. Go to the kitchen and start a kettle with water, and don't be slow about it." Sam scrambles out of the room.

Gram strips off my soaked leggings and socks. She sits me up, pulls off my tee. I try to raise my arms like it doesn't hurt, and she slides on a fleece top that feels too heavy and too perfect all at once. She turns me on my side, folds down the covers, rolls me in. Her nursing is smooth and perfected, as if we do this every day. Over the blanket, she runs her hands along my shins, my thighs, my wrists, my arms. She presses her warmth into my bones. "Ya tell me right now if ya need a hospital. If anything feels broken."

"I just swallowed a little water. That's all."

"Hmmph." She glares at my understatement.

She should. Even now water fills my ears, my nose, my chest. I feel the salt in my pores, in my every battered throb. "I'll be okay."

"I know ya will. I won't lose ya, Rilla. I can't lose more." She looks away, trying to hide the tear at the corner of her eye. She pats my hand. "I'm gonna make ya some tea. We need to wash the salt water out of ya."

Tea. Such a normal thing. Gram's healing. Something I've always depended on. "Tea would be good."

I close my eyes and the room falls peacefully black. I'm too grateful for the mattress under me. Breathing air. Feeling warm. Gratitude surges in me, building tears that seep out from under my closed lids. They trail down to the pillow, each one a tiny river, so small compared to the sea. Almost insignificant. But not.

I'm not sure how much time passes before I open my eyes to Sam sitting at my side. He's pulled my desk chair near the bed. Close, but not too close. "You had us worried there," I tell him, my voice rough.

He lets out a deep sound of relief, half laugh, half heavy sigh. "Sorry about that."

"Don't let it happen again."

He shakes his head, a *tsk* in the movement. "Getting your foot caught in the line is a rookie mistake. You wouldn't catch me doing that; it's like Fishing 101."

I smile, and even that hurts. "I'll keep that in mind."

He leans forward, anchors his elbows to his knees. "Seriously, though. Don't do that again."

"Not planning on it."

Gram comes in, sets a mug next to my bed. Meadowsweet and chamomile for soothing the ache in my muscles, no different than aspirin would. She tucks a hot-water bottle under my blankets. Its rubber warmth bleeds against my side. "Does that feel all right?"

"Yes, perfect."

"Ya sure ya didn't hit your head?"

"Surer than sure."

She puts the back of her hand to my forehead as if the sea brought a fever. "I'm going to call Brower, see what he says about all this." Dr. Brower Walsh is our family doctor, but Gram calls him by his first name since she's known him since he was knee high to a grasshopper. Her words.

"He's gonna tell you I'm fine, Gram. I'm your seal, remember?"

Gram's eyes give me a sly smile. "That may be so, but Sam will stay with ya till I hear from Brower myself. And I'll make soup. Beans and onions. Warm the sea right out of your bones."

"That's exactly what I need."

Gram nods to Sam, and an understanding passes between them. She kisses my forehead, pats my arm again. "Ya stay fine until I come back, ya hear?" Her words crack with worry.

Sam waits a moment after Gram leaves. "What can I do for you?"

"I'm—"

"Don't even tell me you're fine. Even if you are, which I doubt, I'm not going against your grandmother's orders, so you're stuck with me. Might as well make me useful."

My headache sears the space behind my eyes. "Can you pull down the shades?"

"Done." He stands, moves to the window, pulls the blinds and drowns out the sun. He stands at the sill, unmoving.

"Sam?"

He turns, his fingers lingering on the sill. "What's this?"

I try to sit up but feel bruised everywhere. "Cover that. I don't want Gram to see."

His fingers trace the words: **FIND ME. DONT GO!**

"That shirt there." I point to a tee huddled on my desk. His look of confusion confirms that the words are real. "Please just cover it."

He does. When the carving is hidden, I lay my head back down. Just that short outburst drained too much of my energy.

Sam returns to his seat at my bed. "Did you write that?"

I shake my head.

"Who did?"

A tree branch. The long rattling fingers of the maple outside my window. A girl from the deep, the same girl that haunts the shore. Even in my head this sounds unbelievable. Truly mad. The institutional, all-white mad I've feared my whole life. The rocking-in-a-corner mad that is stitched into my DNA. "I don't know."

"You don't know who carved words into your windowsill?"

The heat from my tea carries flowers on its steam. Flowers kissed by bees. Bees exchanging stories.

"I do know, but it's kind of wrapped up in one of my private things."

"I won't press, Rilla. But if you need to talk."

I nod, knowing that talking to Sam is what I need. He can help me connect the girl—her song, her words, her persistence—to Malaga in the way that they must be connected. What would I have to lose? A sternman? Sam is the safest person to talk to because he won't be here after the summer; his roots aren't set down generations deep like the rest of us.

Gram returns and takes my temp old-school, under the tongue. She packs a second water bottle behind my neck. I close my eyes to this simple medicine, and the room is immediately darker, softer. My bones feel too rattled, but they are remembering their places too, as if settling under my skin as they tuck back into position. I hear my grandmother mumble something to Sam. I hear her leave the room.

Sam towels the wet strips of my hair, trying to wring the sea from me still. I sit up too quickly, and pain bolts through my head, up my spine. The way it rips through me brings fear, and I'm a child again, needing my father to tell his soothing stories about the seals that live in the sea and slough off their skins to walk as women onshore. Or the first people, the first fishermen—any of the stories he used to tell. I settle back onto my pillow, my head searing. "Sam?"

"Right here." He repositions the hot-water bottle behind my neck.

"Can you tell me a story?"

"What kind of story?"

"Any kind. When I was little, my dad told me stories whenever I got hurt, to draw my mind away from the pain." I need a story now, and maybe it's just the act of admitting this deep need that brings me calm. My mind begins to drift to the softened place of sleep.

Sam inches his chair closer, his movements a whisper. "Dragons or real life?"

"You choose." The answer sounds like *yew-choo*; my words hold a mumble in their edges.

Sam draws a short breath, lets it free. "Once upon a time there was a king. He was a grandfather, a father . . ."

Grandfather. Father. The words swim together in my head and wash me into blackness. Sleep. A restorative space. I want to hold on to his words. I want to grip at the pieces of his story, but I can't. The sea is pulling me under again, only this time it promises rest and I'm happy to go.

CHAPTER FIFTEEN

Hattie's text is waiting for me when I wake: you okay?

I text back: Fine

Liar

Me: ?

My phone rings immediately. Hattie. She doesn't even let me get in a "hello" before she starts.

"Don't tell me some bullshit about how you're okay. I saw you last night, and you were about the farthest thing from okay."

"You were here?" My brain reaches for this fact but can't pull it up.

"Just got home. But you're kinda proving my point, Rills. You were so out of it you didn't even know I sat by your bed for a gatrillion hours."

"How did y—?"

"Your gram called me. She was freaking out worried about you."

Gram. Of course.

"You freaked the shit out of me, too. Tell me you're okay."

"I am. I mean, I hurt all over, but I'm okay."

"You need to seriously stop stressing. Let your gram take care of you."

"I know."

"Do you? Because you've been going full throttle since your dad passed away, and everyone's worried about you."

"I know, Hatt. I'll be fine. Having you here the other night helped a ton. It was exactly what I needed."

"Then I'm coming over after work today."

"I'll be here."

"And Sam?"

"What about him?"

"Will he be there too?"

"I don't know. Why?"

"Is it a totally inappropriate time to tell you I think he's a hottie?"

I laugh, which makes my side stich with hurt. "Shut up."

"Never."

When I get to the kitchen, Gram eyes my uniform. "Ya will not haul today, Rilla Murphy Brae."

I cringe at Gram using my middle name. It's a fine name; it's Gram's family name. But it means she's triple serious. I adjust my shirt on my shoulders. My arms are sore with even this slight movement. "I won't fish. Don't worry. Couldn't even if I wanted to." Yesterday scared me, and I'm smart enough to know not to work the sea when there's fear in my bones. Still, I need to be on the water again, remind my memory—and my muscles—that I know what I'm doing on the ocean. But I make Gram a promise: "I won't haul."

"Hmph."

"I'm gonna check on the boat, make sure everything's tightened down after yesterday. I might take her for a short spin, but no fishing. I promise."

There's a deep crease in Gram's eyes, like a line carved itself there last night. *Don't go!* the line says. "A promise is your word, Rilla. And ya know your word is all you're worth."

I move to Gram, kiss her just above that worried line. I would do anything to take Gram's worry away. "I give you my word. No hauling. I won't even say the word 'lobster' today." I smile, trying to ease her concern. "Except for right then, when I said 'lobster.'" I bring my hand to my mouth, cover it. "Okay, now for real. I won't say it again all day. I will have exactly zero to do with lobsters."

Gram nudges her way past me, frustrated but convinced. "Fool girl. You're lucky I love ya."

"I am." I move to her, give her a deep hug. Even though my

muscles scream, I hold my grandmother so tight. "I know how lucky I am." Luckier than my father, whose heart gave out on the sea, luckier than so many men who've been lost to the deep. So lucky to have Gram as a mother and grandmother and so much more.

Gram pulls away, swats at me. "Go on and get out of the house, then. I'm not foolish enough to think I could stand in your way."

I slice off a hunk of fresh bread and make my way to the *Rilla Brae*. At the dock, I turn and see Gram watching me from the kitchen. I give her a wave, and my muscles chastise me for the chore. I raise my eyes to my bedroom window, see the reaching arm of the ancient maple tree even as I know it wasn't the tree that knocked at my window. It was the girl.

My girl from the sea and the shore.

The girl from Malaga.

I check all the lines on the *Rilla Brae*, each one tied in cleat hitch knots, pulled secure. Onboard, the chum buckets are clean, tucked neatly into a corner of the deck. The wheelhouse is prepped for fishing, all the instruments cleaned and stored properly. I turn the key and head out to sea. Sam's boat is moored off Malaga. I approach, drop anchor.

Sam's in his skiff by the time I've gathered my bag. "Wanna lift in my salty dog?" His expression as unsure as he is. He coasts his boat to a halt and grabs hold of my fender lines. "Can you climb on?'

"I can." I prove to myself that I can, even if my back hates me for the challenge.

"To the island?"

I nod. "Please."

"You're sure?"

I nod.

Sam doesn't row today; he uses the small five-horsepower engine to cut through the choppy waters. We don't raise our words over the motor's tinny roar. He rides the boat up onto the shore, beaching most of the skiff. Every movement jostles my aching limbs, but I climb out, my feet steadying on the ground.

"How are you feeling?"

"Grateful for your help yesterday." I give my lower back a small stretch. "Today would be very different if you hadn't thought to run the rope through the pulley. I'm indebted."

He doesn't meet my eyes, the scattered shells at his feet holding all his interest. "I'm glad I was there for you."

"Me too."

I've had too much time to think what would have happened if I'd been alone, the way Dad had been.

"I feel like your accident was my fault."

"Your fault?"

The sun on Sam's face brings out the red in his solid cheeks. "I distracted you, talking about a stupid empty lobster trap. That's why it happened."

"Not even." I was the careless one, my mind always in some other space lately.

"Your fall scared the shit out of me."

"I was pretty scared too."

He runs his fingers through his dark hair, and it cascades along the curves of his wide face like always. I feel him searching for words, struggling.

"How long did you stay yesterday?"

"A couple of hours." He looks to the sun spraying over the waves. "Just until your friend Hattie came over."

"Yeah, she called me this morning. I don't even remember her being there."

"You were pretty out of it."

"It was a shock to the system." The near drowning, the rescue. But more, too. The words scratched in wood, the undersea voice I heard as clearly as I hear Sam now. And Reed and his anger. Gram and her unending selflessness.

"Yesterday was crammed with its share of surprises."

"How do you mean?" I watch Sam, how he's intent on a gull diving for fish. "Sam?"

"Nothing. I shouldn't have brought it up."

"Technically you haven't brought anything up yet."

He turns to me then. "Your grandmother told me about your father."

"Oh." I'm not sure if this feels like relief or betrayal.

"She was really upset last night. Told me how you were all she had left. How your mom went away when you were really young. I had no idea, Rilla." He kicks at the broken shells. "I mean, I knew something was going on. . . ."

"What happened to my dad . . . it was recent. I haven't been okay to talk about it with anyone."

"I get that."

"And my mom isn't around because she needed some help from psychiatrists." I wait on his response. I wait for the taunts I heard as a kid, the way Reed called her crazy. But there is only Sam, listening. "I wasn't trying to hide it from you. It was more that I liked that you didn't know."

"Believe me, I'm a big fan of escapism." He picks up a razor shell, the kind Hattie and I would pretend to shave our legs with in the mudflats long before we had leg hair to shave. "But I talked about your dad like he was here, alive. God"—he taps the razor shell to his palm—"I must have sounded so disrespectful."

"You didn't. Not once."

"You have to know I never would've said anything about him if I'd known."

"I know, but I liked you talking about my dad like he was still here. You kept him alive in a way that was . . . unexpected."

"Yeah?"

"Totally. I guess I didn't want you to know about my parents because I didn't want you to treat me differently. My family's complicated."

"Whose isn't?"

No one's. Hattie's always had it harder with her mom. Reed lives with his grandfather because neither of his parents can stay sober even when they want to. It's kind of always been an epidemic among fisherman that no one talks about.

"I'm in Maine because my family got complicated."

"Not a dusty book?"

He gives a small laugh, and I'm grateful for its sound. "Complications and a dusty book."

"Tell me."

"You don't want to hear my story."

"I do." I move to a large rock, my legs needing rest. Sam sits next to me.

Against the harsh crash of the waves, Sam tells me his story. How it took nine years for him to be legally cleared for adoption. How the waiting on Child and Family Services nearly broke him, his family.

"I have a biological aunt who wanted custody. My parents

had no rights when they were foster parents so they had to let my brother and me go."

I know too much about foster care. So many kids I grew up with were raised by their aunts, grandmothers—or strangers who opened their homes to kids needing safe harbor. All because their parents struggled with demons and bad decisions. I haven't seen a lot of happy endings. "How old were you?"

"Eight. My brother and I had just been cleared for adoption, and that triggered the state to go out and look for any blood relatives one last time." He stands, clasps his hands around the back of his neck, the V of his arms sticking out behind each ear. "I'd never been so scared. All of a sudden I was in this new home, in a new state with a woman I didn't even know. And my mom and dad were so far away."

"I can't imagine."

"It's the sadness I always remember. How being away from my parents made a hole in me."

"But she didn't adopt you?"

"No. Turned out, two young boys were too much for her to handle. So the state gave us back to our mom and dad a year later."

"A whole year?"

"The longest year of my life." He plucks a flat rock from the beach, skips the stone into the waves. It pops off the water twice before sinking into a swell.

"And then you were adopted?"

"Not for another four years. Bureaucracy at its finest." He stares out at the ocean like he's seeing something so much bigger than the sea. "My whole family lived those years in fear, petrified that another blood relative would come forward to claim me and my brother."

"But they didn't?"

"No." He shakes his head like he's shaking off the memory. "I only had one family. My mom and dad, my brother. But Child and Family Services couldn't see that. They have to follow rules, protocols. It's a broken system. There's not a lot of room in the laws to accommodate what kids want. Or need." He lets out a deep breath. "I spent most of my childhood living between two worlds, never knowing where I really belonged."

Sam's "after everything."

He turns to me, smiles when he tells me how his adoption freed him, how he wasn't afraid of losing his mom and dad after that day in court. The day he got a forever last name and a forever family. He knew then he'd forever have a place to call home. How in an instant the world became so much bigger for him and he wanted to see it all.

We sit in the connectedness of our stories, our pasts that make today possible, the sea around us.

He picks up an oyster shell, thumbs the iridescent pink

interior. "I think that's why I feel so drawn to what happened on Malaga, how the islanders were taken from the only home they'd ever known all because the government got in the way of people being a family. There's a painful sort of symmetry to our stories." He turns the shell over, rubs at the rough outer surface. "I just wish the people were still here, you know? So I wouldn't have to be."

"I'm glad you're here."

Sam looks at me, a smile in his eyes. "Yeah?"

"I wish it were under different circumstances, but yeah."

"Huh." Sam drops the shell, returns it to the beach. "I like being here because this place holds no memories. The sea is like nothing I've ever known. It's a fresh start. After everything, you know?"

I really can't imagine; the sea has always been my everything. "Is your story the one you told me last night?"

He smiles. "No. That one was about this island. About a grandfather, a—"

"Father."

His face lights. "Ah! You were listening."

I squint to meet his eyes. "Only that part. Sorry."

"Nothing to be sorry for." He comes to my side, shares the rock seat. "I was telling you about the king of Malaga—"

"Wait. A *king*? Or a king in the way common to Maine islands?"

He looks surprised. "You tell me."

"It's pretty traditional for Maine islands to have a king. He's more like a person who settles disputes, less like a crown-wielding monarch."

"You're saying this happens still?"

I nod. "Sure. Head out to Monhegan. Local rule is pretty important when you live year-round with less than a hundred people and you're so remote. I imagine Malaga would have been the same."

Sam waves his hand as a prompt for more.

"It's nothing really," I tell him.

"Something is never nothing."

Small crabs skitter at the waterline, feeding in the space between earth and sea. "It's just custom, part of the island way of life along this coast. It makes total sense if you think about it. Island families depend on one another for enforcing the law, educating children, mediating disputes. But mostly, for survival. Island life out here is hard and cut off from the mainland, even now. The communities are insular, protective."

His eyes squint against the glare of the sun. "So they need a king."

"Well, a ruler, yeah." Doesn't have to be a king, but the idea of a queen is a different conversation. "Usually a man with the deepest island roots serves as the king. But more often, he's the best fisherman, since good fishing is the difference between life and death for islanders, especially during the winter months."

"We know the king of Malaga met with the governor when his party came to the island. He was the voice his community," Sam says.

"Sounds about right." Even though Malaga's particular history is still new to me, the culture of sea life is familiar. Malaga's people were my people. Quiet. Hardworking. Unassuming.

I stare out at the ocean, the way it rushes forth with its determined blue before retreating in a froth of white. Malaga sits on the edge of the world. No wonder its founder chose it for his home.

"James McKenney moved to Malaga around 1870. He was the best fisherman, like you're saying. Had the largest home, with two rooms."

McKenney. Another last name I recognize from this area. Sam's notes told of how some Malaga residents changed the spelling of their names after the eviction, when they attempted to disappear into the mainland population, and how Malaga Island descendants are still here, still fishing the coast. I've gone to school with them, worked the water with them, but no one talks about the island. It's taken a person from away to show me what's been here all along.

"A dig has already happened at McKenney's home site. A

few years ago. The university found bones from fish, birds, and pig—and some fishhooks and ceramics. That site in particular was key to determining how islanders kept livestock out here."

"And he was the king?"

Sam nods. "Yep. He organized the island economy and was fully literate. By all accounts he was an articulate man."

"Where was his home?"

"There." Sam points to a raised ridge near the top of the island. "I've always wondered how much he knew about what was really going on. Like, did he know what the eviction notice really meant for his people?"

"I don't think anyone could've imagined that the residents would be kidnapped and committed to an institution. It's hard to believe even now." I tuck my chin against my gathered knees, the skin there hot, holding the noon sun. "Sam?" I draw up a question from my very own deep. "Was there a girl on the island? Someone around our age? She may have had an infant."

He shakes his head. "Not that I've come across."

All the pictures of children in Sam's journal, the ones at the school, around the island, on the steps of their family homes . . . so many held the caption UNIDENTIFIED CHILDREN.

"But it's possible? Maybe she was lost to history and you just don't have a record of her? Like the old woman in the rocking chair." Forever nameless.

"Anything's possible, Rilla. There's a lot we don't know about the island and its people. There could've been a teenage girl here. Why?"

"Because I think I've seen her." Anxiety makes my head light now that I'm admitting this vision out loud.

"Online?"

No. At my window. On the shore. In the deep. "Here. On the island."

"Here, *here?*"

I smile even as my insides quake. "That's a lot of doubt for not a lot of words."

"Touché." He gives a small laugh, but his eyes look worried. "How do you mean you've seen her?"

There's so much I can't make sense of. So much I need to unearth. And I know I can't do it alone, so I risk telling him more. "I saw her that first day I met you on the island. She's the reason I came ashore. And I've seen her since." I let the words come because I think they're supposed to be spoken. "The thing is . . . I think my mother may have seen her too."

"Oh." His word is a mere push of breath.

"You think I'm imagining it, don't you?"

He shakes his head. "Far from it."

My heart stutters. "Really?"

"Really." Sam stares at the ocean with all its secrets. "I

mean, it's different, sure. But I believe you. If you've seen her, I believe you."

"You said you didn't believe in ghosts."

"I don't, but I believe in you."

There's a rush of emotion that pushes up from somewhere deep in my chest. Something like gratitude and relief. And something more? It washes through me and tears threaten. For someone believing the unbelievable. For someone believing in me so fiercely.

Sam's willingness to take such a huge leap of faith makes my words rush fast: "I think the girl was from here, Sam. I think something happened to her. Something that isn't in your notes or any published article. Something maybe no one knows about."

"Like I said, anything's possible."

And it feels possible. This girl, her story. She wants me to know her. "She's trying to tell me something. I'm sure of it. But I don't know what and I don't know why." I see Sam trying to focus on my words, but his eyes dart behind me for just a second—a quick flash of a movement that's enough to make me turn my head.

Reed's boat approaches.

Out on the water, Reed arcs his arms to get my attention.

"I don't think he's waving for me," Sam says.

"I should see what he wants." I stand. "Can you take me out?"

"Hop in." Sam climbs into his skiff, reaches for the engine pull, but hesitates. "I want to talk about this more if that's something you want."

"I do."

"Then I'm here," Sam tells me.

"No judgment?"

"No judgment."

He twists the engine pull in his hand, still not ready to start the motor. "And, Rilla?"

I meet his eyes.

"My private thing has always felt shameful. Being a kid without a family or roots to call my own, it made me feel lost or unworthy or something. I've never told my private thing to anyone. You make me feel safe enough to risk that stuff."

"You have zero to feel ashamed of. Nothing about what happened to you was your fault."

"Try telling that to the little kid inside me."

"You can tell that little kid that his parents picked him out of all the kids. Because he was special. And worthy. Maybe you should remind that little kid inside how lucky that makes him."

"I think you just did." Sam smiles a perfect smile, one I can't help but return. "So my private thing's safe?"

"The safest." The girl has become my most private thing,

and Sam didn't even question the possibility of her existence. Then or now. "You can trust me."

"I don't doubt it. You've got a way of inspiring trust and making things . . . better. Even with my story of the king—you made it better."

"Better?"

"All the knowledge you have . . . It added to the story I had. Made it richer." He nods toward the island, its rocky edges, its spruce forest. "You make all of this more meaningful, more necessary." Sam pulls the engine cord and the two-stroke motor chokes to life. The noise is too loud to talk over, and I'm not sure what I'd say if he could hear me. *Thank you* rushes through me, but the words aren't big enough. I'm not sure any words are big enough.

When we near Reed's boat, Sam idles the engine, waves a hello to Reed that Reed doesn't return.

"Everything okay?" I ask him.

"Your gram's worried about you. Wants you home."

I nod. "I'll head in."

"I'll follow behind."

"Sounds good." Despite the terrible things Reed said, I know he just wants me safe. No different from Gram.

Sam takes me to the *Rilla Brae* and I climb aboard. "Will you be ready to fish tomorrow?" I ask.

"Will you?"

"Gotta be."

"Then I'm in."

"Five a.m., okay?"

"Okay, but I'll meet you at your house."

"Why? So I'm not alone on the water?" Gram has him watching me, I know. They're all trying to keep me safe.

"No. Because I'm a normal person who likes sleep, and driving to your house will give me about thirty more minutes of it."

I smile. "Fair enough. See you tomorrow."

"Tomorrow."

I head to the wheelhouse, but turn. "Hey, Sam?"

I want to tell him that so many things are better because of him too. Instead, "Thanks again . . . for yesterday."

He winks. "Gotta watch those lines, Rilla. Balance is a tricky thing on a boat."

I smile. A deep one. One I can feel in my chest. "Good to know."

I watch Sam head toward Malaga and feel lighter than I have in weeks. Sam knows about the girl and doesn't question my sanity. It's a start.

I'm soothed by the roaring churn of the *Rilla Brae*'s engine as she rumbles to life. I check all my instruments and head toward home. When I look back at Malaga, Sam's already hiking to the dig site. His figure looks blurry from here, almost shimmering in the sun. And I don't realize what I'm seeing until he breaks hard right, moves toward the stand of spruce trees.

The girl is behind him, following his every step.

Only inches behind him.

I want to scream to Sam. I turn my wheel toward Malaga, an overwhelming need to protect Sam pulsing through me. Did the girl hear my words? Is Sam in trouble now that I've revealed her existence?

Reed's air horn blows two quick bursts behind me and I jump. "Gotta get home," he yells.

I can't tell Reed that I see the girl or that Sam might not be safe. Reed wouldn't be so understanding; he'd tell me again that I was too much like my mother, and that's something I can't hear right now.

I throw a wave to Reed, and when I look to the island again, Sam's still hiking but the girl has vanished. I let go of a deep breath, so deep it feels as if actual weight leaves my body.

I turn my course toward Fairtide.

CHAPTER SIXTEEN

As Reed and I walk the lawn to Fairtide, he reaches for my hand. I let his fingers spider into mine, but he squeezes me too tight. "I'm sorry about what I said, Rilla. About your mother. I shouldn't have called you selfish either; I didn't mean it."

I know. "I know."

"It's just that you've been different lately."

I stop, turn to him. "How so?"

"I had to hear at the wharf about your accident? Word is, you got really hurt." His free hand balls into a fist at his side. "The old Rilla would have wanted to see me, tell me about it in person."

"I didn't call you because I was exhausted. I didn't have a chance to talk to anyone."

"You had time to be with that guy."

I uncurl my fingers from his, cross my arms at my chest.

"I won't have this conversation again." Reed grabs my arm too hard, and I swat him away, whip fast. "Do not grab at me like that."

He throws up his palms. "Sorry." He rakes at his hair. "Sorry."

Reed and I promised tenderness between us always. Reed's house is filled with people pushing loved ones too hard, throwing things that don't want to be thrown. "Let's just go inside so I can see Gram, and then we can talk, okay?"

"Okay."

He lets go a deep breath. Reed reaches for my hand again. I've held Reed's hand so many times in the aftermath of his father beating on him. Or his grandfather. Reed never talked about the bruises that showed up on his face, ribs. It was like he couldn't talk about what had happened even if he wanted to, and he didn't want to. Holding his hand seemed like the only comfort I could give him, even the most recent times, when his knuckles were raw from fighting back. I don't forgive the way he's treated me lately, but we have two years between us, our lives overlapping. I bend my fingers into his.

Gram is at the deck table sorting bulbs. "Flames." She holds up a cluster of tubers. They're only dirt-caked roots now, but they'll grow into the thick orange bloom I found on my boat.

On the girl's tongue.

On my sill.

"My mother had these in her garden nearly a hundred years ago. Every year she'd dig them up and store the plants in our cellar."

"Like mother, like daughter."

Gram winks. She separates a dirty clump of roots, splitting the plant, which will double the blooms. "These were some of my mother's most precious plants."

She has my full attention. "How come?"

Gram shakes her head but doesn't raise her eyes from her task. "They were a gift from someone she'd lost."

"Who?"

Gram considers. "She never said."

I think of the old woman with the Flame Freesia in her crude raised beds. She could have known my great-grandmother. Did they exchange garden secrets? Plants? Did my great-grandmother mourn for the nameless woman who disappeared from history?

Gram wipes her forehead with the back of her gardening glove, leaving a swipe of earth over her eyebrow. "When I was a young girl I was too busy thinking about me. I missed my chance to ask my parents about the things that were most important to them." She sets the plants in her basket, readying to set them into the earth. She's still considering the plant when she tells me, "I'm surprised to see ya back so soon."

"Reed said you wanted me home."

Gram looks to Reed, her eyes quizzical. "I think I said something closer to the fact that I wish ya were resting."

"She will now."

Gram looks up at me like she's peering over glasses, even though she refuses to wear any. "I'm glad to hear it. Can I fix ya anything?"

"No. I'm good. Thank you." I bend to kiss her on the cheek. "Reed and I are just gonna go upstairs so I can lie down."

"Just so long as only one of ya is doing the lying down and Reed knows he needs to use the door from now on. No more climbing down my rose trellis."

A blush rises on Reed's neck. "No, ma'am. I mean yes, ma'am."

Gram waves him off. "Don't ya 'ma'am' me."

Reed and I head inside, upstairs. I'm only two steps into my room when my annoyance bubbles over at Reed making me leave Sam and Malaga for nothing. "Gram wasn't looking for me at all, was she? Why did you make me come home?"

"Because I needed to see you."

"So why didn't you just say that?"

"Because I wasn't sure if you'd care."

I go to the window, the graffiti message carved into my sill. If Reed could lie to get me away from Sam, could he have carved

a plea into the wood at my window? My mind reaches for anything that isn't unexplainable. I lift the T-shirt to expose half of
the scars etched there: **DONT GO!** I point to the words. "Did
you do that?"

"Um, no, Rilla. I did not deface your window."

"Someone did."

"And it had to be me because it doesn't have an apostrophe
and I'm the dumb kid with no diploma, is that it?"

I feel my face twitch with shock. "No. That never crossed
my mind. I thought it was you because you don't want me to
leave for school. I thought maybe you came by, you know. Maybe
you were stoned and maybe you had your pocketknife with you."

"I've never hidden the fact that I don't want you to leave, but
that"—he nods to the carving—"that's crazy." Crazy. The word
he used to describe my mother. The terrible word all the kids
used to yell at me on the playground.

"Who else has been in your room?"

I hear the question behind his question. "What is that even
supposed to imply?"

"Hattie said that kid was sitting by your bed yesterday when
she got here." His eyes flicker with that same caged aggression
they hold after he survives a fight at home.

"Sam. You know his name is Sam, and he was only here
because he brought me here, Reed. He saved me from drowning.

Gram probably thought he had the right to stay and make sure I was okay."

I see how much rage Reed is trying to tame. The pulsing vein in his forehead, his fists pumping open and closed as if in rhythm with his heart valves. "You should've called me after."

"The last time you were over made it seem like you wouldn't want to hear from me."

"It was a fight, Rills. That's all."

Reed has lived his life with fights surrounding him. They're easier for him to shake, I think. "Maybe I should've, but I knew you'd be hauling today and I needed—"

"To see Sam."

"Yes. To thank him. He. Saved. My. Life. Without him I wouldn't be here talking to you right now."

This seems to calm him some. "What happened?" He moves to the bed, invites me to sit next to him. I slide my shirt to hide the carving and join him.

I tell Reed about the rope around my ankle, how I'd been distracted, how the trap hauled me overboard and dragged me under. Nothing about this story is new to Reed or to any fisherman. It's just that it was *my* foot. My accident. My trap.

He gathers me to him, so close, too tight. I have to pull away. "I'm still really sore."

"Right, yeah. Sorry."

"It's okay."

"No. I'm sorry I wasn't there for you. Yesterday. And before the accident. If I'd been on the boat with you that wouldn't have happened."

"You can't know that."

"I can, Rill. I'd do anything to protect you."

A snicker slips from my lips. "You're stoned every single time you go out on your boat lately."

"So?"

"So you can't think that's safe."

He stands, digs his fingers through his hair with both hands, scratching at his scalp. "I don't want to talk about that, okay? I want to talk about you and me and fishing. Can we do that?"

"I'm good with the you and me part, but I won't talk fishing."

He shoves his hands in his front pockets. The motion tugs his jeans lower, showing the lip of his lean, tan stomach. "I think that has to change."

"Why?"

"Because I think we should buy the co-op."

"The co-op? I didn't realize Hoopah was selling."

"He's not. Not now, but he will, Rill. He's got to retire, and you know his kids don't want it. We could buy it."

"With what money?"

"If you stay, we can fish together, save up money. You don't need school when you've got a future right here."

I feel heat build at the base of my neck. This is why he pulled me off Malaga? This is why he interrupted my conversation with Sam? So we could fight about school? Again.

"It'll be our family business, Rill. Something to pass on to our kids."

"Reed, the conversation you're trying to have is for, like, ten years from now."

"I want to take care of you."

How has Reed become a person who thinks I need someone to take care of me? It sounds like he's saying I'm not strong enough to fish alone and it feels too much like his grandfather's thinking. I stand to pace, my room suddenly feeling too small.

"Don't you love me, Rill?"

"Of course."

"Then stay. If you really loved me, you'd stay for me."

I stop, search his eyes. "You don't really think that?"

"I do."

"It's the opposite of the truth. I'm leaving *because* I love you. If I stay I'll regret it, and I don't want regrets."

"So now I'm a regret?"

"You know what I mean."

"No, I don't. I feel like I don't even know you anymore. Like you're gonna go to Rhode Island and not come back."

"I'm coming back."

"What if I don't trust you to come back?"

What? "You don't trust me to come home to the only family I have left?"

Something snaps in him. Something buried too long. "No. I don't trust you, okay?"

"Um, no. Nothing about that is okay."

The lines in his face grow deeper as they gather anger. Or suspicion. Maybe both. "I don't trust you with *Sam*"—he slurs his name—"or with remembering any of us after you go away and fill your head thinking you're better than the people you left behind. You're not better than me, Rill. You don't get to judge me because I didn't finish school. So what if I chose work instead? So what if I like to get high?"

"Where is this coming from? I don't think I'm better than you."

"Bullshit." Reed paces now. "You've always thought you were smarter than everyone on this peninsula, with college and your scholarship." He spits these words like they're terrible things. "But you're the one with the crazy in your family, Rill. Not me. I'm offering to take care of you. I'm telling you not to run off the way your fucked-up mother did. Stay here. Where you belong."

I take a big step back. "My *fucked-up* mother?" Anger rises. Is this for real?

"You know what I mean, Rill. Come on. She's in a nuthouse. Or she was anyway."

"Reed, you need to go."

"If I leave now, I'm gone for good." He's making me a promise now, this boy built of anger and fear and something else. A need to control? This boy has a part of him that hates me. Has it always been this way? I scrub at my arms, rubbing off the sting of his callousness.

"If that's what you have to do." I move to the door.

"So you're just off to Rhode Island, then, no matter what I want? You'll just run away. Fuck, Rill, you're as nuts as she is. How did I not see it before now?" He shakes his head at me. Like I'm ridiculous. Like I'm missing the obvious thing right in front of me.

And maybe I am. Because Reed's anger toward me can't be new.

"Whatever." He huffs, climbs out the window, his sneaker stepping right over my shirt and the words etched into the wooden sill.

Gone, just like that.

I text Hattie: I think Reed and I broke up

Hattie: For reals? *hides smile*

Me: Think so. He stormed off hating me so . . .

Hattie: So he's an ass

Hattie: I'm coming over

Me: Maybe not tonight

Hattie: You okay?

Me: Think so

Hattie: You're better without him

Maybe she's right. Because everything Reed said tonight feels too wrong.

When I hear Reed's boat fade into the distance, I need air. I leave my room and see Gram sitting on the bottom step of the attic stairway, the door wide open. The perfume of oil on canvas mixes with the salt air that always lurks close to my home. The paint smell is as familiar as my childhood, the way I'd find its echo on Gram's fingers. The oils are heavier here. Concentrated. I steal a look up the plain wood stairs, so steep and narrow. The room upstairs is as magical as Narnia to me, and my curiosity about the space is as strong today as it was when I was little. I catch only a glimpse of a canvas, its visible edges darkened with greens and blues. It is the sea in our attic.

"Sit." Gram pats the narrow, worn step next to her, and I do, turning my back to the mysteries of the third floor.

"Did you hear?"

"I did."

"I don't know where it came from. It was like he'd been holding on to all this resentment and then just exploded."

"Sounds like the truth." Gram takes my hand. "Hearing distrust between two people is never easy. But I think he's right, Rill. Ya two aren't kids anymore. Maybe ya both needed to say the things that were said."

"You think he needed to compare me to my mother?"

"No. That was unnecessary, and I'd bet on Reed realizing that right about now, if he hasn't already."

"Do you think he's right? That I'm like her? That me leaving makes me like her?"

"Your mother left to protect ya, Rilla. She didn't run away. The deepest love is a mother's love, and your mother knew she couldn't care for ya. She needed to get herself right first."

"But she never came back."

She strokes my hand. "Maybe that just wasn't possible. Ya won't find a thing on this earth more complicated than humans, and it's not our place to judge one another. People have to deal with their particular complications the best way they know how, even when their actions hurt us most of all."

"I don't want you to ever think I'd leave you the way she left me."

Gram coaxes my head to her shoulder. "I know ya will come home, Rilla. You're my seal."

"Do you think Dad trusted me to come home?"

"Your father trusted ya with his life."

"Maybe he shouldn't have."

Gram pulls me from her, gets a good look at my eyes, which are watering now. "Why would ya go and say a thing like that?"

"Because I couldn't save his life. If he'd trusted someone better, more reliable than me, then maybe he'd still be here." The sadness of this truth fills my chest.

"That's the last time you're allowed to say that, Rilla Brae. And you're not allowed to go on thinking it. Your father died because it was his time. He died at sea doing work that he loved and was still strong enough to do. Few men can say they've been gifted that privilege."

"There's no privilege in death."

"Not in death, Rilla. But in living life the way ya want to live it. Keeping your heart filled with enough joy to share it with everyone ya meet."

"I didn't feel a lot of joy in Reed's heart."

"No."

"How can he think that's love? Wanting me to live a life he plans for me?"

"Reed hasn't had a lot of good role models when it comes to love."

She's right. And I know that's all I should be thinking about as she holds me to her warm shoulder, but I can't stop seeing Reed escape through the window, stepping on the words carved into the wood in my bedroom. FIND ME. DONT GO! I burrow deeper against Gram. She hums a song under her breath. I recognize it as The Who, "Behind Blue Eyes." I close my eyes to the whisper of her tune, so familiar, so Gram. In the dark space behind my lids I see words painted there. FIND ME. DONT GO!

Gram rocks me and the words become brighter, stronger.

Electric.

The words pound against my skull with their growing brightness, their electric taunt: FIND ME. DONT GO! Pulsing. Banging. Forcing pressure against my skull. I press my hand to my head to push back the searing pain.

Then the words change.

The letters morph into new shapes, the long sweeping sides rearranging themselves into something new, something different. They dart everywhere, a scramble in my mind. Until they reorder, settle into something new:

IM HERE.

The words the girl whispered to me. I dart open my eyes and the hallway pierces with a shiver—a winter cold that stings the flesh of my cheeks with its bite. The cold wraps me, sending a chill into my bones, ice into my blood. I try to stand, to warm, but my legs collapse under me. I am on the floor, Gram bending over me. Her voice joins me, her words dull and distant, taking a long time to reach me. *Are ya okay? Are ya okay?* I want to tell her yes. I want to be okay. But I can't speak.

The *crack* of the slamming attic door sends out a bolt of thunder. IM HERE scrawls upon the wood's face in a yellow glow. The same blistering words pulse in my brain. How are they here? I reach up to touch the door, but Gram takes my hand and helps me to stand. She leads me to my room, stumbling. Because I can't take my eyes from the attic, waiting for the girl to walk out. She's here. I can feel her. Her cold breath. Her words. She is here with me and Gram, in this house.

Gram guides me to my bed, settles me down.

"Rilla. There is something not right."

"Something's not right." It is the closest I come to telling Gram the truth before my mind swirls with light, as if I stood too fast. The whole room swims with a scorching gold. It pulls at me, around me. Beats of sizzling light. Embers. The light is fire, singeing the air in my room with crackling whistles, popping embers from a blaze. The sparks zip past me, around Gram. I squeeze her hand, needing to keep her safe. She calls to me from a distant place, but I'm so far away. I'm in a room of flame. I let go of my gram. I reach for a spark, capture it in my hand. The fire is a burning cold. The ember squirms in my palm, morphs into IM HERE. These two words scrawl across my skin as my room pops with the crackling fire, the flames lighting the room orange.

But there is no heat. Only cold. I shake the embers free from my palm, trying to erase their words. IM HERE. I want the girl to be here and I don't. Not with Gram.

Not now.

The air's too thick, too frozen. It's hard to breathe. I call for Gram, and the words drop out of the flames, searing through the layers of my flesh and setting fire into my bones.

IM HERE IM HERE IM HERE.

CHAPTER SEVENTEEN

When Gram wakes me, she has the doctor by her side. I sit up, see the sun fading from the day. The light is gone from the room, the air heavy warm with summer. I cast my eyes to the windowsill, to the rocking chair. I turn to the pillow beside me even as I know the girl isn't here again.

"Hello, Rilla." Dr. Brower Walsh stands at my bed, all lean giant with his tidy haircut and wide brown eyes. Doc Brower makes house calls for only a few families, people his grandfather treated when he was the area doctor and traveled from house to house. "Your grandmother tells me that you had an accident."

My head throbs. "Yesterday."

"You gave her quite a scare." He holds up two fingers, looks to my neck. "May I?" I nod and he sets his fingers above my collarbone, looks down as he counts to some number in his head. "Good. Good." Two hands now—all fingertips maneuvering around the contours of my neck, ears, skull. "Any headaches?"

I think of the burning light assaulting my brain, the strands of ember words searing there. That was no headache. "Earlier with Gram, I felt a little dizzy."

"Her eyes practically rolled into the back of her head." Gram's voice is twisted, worry making her words low and shaky.

"*Mmm-hmmm.*" Dr. Brower removes a thin instrument from his bag. "I'd like to check your eyes. Follow the red light." I do. My eyes track back and forth. Left to right. Right to left. "Do you happen to remember if you hit your head when you fell overboard?"

I remember so much, the moments playing in slow motion in my brain. The bubbles spraying around me as I was plunged into the deep. The race to cut through the rope binding my ankle. The girl yelling for me, telling me not to go. The underwater squeezing my lungs. The darkness that stretched on forever. "I didn't hit my head."

"No other issues since your spell in the water?"

"Not that I can think of." Not that I can talk about.

"She had a fight with Reed just before she collapsed." Gram is reaching.

"Ah." Dr. Brower nods, checks the range of all my joints. Elbows, knees, ankles, wrists.

"How are you sleeping?"

"Not great."

He presses the stethoscope behind my ears. "And your diet?"

"Good."

He looks to Gram for confirmation. She nods. "No changes."

He surrenders his stethoscope to its perch around his neck and takes my hand, his touch pressing gently against the burn that's still healing at my wrist. "Is there anything else going on that you want to tell me about, Rilla?"

"No, nothing."

"What happened here?" He taps at the very edge of my bandage.

"It was an accident. I singed it on my engine."

"May I take a look?"

I nod, knowing he's looking for signs of self-harm.

He removes the bandage slowly. "Yes, that's healing nicely." He wraps my wrist gently, expertly, before resting my arm at my side. "I think you may have experienced a stress-induced anxiety attack, or panic attack. That dizziness you felt, was it accompanied by a racing heart? Sweaty palms?"

"Yes." Even though I know this isn't anxiety. I've had a panic attack before, when my entire body filled with my heartbeat and I wanted to flee from my own skin. This isn't that. This is my brain trying to make sense of something that isn't as natural as the fight or flight instinct.

"I'll prescribe you some antianxiety medication. You can take one when you feel like you're getting overwhelmed. They do tend to make people drowsy, though, so I don't recommend that you use them while out at sea, okay?"

"Okay."

He takes out a small pad, scribbles some words before tearing off the top leaf of paper. "This medication might also help you sleep because it can calm the mind." He pats my leg. "Take one only if you need it."

Gram reaches for the prescription and I don't see a hint of argument in her eyes, which scares me more than the visions. Normally Gram would argue that lavender or chamomile would be enough to calm my mind. Instead, Gram clutches the prescription to her heart, letting me know we are both in out of our depths.

Doc Brower throws closed the clasp on his traveling medicine bag, its leather worn enough to have been inherited from his grandfather's practice. "A good night's sleep is critical, Rilla. Especially after losing your father. The death of a loved one is one of the greatest stresses that the human mind can endure. Be easy on yourself. Try not to do too much."

"I'll try."

Doc Brower reaches for my hand. "We need you to be good and healthy before you head to college and make this peninsula proud."

His words are so close to something my father would say that they make sadness shoot through my core. "Yes, sir."

He squeezes my hand. "Take care, now. You can call if you need anything at all."

I need so much, but nothing the doctor can help me with.

Gram walks Doc Brower out of my bedroom and switches off the overhead light as she leaves. She doesn't return until she has my prescription bottle in hand. She sets down a fresh glass of water before twisting at the medicine's cap. She taps out a small green pill. She sets it under my bedside lamp. Then she kisses me on the forehead and leaves a stamp of warmth there. "Ya need your rest, Rilla. I'll be right here if ya need me."

"I'll be fine, Gram."

She pats at my hand. "I know ya will."

Gram sits on the rocking chair, her worry forcing her back so straight. I roll the pill in my hand. It is small and round and chalky. It's green, not red. Did my mother start with the green pills? My mother. Reed's angry words swim at me, joined by the ember words scrawling across the attic door, filling my room. The memory of being pulled into the deep.

I take the pill, swallow it without water.

I lower my head to my pillow and my mind races with Dad's funeral, Malaga's history, the girl with the song. Gram's attic and the wood grain that rearranged to tell me IM HERE. And then.

Then the scenes quiet. My mind fogs with some internal lullaby. The bombarding images turn to black. An all-consuming black. Soothing. So opposite the institutional place I've always feared. I walk into this blackness knowing I'm safe. Knowing the blackness is there to hold me. Comfort me.

I give over my trust.

I surrender my independence.

I let the black carry me off.

I wake from another world. The pill Doc Brower prescribed me knocked me out. I even slept through my alarm, apparently, since I feel Gram prodding me in the arm to open my eyes.

"I've been trying to wake ya for nearly five minutes, Rilla. Are ya all right?"

"Fine. Yes. All good." I give Gram the reassurance she needs. "I just needed sleep, like the doc said."

Gram's eyes are creased with worry. "Sam's downstairs."

"I'm up." I sit against my headboard despite the lasting ache trapped in my back.

"How are ya feeling?"

"I feel great." I rub at the corners of my eyes. "I slept great." No dreams, no interruptions.

"That's a balm for my heart." Gram pats me on the shin. "The medicine helped, then?"

"Definitely."

Gram squeezes my shin. "Ya feel like having some breakfast?"

"I'm starving." Gram has always equated an appetite as a sign of good health.

"I'll fix something. Can ya come down?"

I nod. "Of course."

Gram smiles as she leaves, closing the door gently behind her. I wait until I hear her footsteps on the stairs before I go to the windowsill. The window is closed, locked from the inside. I move the shirt that clings to the sill. Just below the words **FIND ME** and **DONT GO!** are scratched two additional words. Familiar now. **IM HERE**

FIND ME

DONT GO!

IM HERE

I let my thumb trace the thin ridges of the words. I don't know how the words are scrawled here, how the girl can visit me and mark my world in this way, but I know the words are hers. And I make a promise to find her.

I look out at Malaga and hold my hand against the glass. "I know you're here." I press my forehead to the cool glass and give in. "But why?"

So much of me doesn't want her to answer.

Too much of me needs her to answer.

I exhale hard against the window, causing a spray of fog to spread across the glass. I raise my finger, write: WHO R U? into the circle of steam. I return my forehead to the glass, maybe waiting for an answer. Or maybe I'm just relieved the morning feels so still and my bones feel so rested. But there's an emptiness in me that I know belongs to my mother. It's the same emptiness I felt when friends had their mothers picking them up from school, throwing them birthday parties—an absence. For the first time since I was six, I wish my mother were here. I wouldn't ask her to explain her choices, her leaving. I'd only ask her to talk me through what's happening, let me know how close I am to the edge.

I dress for normal. White tee, black leggings. I pinch my cheeks so the red will rise. I stretch my face into a smile. Normal. Normal enough for Gram to let me slip out onto the boat.

She's with Sam, eating cubed watermelon at the table, by the time I get to the kitchen.

"There's your tea there." Gram nods toward an empty mug next to the kettle, but keeps her eyes trained on me. I pour a cup, bring my mug under my nose, breathe in the clover leaf and orange rind. For clearing the blood and the lungs. I take a sip and let the hot liquid river its ways to my stomach.

"Sam tells me ya two have plans to go buggin' today."

"Have to. Some pots have been soaking for four days now."

"Is that a long time for a trap to soak?" Sam asks.

I nod. "Ninety-two hours is the longest the law says a trap can stay in the water. Any longer than that and the lobsters won't have any food to survive."

Gram *tsk*s. "Maybe we should be thinking about your wellness, Rilla, not those bugs."

"I feel okay, Gram. Really." I grab the jam from the fridge, the peanut butter from the shelf.

"We already made lunch," Sam says. "Egg salad with celery."

"My favorite." I spear at a watermelon cube on Gram's plate. "We should get going, then."

Sam nods. "Ready when you are." He stands to clear the dishes.

"Ya stay with Rilla at all times." Gram folds her paper napkin, smooths it against the table.

"You have my word."

"Around here that means something, Sam Taylor. Your word is a contract."

He nods his understanding. "You have my contract. Rilla will not be alone on the boat today, and we'll be extra careful."

"Do I get to weigh in on this at all?"

Gram stands, steadies her hip against the table. "Not right now ya don't. Ya just focus on keeping your feet on that boat today, keeping your mind clear. Can ya do that?"

"I can, Gram. Promise." I kiss her on the head, then pull the *Rilla Brae*'s keys from their holder. Today Gram has threaded a wisteria vine around the chain. For love and longevity. I double back, kiss her again. "Thank you, Gram."

"Ya come home safe."

"Always."

Sam and I head across the lawn. Today's waves barely break into rolling whitecaps. There is only a soft wind. The air seems still, like it too is recovering.

"So . . . did you really pass out last night?"

"Um, no. Is that the story Gram's selling you?"

"The long and short of it."

"I had a headache, that's all. But then I slept like a rock. I feel good." It's not entirely untrue. We reach the dock and I climb aboard. Sam unties the ropes from their cleats.

"Did it have something to do with that girl? Did you see her again?"

I freeze. It's strange hearing Sam talk about my girl, but I don't overthink the consequences of letting the fullest truth swim out: "Yes." I can't say how she conjured the blinding embers of light or how she wrote more words in my sill. I know only that she's here. Somewhere. "I need to find her, Sam."

"We will." He looks toward the house where Gram is on the deck, arms planted at her hips. "But first we fish, okay?"

"Okay." It takes me a second to start the engine. It seems like an impossible gift that Sam will help me find the girl, that he doesn't judge me or doubt me. Then there's a movement on the shore, a hovering. A blue heron sweeps down to the water, her prehistoric wings parting the air with grace. She lands, stands statue still in the shallow tide, waiting for her prey.

"Did you know that the heron is a bird of the *in-between*?"

I turn to Sam, my eyes all question.

"Herons prefer to hunt at twilight, which is a symbolic time of 'in-between' since it's not night, not day. And the heron's at home on earth, in the water, and in the air. Some American Indians see this as a sign of liminality—of easily crossing into the space that is neither here nor there."

The heron's head twitches, her gaze finding us. "My dad taught me that blue herons were lucky."

"That too." Sam unties the final rope, gathering it into a circle hung at his wrist. He lays the bundle on the dock, steps over it to board the *Rilla Brae*. "Maybe it's a sign that we'll have luck with the in-between."

The heron pushes upward and lifts to the bluest sky, her wings finding their glide. "I hope so."

*　*　*

Something in our first pot is flailing when Sam hauls it to the rail. "What is that?"

I move to the trap, spring the coils. "Puffer shark." I grab for the small fish and toss her to the deep. "Gotta get her back in the water before she takes a gulp of air and blows up like a balloon."

"Would it really do that?" He moves to the lobsters, throwing out three tiny ones without even measuring.

"In the ocean they swallow water to blow up four times their size. To ward off predators." I measure a keeper, band her, and toss her in the tanks. "If a puffer shark's out of the sea too long, they'll breathe air, and then they can't swim for hours. They just float on the surface in a helpless ball."

"Does it hurt them?" Sam rebaits the trap.

"Dunno for sure. I've seen young kids who keep them out of the water for fun so they can watch them bob, but it was always my dad's basic rule that we don't kill or harm anything we're not here to catch."

"I like your dad."

Still present tense. Even now. "Me too."

Sam and I catch a good rhythm, and we're through with all of our pots by early afternoon. A lot of hungry lobsters found our cages in the time they soaked, and we head to the co-op, where Sam unloads with Hoopah.

"Rumor has it ya fell in the drink," Hoopah calls to me as I dump the bait bucket, the screeching gulls diving for remnants.

"I may have taken a little swim." It's best to make light of what happened yesterday so no one gives it too much thought. It may be fishing superstition, but we all know it's better not to call too much attention to the near misses at sea.

"It might be best not ta swim with a rope grabbing at ya ankle, but that's just me." He gives me a wink, one that tells me he's glad I'm safe.

"I'll remember that next time."

"You'd better. Ya fathah would want ya fishing these waters for a lotta years to come, Rilla."

"I plan on it." Despite Reed believing otherwise.

Sam hands me the slip, his face trying to contain the biggest smile. "Five hundred and eighteen pounds," he whispers. "Boo. Yah!" He doesn't whisper the last part.

"Damn." I take the slip, double-check the number.

"Our best haul yet, huh?"

It's another superstition that keeps me from calling any haul the best haul. "It's impressive."

He wipes his hands on the bib of his rubber overalls. "I think I might change my major to fishing."

"Ha! We'll make a salty dog of you yet."

"I think maybe you already have. This fishing stuff gets in your blood."

It does. "Sure does."

I push at the throttle and the engine hums. The salt breeze swirls around us as I head through the sea of buoys bobbing their colorful necks out of the glistening Atlantic.

We're about a half mile from home when Sam joins me in the wheelhouse. "Hey, Rilla?"

"Yeah?"

"Do you think we could anchor out here for a little while?"

"Too deep to anchor here. What's up?"

"Nothing." Sam gazes out at the expanse of blue where the horizon and sea bend to meet each other. "I just wanted to float for a while. I've never done that."

I check my gauges, my depth finder. The only boat traffic is far off the port bow, so I cut the engine. "We can float." It was one of the things I liked to do most with my dad. Sit in the waves and watch for marine animals. As if they know, a pod of dolphins swim by, their sleek backs lifting in and out of the water in precise rhythm. Two juveniles play at the rear, teasing us with their backward swimming and head nods.

Sam watches, awe lighting his features. "That is by far one of the coolest things I have ever seen."

I smile. "It's pretty cool."

"In Tucson the sky is so big and blue that sometimes it's hard to believe it's real. But here, it's like there's a blue sky and then another one just below it, one that's alive and breathing."

"I think you should change your major to poetry."

Sam laughs. "A fishing poet?"

"It's honest work."

"I'll consider it."

When the last of the dolphin pod disappears, I take a seat next to where Sam's got his feet up on the cooler. I lean forward and rest my elbows over my knees. I let the sea fall around me, the humidity curling the tiny hairs around my face. The spray from the waves coats my skin with wet and salt. I lick at my lips, draw the salt onto my tongue.

"I think I'd like to get to the desert someday."

"See the ocean of sand."

"With sage plants instead of waves."

"And coyotes howling instead of wind."

"That too."

"Look me up when you do."

I laugh. "Will do. Considering you're the one person I'll know there."

We let the waves rock us for some time before Sam says, "I think I might really have the ocean in my blood. Being out here feels like coming home."

"Same."

"I'm also kind of afraid of it, if I'm being honest. It's still so wild. But don't tell your grandmother that the sea intimidates me or she'll never trust me on the water with you again."

"Your secret's safe." I tilt my head back, let the sun reach inside of me.

"You know that book I found in my parents' shed? It had this section on men fishing off this coast, how they didn't even need fishing gear to pull cod from the ocean. They could just lean overboard and grab a six-foot codfish out of the ocean with their bare hands."

"Sure. That's how Cape Cod got its name."

"Yeah?"

"Yep. And Gram says that her great-grandfather used to fish by throwing a simple net over the side of his boat. No hook, no bait."

"For real?"

"For real. And that was after most of the cod stocks had been reduced."

"Do you think it was that way for the Malaga fishermen?"

I remember the open dory at the shore when I first saw the girl. It was big enough for four men, men who would pull their catch up and over its edges. "I do. I think the fishing was different then. Less people. Fuller ocean."

Sam leans forward, assumes my exact position. "I looked for your girl last night. I read and reread every article written about the island, even accessed the state archives and searched the records of the Maine School for the Feeble-Minded."

"How'd you manage that?"

"University perk."

"Anything?"

Sam shakes his head, unable to hide his disappointment.

But I know her story exists somewhere. "My gram always says that bees bring stories."

He squints, looks at me. "How's that?"

"She taught me that bees bring stories on their wings, deposit them into plants as they pollinate. Then humans eat the plant, share the stories."

Sam sits back, a smile rolling over his features. "I like that."

"She believes that stories connect us, make us appreciate all the shared parts of being human."

"I feel the same way about the earth. That it keeps our stories."

"Exactly. And what if . . . what if the girl has a story that can't be told through the archives or your dig site?" How far would she go to crawl under my skin, make me know her truth? "What if the girl from the island has a story she's trying to tell me?" The girl from the sea, the girl with her song. Is she trying to tell me not to make a mistake?

DON'T GO!

Or is she trying to tell me about a wrong that was done to her?

IM HERE

"I'd like to know her story," he says.

"Me too."

"Can you tell me what you know?"

I stretch my gaze to the sea, to the blue horizon with its straight line and perfect predictability. And I let go.

I tell Sam about her voice singing from the shore, singing from the deep. I tell him about the scratches in my sill, the flower she left on my boat. I tell him about the baby's wail, the fingers at my window, the girl in my bed with her matted hair, the cut on her lip, the raw of her fingertips. I tell him everything because we're supposed to share our stories. Some so they bring joy. Some so we don't repeat our mistakes.

I slog up the stairs when I get home, my muscles tired, even if my head feels lighter for sharing with Sam. I run my fingers through the divots of scratched wood at my sill.

DON'T GO!

"I have to," I tell her. "I have to go." I need to see the bigger world.

Then I trace **IM HERE** and press my palm over the two words, honoring them.

"I know," I tell her. I know.

CHAPTER EIGHTEEN

The next morning, I drop anchor off Malaga Island. I turn off the VHF, can't hear Reed's *All in?* I don't know how I'd answer his call now, if he'd even make one at all. I haven't answered Reed's text, his apologies.

"You're sure you don't need to pull traps today?" Sam asks.

"I'm sure. I'd rather be out here, if that's okay. My muscles could use a rest after the last few days."

Sam nods like all of this—everything I've been through lately—is perfectly acceptable and sane.

He rows to shore and we unload, me with a backpack heavy with food and water, Sam with his shoulder bag stuffed with tools. We hike to the dig site, set down our belongings.

The sun is already warm above us, and the gulls are pecking at the water, darting with the retracting high tide. I tuck my fingers into my lower back and arch to stretch. My muscles are still calming after being dragged down through the ocean, then hauling such a strong catch yesterday. My eyes scan the forest edge, the rock face of the island. There's no movement in the trees, no wind to bend them with its sway. I catalog all the things I know: the sea, the sky, the granite ledge beneath my feet.

And the things I don't know: how the girl could be here still, how I can see her, hear her. "Could I ask you to walk up through the trees with me without sounding too weird?"

"Only if you tell me what you're looking for."

"That first day, I heard an infant crying. I saw the girl run into the forest. I think . . ." What do I think? That she could be camping here? Living here? "I think maybe she's there somehow." *Somehow.*

"Let's go."

It's an easy invitation despite how strange this information must sound to him.

We walk to the woods, and I search the tree line, the low spruce branches that reach out, almost naked because they can't get enough sun at their bottoms. I look for anything. Hanging wash. Caught fish. Blankets warming. Anything to tell me that my girl lives here, that she is human and not a ghost.

We hike the length of the forest but find nothing. Not a hint of campfire, no area of needles disturbed. No girl. No baby. When we round high on the cliffside of the island, we leave the dense forest at our backs. Sam points to a patch of ground. "That's where the university wants to set up the next dig."

"Why there?"

"We know from photos that a boatbuilder's home sat on the ridge there." He scrambles down to this future dig site, and I follow.

I can see Fairtide from here, my closed window, the trellis just below it. The skin along my spine pops with gooseflesh as if I've been here before. I feel the weight of memory like years sitting in my bones. Me, staring at Fairtide. Staring at the house's windows as they flickered with candlelight. An instant stretches into years. And I am here, watching Fairtide's green lawn, its dock. Me never taking my eyes from the house, the home, its people. It is a tsunami of a déjà vu.

And then it's gone.

And I know the memory isn't mine.

My legs feel shaky, unsure of their strength. My head spins, knowing this girl has watched my home for decades. She watched my mother here, maybe even my gram, the men and women of my family who came before. My flesh bumps cold, knowing that we are connected, me and this girl. But how?

Sam turns to walk to his dig site. I'm not ready to leave this spot. Not yet. "You go ahead. I'll catch up."

Sam leaves me where a craftsman made his home. The air

feels thick in this place, pressing against me on all sides as if holding me upright. There's an odd smoke that fills my lungs. I cough out the burn that sits in my throat, and the air around me smells of death holding its breath.

I pick up a stick from the ground and I write what I know. I scratch the two words into the dirt. YOU'RE HERE. I place the stick below the words, underlining them. Then I turn toward Sam. I move quickly, watching my footing over the uneven ground as I jog to him. The granite juts out in places, surrenders into bowls at other points. Sam's whistling a tune only feet in front of me as I close the distant between us. It is unmistakably "Pinball Wizard." Sam carries this bit of Gram and her eccentricities out here, lets her favorite song live in the wind. His footsteps seem carefree, childlike. Dad used to say that you could gauge a person's happiness by the heaviness of their step. Did Dad ever walk on this island? Did his feet grip the hard granite underneath each step the way mine do now? Sam drops below my sight line as he makes his descent to the dig site. He takes his whistle, The Who's song, with him.

I'm about to call to him, tease him for his choice of music, when I'm slammed to a stop. The wind pushes me, or something else. Hands. Two strong hands at my chest. They shove at me, thrusting me off-balance. Their push is hard and deliberate. I fall onto the hard rise of my tailbone and pain sears my spine. My eyes search the island, but I can't see anyone.

Could it be my girl?

My heart thunders. I scramble to my knees, force myself upright. I step toward Sam, but the thick, hard hands rake across my throat, squeezing my air. I choke. These hands find my windpipe and press. Too hard. So hard. I try to pull away, but the hands rip at my shoulders, my hips, my hair.

They pin me to the granite rock, a hulking mass pressing out all my breath. I try to choke out Sam's name, but the words can't make sound. I gag, try to breathe. Hands are on my shirt, pulling, tearing. I scream.

The scream ripping from me isn't mine.

It's from the wind, or the trees. So similar to the baby's cry.

The screaming rises around me, magnifying. It drowns out the sea and the gulls. Fear pulses within my ears. I smell the thick tar of tobacco, dusty as if trapped in facial hair. The invisible man smells of rage and hate, and it makes my tongue burn. I beat at him with my arms, but his hips press too close to mine. He holds me down, my legs pinned, my one arm restrained. He wrestles me with his rabid strength. And there's another scream. I want it to be Sam. I want him to be here, to help me. But it's the baby's wail. My ears fill with the wretched screech. My fingers find the man's hands, and I claw at them. Flesh packs under my nails as I dig. Time slows, and I feel his blood trickle onto my own. The man traps my free arm, pins it. My wrists are bound by his strength, the skin on my hands scraping as they scratch against the coarse granite.

Then I see him.

His shoulders blocking the sun.

Wide shoulders, all muscle.

Sam's shoulders. His hands are on me, his face searching mine. "Rilla!" he calls. "Rilla!" His voice is loud and echoing, as if he's trying to wake me from a dream. I flail at him, my fists crashing against his chest, his head. My legs kick at his side. Sam falls to his knees on the ground next to me. "Rilla?" His voice is so soft now. I punch at his figure, scream at him until he's washed of color, out of breath.

"What did you do?" I yell. "What was that?"

"You were screaming, so I came running, and then you attacked me."

"*I* attacked *you?*"

He shakes his head, surrenders his hands. His palms are clean, unscathed. Where are the scratches I left? The blood I felt dripping down my arms? I search my own hands, looking for cuts. For proof. "Rilla. What happened?" His voice breaks with tenderness.

I bring myself to kneel. "I was pulled down. Something . . . no, someone knocked me down. Held me down." My throat burns from the pressure there only seconds ago.

Sam gathers me in his arms, and I can hear his heartbeat thud. I let him hold me, his hands so different from the ones I felt only moments ago. "There's no one here, Rilla. You're safe. I promise."

"It was so real, Sam."

"I believe you."

"How?" Anger rises in me for feeling so helpless. For another person's weight stealing all my strength. "How can you believe me?"

"The way you were calling for me." He takes a stuttered breath. "Like someone was hurting you."

"They were." I can't explain it, can't put it into words. "Something's here, Sam. On this island. Something is trapped here."

I press my gaze to Fairtide, to the color of Gram's gardens. Gather what's real.

"It's okay now. Just breathe."

The hands were on my chest, grabbing at my throat, my hair. I check my shirt for the rip I know I'll find there, but the front is clean. My leggings too.

"Did you see someone?" Sam is careful with his words, like he doesn't want to push me.

"No." I shake my head. "I felt . . . there was . . ." I bring my hand to my temples. "It was more like a memory."

"This happened to you before?"

"No. Not my memory." I watch Fairtide, unsure how this spot can seem so familiar to me. "It was like I was trapped inside someone else's memory. The girl's memory." I know how strange this sounds, how strange I must have looked. And yet.

"How is that possible?"

"I don't know. I'm not sure it is." I rub at my wrapped wrist, the bones I felt scrape across the rocks. "But someone attacked me, Sam. I felt his weight on me, the smell of his tobacco. I didn't make this up."

He reaches for my hand. "I'm not saying you made anything up, Rilla. I believe you."

My mind's not slipping. I *felt* that attack. I felt the man's strength. And more than that, I felt his anger, his intention. "I think he may have hurt her, Sam."

"I'm just glad you're okay."

"Am I? Is this what okay looks like?"

Sam squeezes my hand. "We'll figure this out, Rilla. I swear. But I promised your gram I'd keep you safe, and I'm pretty weirded out right now." He scans the island. "Are you good to walk back to the site? You can sit, get some water."

"Yes." I stand, Sam helping me up. I steal one more look

toward Fairtide. Its sloping lawns, the dormers in its roof, my bedroom window. We walk past the dirt patch holding the two words I inscribed there: YOU'RE HERE.

The invisible man is real.

The girl is real.

They are connected.

To each other. To me.

When we reach the dig site, Sam invites me to sit.

"I'd actually prefer to stand." I pace the length of the excavated earth.

He rummages in his pack for a bottle of water and hands it to me.

I gulp at the water, still so cold. I wipe at my lips with the back of my hand, watch as a paddling of mallard ducks swim atop the rolling waves, their dark feathers buoyed against the sea-glass-green ocean. "I saw her here with you, Sam. The girl."

"With me?"

"She followed you up to the dig site when I went home with Reed the other day. She was behind you."

He rubs at the skin on his forearms. "That's creepy."

"I realize, believe me." I look behind me, fearing my attacker. Not that I'd see him, but still. "Sam? Is it possible the girl lived on the island but wasn't here when census workers came? There's that note in your journal about how some islanders worked on the mainland."

"That's true, they did."

"She could have been on the mainland. Maybe that's why there aren't any photos of her."

Sam nods. "Possible." Sam considers this reality like we're not talking about a spirit that haunts me. "I'm not sure we'll ever conclusively know everything about the settlement, Rilla. So much has been lost to time. But your girl could have lived here. There are discrepancies almost everywhere in the record keeping. Even today sources can't agree on how many graves were removed from the island or how many residents were forcibly committed to the state asylum—and those are pretty major occurrences. The state failing to document a resident or two seems totally feasible," Sam says.

I think of another of Sam's notes, how one of the bodies— the body of a child—was lost overboard when the state ferried the graves off the island. "Or two? You mean her baby."

"You say she has one."

"I'm not sure. I know I've heard an infant cry more than once. A terrible cry." My skin burns with the heat of bruises setting into my skin, the attack with me still.

"Maybe your girl gave birth after the census workers were here. Population was determined in July of 1931, but the evacuation didn't happen until the following year."

"Plenty of time for a baby to be born." My mind latches on to this possibility.

"Except." Sam's face falls. "There was the threat of imprisonment if the residents didn't show on the day the census was taken. Remember?"

I do. The newspaper clippings in Sam's research journal. The warning notice posted on the island and mainland weeks before the day of the census. Islanders would have feared that threat, same as any free person. What would cause the girl to defy the government? The law? "What if she couldn't be here?"

"Couldn't?"

"What if she had her baby on the exact day the census workers came?"

"Then we'd have records of her and the baby."

"Unless she wasn't here when the child was born." The wind sings about my ear. FIND ME, it pleads.

"You're thinking she was in the hospital?"

"No." I quicken my pacing. "Malaga women would've had their babies at home. And with the hate building toward the residents, I'm not sure the hospital would've admitted her."

"So then . . . what?"

What? I have no idea. "I don't know. I'm only speculating. But what if she was a domestic worker and was on the mainland when her baby came? Or on her boat? An island woman would've been strong enough to endure childbirth alone."

"You think?"

"Any girl would have seen a half-dozen babies born on the island during her lifetime. Girls would have helped with births—or at least the cleanup."

Sam considers. "It's a good theory."

"But it's just a theory." I need more. The girl wants me to know more.

Sam's eyes drop with sadness. "A theory is likely as close as we'll ever get to the truth."

The girl isn't always with the child and I've never seen the infant's face. Perhaps it's something else she's carrying. But then, no. I heard the child's wailing. Even that first day I knew that cry was unmistakably that of a baby's. "She had a child." I know this as clear as I know my own name. "I think maybe that's what she's trying to tell me." I stop, look at Sam. "Does that sound impossible?"

He stands, comes to me, takes my hands in his. "I think everything that happened out here was unforgiveable. It's honestly hard to get my head around it most days. But the scientist in me wants proof."

"Proof?"

He nods. "I wish we had something, Rilla. Anything to tie your girl to the island."

"You have me. Everything I've told you."

"Then that'll have to be enough." He lets go of my hands, and his absence makes my skin go cold. He bends at his knee and rests a palm to the earth, as if listening to its story. I imagine it vibrating with the hum of bees. "I was at a friend's birthday party when I got my first kiss."

My head shoots up at the randomness of this information.

"Johanna Light. I'll never forget that kiss. She was so beautiful." He gives a short laugh.

"Sounds like a good kiss."

"It was the best. That first kiss. It ripped through me like a thunderbolt."

"Why are you telling me this?"

"Because the weird thing is that the kiss happened when I was living with my aunt. But when I was returned home months later, my mother knew about the kiss."

"Someone told her?"

He shakes his head. "No. She said she saw it. Like *watched* it."

"Weird."

"No, Rilla. You don't understand. There was a whole state between me and my mom then but she told me that she was on the couch, closing her eyes for a short summer nap, and she saw me kiss Johanna Light. She described everything—Johanna's dress, the tree we stood under, the other kids fooling at the tire swing near the birthday table filled with chips and drinks. She even saw the yellow balloons tied to the table's legs." He steals a breath. "Man, I hadn't remembered the yellow balloons until just now."

"I don't get it."

"My mom said that's the way love worked. That when someone you love feels this ultimate joy—or sadness—the people you love feel it too."

I brush at the bumps rising on my forearms.

"She said love meant our hearts and minds were connected even when we weren't together."

I can't help but wonder if my own mother has seen snippets of my life in her dreams.

"It happened one other time, when my brother had to go to the hospital. She knew every detail of his accident. As if she'd been there."

"There aren't a lot of people who would believe those stories."

"But you do, right?"

"I do."

Sam smiles. "My mom always said my brother and I were born from her heart since she didn't give birth to us, you know."

My heart skips with a lovely pain. "That's beautiful."

"I've always thought so. But everything my mother taught me about love makes sense here, too. Maybe this girl's heart is connected to yours somehow. Maybe that's why you can see her."

I think it.

I fear it.

I know it.

Want it.

The crisp whine of a calling gull cuts through the silence that settles over us.

"And you . . . ?" Sam stops, waves away the thought. "Nah, forget it."

"What? You can ask. Nothing is too weird now."

"You'd mentioned maybe your mother saw the girl too?"

I sit, pull my knees closer to my chest, holding this possibility in my heart. It is a reason for my mother leaving. A reason that isn't me. "I think maybe she did."

"Do you think your mother was attacked? That hers is the memory you felt?"

"No." I know this even if I don't know how I know. "It was the girl's memory. But I think the girl visited my mother somehow. My mother used to call them Water People, the people she thought lived in the ocean. But maybe there was only one Water Person."

One girl reaching out to my mother.

"The last time I saw my mother, she was collecting stones from the sea."

My mother's hands so delicate.

"I watched her in the surf, how she filled her pockets with those stones. I remember being so excited for her to bring me all her treasures."

Rocks trampled by dinosaurs, squeezed by continents of ice.

Broken glass from a pirate ship, purple and exotic.

"She used to collect broken bits of clay from the shore and tell me tales of how the Water People left their pots behind."

"Whoa."

"But on her last night here those discarded pieces weren't enough. My mother added rocks to the pockets of her skirt. Small ones at first. I was only six when I watched her walk straight into the waves, carrying so much extra weight. I knew she was going to the Water People, and I'd never been so scared." My breath hitches. "I knew she wanted them more than me. She was *choosing* them over me, and all I could do was watch. She was leaving me behind, and I didn't know how to make her stay."

"Rilla." Sam reaches for my hand. I feel his warmth wrap my fingers.

"My gram called an ambulance, and they brought her to the hospital. But she's stayed away for twelve years. Maybe she never wanted to be with me at all."

"I can't believe that's true."

I did. All these years. Until now.

Sam squeezes my hand.

"Now I think maybe she wanted to protect me from her, or maybe my mother thought she took the Water People with her—you know? To keep me safe." Protected. "But I think she saw my girl. I think my mother was trying to find my girl."

"Same as you."

Same, but different, too.

"Just promise me you won't walk into the sea like that."

"I won't." I would never. But maybe my mother thought that once too.

At home, I research everything about the boatbuilder's family. There's a photo of him and his wife at the front door of their small one-room house, two children at their feet. Their clothes are clean but worn. The children are shoeless. The man has his arm around his wife's waist, as if to protect her. UNIDENTIFIED CHILDREN, the photo says. Like so many others. I wait for the song to rise, but its melody never fills the air. I wait for some connection to speak to me, but there's nothing.

Only the hard wind churning up from a swelled sea.

I fall asleep with the images of Malaga all around me.

I dream of swimming.

I poke my seal-slick head from the water, and an old dory coasts along the waves. The girl's inside, rowing from the peninsula to the island. I swim behind her. The sides of her boat are low like the one Sam described from the book he discovered when he was twelve in the desert, low enough to scoop fish from the sea. I swim my head higher and see the fat bundle on the empty seat at the back of the boat. I think it's the girl's baby until I see the rounded cloth tied at her breast, the child at her heart. As the girl pulls the oars against the sea, she leans back, her infant rounding toward the moon. And in the spray of light that the moon lends the surface of the sea, I notice the blooms of the Flame plant, their bright orange flowers like fire in the boat, its bulbs and roots wrapped in burlap as if the uprooted plant were a gift.

When I wake I go straight to Gram's front garden and let my fingers stroke the soft emerging bud of the Flame plant— the plant named for fire. I break off a flowering stem to show Sam. Because it's in this garden that I realize I shouldn't be looking for a girl.

We need to be looking for a plant.

CHAPTER NINETEEN

I want nothing more than to search the island for the Flame Freesia at first light, but I have to haul traps. Sam sets the gaff hook on the first buoy in our string and starts to pull. Immediately I know something is wrong. There's no tug at the opposite end of the line. The rope slicks too quickly through the pulley, pulling up only seaweed.

"What happened?"

"We lost a string." One string, three traps.

"How?"

I pull up the rope, fan my thumb over the sprig of tufted rope that sprays wild as a snipped braid. "Someone cut the line."

"What? Why?"

"Happens all the time. It's a shitty way to settle a dispute." I scan the sea for other boats, one that might be watching too closely, but of course there's no one. Cowards never stick around.

"You think it was Benner? Retaliation for what you did to his traps?"

"Most likely." But a small worry grows inside of me that this sabotage could have been Reed because of the things he said—the argument that may have been too harsh for us to come back from. I shake off the thought. "There's no better way to tell someone they don't belong on the water." I set my course for the next buoy, my rage building toward Benner. "We need to check the next string."

The next string is fine. The next thirty strings are fine. Sam and I band the keepers and it's almost a good enough haul to calm my anger for anyone messing with my traps. Until Sam pulls a slack rope at the end of our run.

"Rilla?"

I join him at pulley. The last line is cut, just like the first line.

"This isn't a coincidence, is it?"

"I'd say that's about as far from a coincidence as you can get." It's Benner telling me girls don't belong at sea. I know it the way any lobster fisherman would know.

"What happens to the traps?"

"They're ghost traps now. They'll sit on the bottom of the sea forever."

"With lobsters inside?"

"The tiny ones might crawl out, but the big ones get stuck in there."

"And they die?"

"Sometimes. Sometimes the trapped lobsters attract new lobsters to climb in and one cannibalizes the other. No one really knows how long something like that can go on."

"Not good."

"Arizonians and their understatements." I toss the buoy into the back of the boat to join the severed line from the first string. "The sea bottom is littered with ghost traps."

"I'm sorry, Rilla."

I thrust forward on the throttle. "Nothing you need to be apologizing for unless you're the one who cut my line."

"You're joking, right?"

"There isn't a lobster boat captain alive who would joke about ghost traps."

We deliver our haul to the co-op, and it's decent. Four hundred and six pounds. "I'm gonna go grab a check for this." I wave the sales slip at Sam. "Mind waiting on the boat?"

"I'll hose her down."

I nod and head toward the office.

Hoopah's smile welcomes me inside. "Good ta see ya."

"It's good to be seen."

"Whatcha got there?"

"Today's slip. Just need to get paid out today."

His brow creases. "That's not like ya. Don't want the check sent to ya account?"

"Not for this haul."

He nods toward my slip, and I hand it to him. He studies the value. "Ayuh. A good day, Rilla." Hoopah flips the checkbook open to a new page and uses a calculator to multiply my catch weight by today's price per pound.

"Make it out to Sam Taylor."

Hoopah nods. "If that's what ya want." He writes out a check and signs his name. He tears it off, hands it to me. "You'd make any father proud, Rilla."

I fold the check, slip it in my coveralls. "You haven't heard any chatter on the docks, have you?"

"Nothing but chattah."

"Two of my strings were cut today."

He narrows his eyes. "That so?"

I nod. "I know you likely won't hear anything, but just in case."

He scratches at nonexistent facial hair on his chin. "I've got my suspect."

"Me too."

"Ya watch ya'self now."

"Always."

He nods. "Ayuh."

On my way back to the wharf, I see Reed and his grandfather stacking new traps onto his grandfather's boat. They're shining green and don't carry a lick of clinging seaweed. I stare at Reed, know he sees me. And I don't mistake how he doesn't wave, doesn't even raise his head in a nod. I hate the way my suspicion flares for Reed being partly responsible for my six traps being lost to the sea.

I go to my boat, where I slip Sam his pay.

"What's this?" He unfolds the check. "Good God, that's a lot of money. Why are you giving me so much money?"

I turn over the engine. "That's a paycheck, Sam Taylor."

"That's a ridiculously big paycheck."

"You got lucky. The next time might not be the same."

"How do you mean?"

I throw the *Rilla Brae* into gear and leave Reed and his grandfather and the docks behind. My angry suspicions won't leave me. "My dad always paid me on the seventh day of work. The full price of the seventh-day haul. On a good seventh day, you make more. On a bad seventh day, not so much."

"This is too much."

"It won't feel like it next time when you get half of that." I putter through the No Wake Zone and head toward Malaga. "Besides, that's the way it's done on this boat, and you're on this boat. A lot of other captains will average out the week's catch and give the sternman a fixed percent. But my dad was different."

Sam slips the check into his jeans pocket. "Rule number one: Captain's always right, right?"

"There's a lot I've been wrong about. But I'm hoping today I'll get something right." I tell him about my dream and the flower and my hunch.

My body is electric with hope as Sam and I scour the island for the Flame Freesia. My dream had to mean something, the girl transporting the very plant that Gram's mother held so dear. It connects my family to the island in a small way. Connects my family to the girl, even if it was just a dream.

Though it feels too much like bees carrying their stories. This flower, carrying a story.

We grid the surface of the island with our footsteps, no different from how Sam grids his dig sites. We walk normally at first, our excitement not wanting us to be slow about the search. When our hunt turns up nothing, we get down on our hands and knees, scour again.

"I don't know how this can be." I'm exhausted. Deflated. I sit with my knees pulled against my chest. "I really thought we'd find it."

"Finding the echoes people leave behind isn't always easy."

"But I was so sure. Really sure."

"My professor tells us not to expect anything from the earth so we'll be that much more rewarded by what we do find. She says hyped digs can be the most disappointing."

"Like today."

"But there's always tomorrow," Sam says.

Tomorrows always arrive lighter.

When we get back to Fairtide, I'm not ready to go inside or give up. I'm frustrated by the cut traps and our inability to find the flower I was sure would be on the island. My chest is too tight to pull a deep breath into my lungs. I need a swim.

"Would you mind bringing up the cooler? I'll be in. I just need five."

"Sure thing." Sam lifts the cooler onto his shoulder and starts across Fairtide's green. I wave to Gram to tell her everything is all right. I kick off my rubber boots and stand at the dock's edge. It's strange how I miss the girl; how I was so certain I'd find her today, or a clue from her at least. But my optimism was stupid, because the flower could never survive on the island without someone to care for its roots the way Gram does. Sadness rises with the feeling of failing the girl, and my family.

The waves are dark in the early evening, their rolling motion churning oil-black seaweed in its grip, spitting up the sea with its weeds and seafoam. I inch forward, my toes gripping the edge of the dock. The waves splash against the pilings, jumping up, wetting my toes. The water sings to me, its waves a melody. Calling to me.

> *Come here, come here*
> *My dear, my dear.*
> *Won't you come here and be my dear.*
> *Be near, my dear.*
> *I'm here, I'm here.*
> *Won't you come near and find me, dear?*

The song rises across the backs of the waves, its words like dolphins playing, beckoning me.

I am the dear.

The girl wants me near.

Did my mother hear this same summons so long ago?

Is that what she heard when she packed all those stones into the pockets of her long yellow skirt, its hem dark with seawater? My heart surges, remembering how much I feared my mother that night, but I don't feel that fear now. The song brings peace.

The song of the Water People.

Come here, come here
I'm here, I'm here.
Come to the sea and find me, dear.

It's an invitation carried on rolling waves.
Calling to me.
I want to be with the Water People. The Water Girl.

Be near, be near
My dear, my dear.
Be with the waves and find me here.

I strip down to my T-shirt and hold a breath. I dive. The
ocean rushes its ice all around me. I propel my body under
the crashing waves, listening for the underwater song. I want
the girl to be here. I want her lullaby to call me. Only me. I
swim through the black world of the ocean, let the cold press
into my chest.

When I finally surface, I slick my hair back along my scalp
and take a breath that expands my lungs, skin, everything.

The sun is gone now. The fat white moon hangs directly
above. Darkness floats everywhere. How long was I underwater? A boat bobs close to the shore. Approaching. So
familiar. I twist toward Fairtide, the water swirling around

me. Our dock is shorter somehow, made of wood now. The *Rilla Brae* is gone.

The small boat rows to Fairtide's dock. A rope is thrown from inside the boat. And then the girl. She steps onto Fairtide's dock, her fingers fastening a quick running bowline knot. She hoists a bundle from her boat and settles it onto her back. She starts toward our deck, which is impossibly no longer there. I follow the beautiful girl in her white dress. She knocks on Gram's door. Our back door. But it's not Gram who answers.

A tall, frail woman peeks out of the slit of doorway. I can only see half of her face, though I know she is Gram's mother, so similar to her hanging portrait above our living room fireplace.

My great-grandmother. The wood dock. The girl with her perfect black braids. The oil lamplight bouncing at my great-grandmother's features as she holds the flame to the darkness. All signs of decades ago.

"Good evening, Mrs. Murphy."

"Agnes. Good evening."

Agnes! My girl. A name.

A shiver crawls over my skin.

My gram's mother opens the door wider. I don't miss how she looks to the night, as if suspicious that someone could be watching. I feel heat push forth from the house, our kitchen stove warming bones even then.

"Only one tonight," Gram's mother says, handing over a bundle. The girl rests it in the crook of her free arm.

"For you, Mrs. Murphy." Agnes passes her package through the door.

"You always do such a nice job cleaning, Agnes. I don't know how you get those tea stains out."

"The secret is the salt water, ma'am."

Flickers of light coat my great-grandmother's features as she lowers her gaze. "Agnes? Is that her?"

"My baby, ma'am." Agnes shifts her arms, and it is only then I see the infant strapped to her chest.

"Wait here, dear. I have a gift for you." Gram's mother disappears from the open door to expose a sliver of our kitchen, the windows just as they are now, the stove anchoring the space. She returns, a small swatch of fabric stretched over one hand. "It is a meager token, only a bonnet. I knitted it myself."

"It is lovely, Mrs. Murphy." Agnes's voice lifts, joy floating her words.

"May I?" Gram's mother nods toward the infant's small head.

"Of course." Agnes brings the infant out from her middle, but only some, as if her heart can't stand to feel distance from the tiny child.

Gram's mother settles the bonnet onto the baby's head. "Eleanor is a fine girl, Agnes. You should be very proud."

Eleanor?

Agnes nods, her eyes only on her child. The infant coos then, no different from a little bird.

The air warps. *Eleanor?*

"She looks pale, Agnes. Is she well?"

Agnes's back straightens. She pulls the child closer. "Pale, ma'am?"

"Her skin, Agnes. Her skin is quite light compared to yours."

There's a lift in Agnes's shoulders. "Yes, Mrs. Brae. My husband hails from Ireland. His skin does not like the sun." There is a laugh in this last statement. Love sewn in her words.

"Yes, well. What a blood endowment for the youngster[5] in this hateful climate."

Agnes looks to her child. "I don't understand, Mrs. Brae."

My great-grandmother looks at Agnes with something like sorrow. "Agnes." She wrings her hands. "I have to ask you to leave the linens at the back of the door from now on. I will be unable to answer should you knock." She points to a spot near Agnes's feet. "I'll set a box there, for you to leave the clean things within."

Agnes nods. "Certainly, ma'am."

Gram's mother hands something to Agnes. The jingle of coins. "I fear I will not see you again, dear."

"I will always be close," Agnes says. "Malaga is no distance at all."

"Yes." My great-grandmother's face softens in the light. "I wish you and your family well. Be safe. You are a fine mother, Agnes."

"It is fine to be a mother, Mrs. Murphy. I wish the same for you one day." Agnes lifts the new parcel into her hands, a neat cloth wrap of dirty linens. She carries her child and her work back to her boat. A tune rises, one that is so familiar now. She sings this song to the child named Eleanor at her breast. *Come here, come here, my dear, my dear.*

And I call to Agnes over her song. I scream the words she has carved into my room, the words she sang in the sea: "I'm here! I'm here!"

Agnes sings to the sea, to the child. She doesn't hear me, can't see me. She doesn't break her rhythm as she pulls her oars through the heaving swells, her boat headed toward Malaga.

My head warps with the thoughts racing too fast. The name Eleanor. My great-grandmother knowing my girl. The girl from Malaga. I dive to follow her, and the ocean rushes around me.

The waves bring my name, no different than they've brought Agnes's song. *"Rilla!"* The sound carries through the thick of water, stretches into a melody.

Agnes. I push out a breath and bubbles burst around my lips.

"Rilla!" My name again, called from the water's edge. "Rilla!"

The sound is wonky, the syllables shimmering through to the underwater.

I swim to the sound. My heart thunders for the chance to know Agnes, ask after her child. Ask if the baby is my grandmother.

But when my head breaks the surface of the water, the world slips around me. "Rilla!" It is Sam's voice.

"Sam!" Water fills my throat, scratches with its salt. Sam is on Fairtide's dock. Fairtide's aluminum dock. I cough up the seawater.

"Dinner's ready." Sam says it like no time has elapsed. Like I didn't just visit the past. He boards the *Rilla Brae* and grabs a towel.

I tread in the water, unable to leave the sea that's transported me through time. I want to dive underwater, find Agnes again, swim through years. I take a breath, ready for the plunge.

"Rilla?" Sam waves the towel for me.

I see the worried look on his face, how his eyes plead for me to be okay.

"You good?"

I turn to look at Malaga, so beautiful in the afternoon light. There is so much light now. And even though I can't explain how it's possible, I feel good. Settled. I feel the truth of it in my bones. As much as I want to follow Agnes into the past, I want to be in the present with Sam more. I climb the swim ladder and press the cotton against my face, dry my eyes. "I met her, Sam."

"Who?"

"Agnes. My girl."

CHAPTER TWENTY

After dinner, I tell Sam about Agnes's visit to Fairtide, how she brought laundered linens and her newborn.

"Eleanor," I tell him.

"Your grandmother's name?"

"That's why she's here, Sam."

We sit in silence for a long time, watching the moon rise above the trees on Malaga.

My mind hums, filled with bees. Calling up the story of Agnes so that it will never be buried again.

When I head inside, I find Reed in my room. He rises from my rocking chair, a piece of paper in his hand.

"Hey." He says this small word like he didn't say such huge things the last time he was here.

"Hey."

"I've been waiting for you for a while."

"You could have joined us." Even as I say it I know it's not what I would have wanted.

"I didn't come here to see Sam. I just needed . . . wanted to say sorry. For everything I said about your mom and you. I was a shit, Rill. You didn't deserve that."

"I didn't." No one does.

Reed hands me the paper like a peace offering. "Thought you might like this."

At the top of the form is Reed's name, computer generated.

"It's my GED. Only the first exam, but still, I passed."

Despite everything, pride surges in me. "This is great, Reed, really."

"It's what you wanted, right? Education's important to you, Rill."

"It is, but I want you to get your diploma for you, not me."

I sit on the edge of my bed and catch Malaga's trees peeking through my window's view. I wonder if Agnes is on the island tonight. Or closer, maybe. Could she be here now? Something about that possibility warms me.

"I still love you, Rill."

"I'll always love you, Reed."

He combs his fingers through his hair, lets out a shallow breath. "That doesn't sound promising."

I remember Reed's anger, how it overwhelmed him the last time he was in my room. The fisherman in me wants to ask him if he cut my traps. But the girl in me knows it doesn't matter.

Two years.

So many private things.

"You said a lot of things when you were here last, and maybe that's enough." Even as I know it's time to move on, I want to go to him and hold him, the same way I've done so many times. But the space between us feels too distant to close. "I'll expect a copy of your diploma, of course." I try for light, supportive. I try to remember all the good things I love about Reed.

"So that's it? We're done?"

I search his eyes. I can't ever forgive him for the things he said about me or my mother, and I hate the way I suspect his capacity for becoming too much like his grandfather. But mostly, I don't have the energy to fight with Reed anymore. "I think that's the way it has to be. I think it's what you want too, if you're really honest with yourself."

"It's not what I want."

"It's what I need."

Reed nods, a small one. He walks behind me to the door. Not the trellis, the door. "Will I see you around?"

I turn. "Of course."

He lowers his head and steps out into the hallway. I hear his words as he walks away: "Counting the minutes."

Sadness rises in me. And relief, too. My thoughts wrestle somewhere between my past and future. An in-between place, Sam would say.

I go to the window and stare out at Malaga.

I press my hand to the carved messages Agnes left for me. I watch for any sign of her, but she doesn't come. She lets the quiet settle around me. She lets me let go. Of Reed. Of pieces of my past. Of fear.

CHAPTER TWENTY-ONE

Sam's car arrives right at five o'clock the next morning. I dress, pull my hair into a messy ponytail. I head down the stairs, past the black-and-white photographs that hang along the stairwell. My ancestors peer at me through the sepia-toned edges of the past.

Sinclair and Thomas Murphy in their WWII uniforms before they left for Normandy. My frail great-grandmother at the water's edge, Malaga behind her in the middle distance. The photo of my gram, the earliest photo I've ever seen of her. She's an infant, bundled near the fire, her face satisfied with sleep. There's a small Christmas pine on the table behind infant Gram, presents wrapped with plain paper, twine bows.

I stare at her photo now as I did last night, knowing she's the connection to Agnes. Did my great-grandmother name my gram after the child from Malaga? Did something so terrible happen to Agnes's infant that my great-grandmother wanted to honor her memory? Or could Agnes have given birth to my grandmother?

I squint to the photograph, notice a carving on the button set at the bonnet's neck. Only three lines are visible, the horizontal lines of the *E*.

For Eleanor.

The black-and-white photo is too deteriorated to know for sure if my grandmother wears the same bonnet my great-grandmother gifted the child Agnes held in her arms.

I go to the kitchen, where Sam waits with Gram. The room is a fog of steamed oats.

"How ya feeling this morning?" It's a question Gram can't stop asking, and I really can't blame her, considering.

"Right as rain." I kiss Gram on the cheek and feel the warmth of her soft skin. Her skin. What was it that her mother said about the infant Eleanor's skin? *A blood endowment for the youngster in this hateful climate.* Gram's mother knew about the racial tension building toward Malaga residents. The awfulness of everything that happened to the islanders swarms me. It's why my great-grandmother wouldn't open the door to Agnes. Because of the color of her skin. And the growing intolerance toward the people of Malaga.

There's so much I want to tell Gram, ask Gram. But how?

How do I tell her anything when I only have questions? And how would she feel about the possibility that our family—the Brae and Murphy lines that she's so proud of—might not be our blood family at all? Our ancestors—Sinclair and Thomas Murphy, everyone who came before—what if we aren't blood kin? Because that's our story if my gram was the infant tucked so close to Agnes's heart.

And if Gram was the infant in Agnes's arms, who brought her to Fairtide? And why?

"Be safe out on the water today," Gram says.

Be safe. They are the same words my great-grandmother told Agnes.

They're the words every fishing family extends like a prayer.

I grab the keys to the *Rilla Brae*, and Sam follows me to the dock. The mist is low on the water today. Its haze creeps in front of us, summoning us toward the island, the same way fog brought the Water People to my mother. Called her to the Water People.

My grip tightens on the wheel of the *Rilla Brae*, prepared now for the unexpected. I scan the sea around me, a gray and unyielding mass. There is so much more underneath, not just the ecosystem I've studied my entire life, but the otherworldliness that lurks just below the surface.

The just-waking sun guides us to the shores of Malaga. The

dawn, a time of the in-between. The tide is low and our boots get pulled by tidal mud, each step suctioned by the grabbing, wet earth. The air is layered with the smell of clams and salt. I pull it into my lungs, my blood, letting it wake all my senses.

Sam and I walk the beach and then the granite rise of the island.

Today the king's shack is here, the unmistakably large two-room house. I don't know how its structure greets me in the morning light, but I can see racks of salted cod hanging and drying in the sea air, vegetable gardens throwing out vining crops, creeping tomatoes. The door opens, and a child steps outside. He's a young boy with high boots and standing-up hair. His shirt is too big for his small body, and the open neck exposes his collarbone. I recognize him from the photos of unidentified children at the schoolhouse. My heart reaches for him.

The boy runs to the back of the house, calling for Aggie. My breath stills, waiting for her to come.

"What is it?" Sam asks.

"Don't you see?"

"See what?"

"The king's house." My words are a whisper. "The little boy."

I draw in the smell of smoke. It rises from the chimney, curling into a twist as it reaches for the dull morning sky. The smoke makes the scent of boiling fish rise, and something else, too. Something as thick and starchy as the clouds crowding the sky. Potatoes, I think. Fish and potato stew. The little boy darts out from behind the house and runs off in the direction of the boatbuilder's house.

I point in the eager boy's direction, but only with a small flick of my finger, oddly afraid someone will think me rude for pointing at this boy who doesn't see we're here. "There." My fingers fumble for the side of Sam's shirt and tug at it so that his eyes can follow the boy.

But then the child is gone.

"I don't see him, Rilla." Sam keeps his voice low.

I turn to the house, but it has vanished too. Only the starch clings to the air, an echo of fish and potatoes and fire. "He ran off. Toward the carpenter's house." That place where I was attacked. I fear for the boy.

"Can you see him still?"

I will my eyes to re-see, re-conjure. "No. Everything's gone now."

Sam takes my hand, and I'm so fully aware of my body in this moment. I want to tell my limbs to return to that other place, the in-between place where a boy can run in front of me, run out from the past. "What else can you remember, Rilla? This is important."

The sky begins to gather light. Soft at first, a painted promise of the sun.

"You saw the house and the boy for a reason. There has to be a reason."

"How is this possible, Sam? I'm literally seeing things that aren't there."

"What's happening to you, Rilla, it's special. Only you can see the islanders, their past. That has to mean something." His voice is so soft, as if he doesn't want to wake the people that might be on Malaga still. The Water People. The Island People. "I envy you." He seems to realize he's holding my hand and lets it go.

"You envy me?"

He thrusts his hands in his pockets. "The reason I dig in the dirt is so the past will talk to me. But you're *there*, Rilla. Something is taking you there."

"Or someone."

"Not just someone. Agnes."

"That's what the little boy said, just now." I bring up this additional detail for Sam. "He ran out of the house yelling for Aggie. The boy was running to the site of the boatbuilder's house, like he knew he'd find Agnes in that place."

Sam hikes his pack higher on his back. "We need to dig there." I hear the excitement in his voice, like he knows the earth will help us.

As we approach the spot where I was attacked, my heart races. My skin fires with fear. I take small steps, waiting for those invisible hands. And then I find my words, scratched into the dirt, a twig as their underline.

YOU'RE HERE.

Above them, a blooming Flame Freesia.

Its bright orange cups glow in the rising sun. I bend to this fiery orange mound, steady a soft bloom between my two fingers.

Sam falls to his knees next to me. "This wasn't here yesterday."

I shake my head. "But it's here now."

"And there." Sam points to another flaming orange plant just down the slope, it's green mound showing off a healthy spray of blooms.

"How did we not see these before?"

"I don't think we missed anything, Rilla. I think they're a new trail. Look." He nods to the handful of plants leading toward the water on the opposite side of the beach. The south side, the one that holds deadly rips. The plants are all blooming, thriving. They're scattered from one another, a dozen feet or more between each burst of bloom. Sam is right; they're a trail. "Agnes left us a map of flowers."

"A floral footprint."

My skin wraps my bones in cold.

We walk slowly along the jagged line of Flames. The sun rises to shed its full light. I drop my bag at the last bloom. "Here."

Sam lowers his pack, cordons off a new dig site with his stakes and twine, creating a neat rectangle that is so similar to the tidy vegetable gardens that once fed island families.

It takes hours just to peel back the first inches of dirt, our trowels and brushes intent on finding the clues that will lead us to Agnes. By midday the sun ducks behind the clouds, which threaten rain.

"Will you tell your professor about what we're doing here? Following clues like this?"

Sam sits back on his ankles, shakes his head. "I think this is definitely our private thing."

I like the idea of a shared private thing with Sam. I lean toward the center of our excavation site, brush away the dirt, speck by impossibly tiny speck.

It's Sam who discovers the bowl of a pipe. He brushes it free from generations of silt, holds it up with his gloved hand. "The islanders were scorned as degenerates because of their use of tea and tobacco."

"What weren't they judged for?"

"Too right."

I think of the old man and that beautiful chair he brought to my gram, my dad. Was he from the island? Was he too ashamed of his past to name the place he was from? I want to believe my family helped his family, the island people. Or at least let them be free.

We dig all day. My back aches from bending over the earth, carving out its secrets. We find only buttons, more battered pottery.

The moon joins us before I'm prepared to meet it.

"We should be heading back."

I nod, reluctant. "I have to haul tomorrow."

"We can come in the afternoon."

It's a small consolation.

At home, Gram's left a note that she's at Brenda Sherfey's for their monthly Garden Club dinner. It's late, but I'm glad to find the house quiet. My clothes are filthy, and I don't have the answers for the questions Gram would likely ask about why I've been gone past dark. Why I didn't radio in.

I go to my bay window. I trace my fingers over the scratched marks.

IM HERE
DONT GO!
FIND ME

I pull scissors from my desk and use their sharpened point to carve my promise under her message. **I WILL FIND YOU AGNES.**

It no longer matters that we're separated by decades.

It matters only that I unearth her story.

I shower and make tea that would have marked me as degenerate in Malaga's time. I go to the lawn, wanting to be on Malaga's shores.

I watch the quiet island, knowing Gram's parents would have witnessed the persecution of Malaga residents. My great-grandparents were part of a community that wiped out another community. Gram has to know something about the island people. Or how she got her name. Her mother must have shared some piece of this story. Maybe Gram needs help calling it up.

But even as I decide to approach Gram again, I'm afraid of all the possible answers. What if her father carried his rage and prejudice to the island? What if his boat was the one that carried the abducted islanders to the mainland? What if my great-grandfather was one of the men to commit eight innocent people to the state insane asylum? Someone had to sign those orders of commitment.

But no articles name those people.

No articles speak of the shame of their actions.

The storm that's been threatening all day finally cracks open the sky. The rain runs in sheets hard enough to raise the sea. I let the cold pellets pick at my skin, form small river pathways down the length of my hair. The rain swells the grass. I stare through the veil of water, consumed by lonely Malaga. I blink away the drops that collect along my lashes.

Rain would've been a gift to islanders, fresh water in a sea of undrinkable water. The pottery we found would have held this precious resource. I squeeze my eyes shut, willing my body to go back to the place where a young boy called Aggie's name.

But it's Gram I hear calling. "Rilla!"

Her voice is distorted. The rain slicks against her words. "Come in before there's lightning!" I can't see Gram in the doorway because the rain falls in torrents now, filling the sea with its rush. I don't want to pull away. I want the ocean to overflow and have it carry me to this yesterday place, when Malaga was home to dozens of people. It feels like a long time and no time at all before I head inside, grab a dish towel to wring out my hair. I'm surprised Gram isn't in the kitchen, prepared to warm me.

"Gram?" There's no answer to my call. I light a burner, let the *whoosh* of gas bring flame. I grind a lemon peel, knowing Gram has retired to her attic, her place of repair.

The kettle screams, and I pull it from the heat. I pour the hot water into the mug, the scent of sharp citrus rising on steam.

"Rilla!" Gram's voice curdles the air in the kitchen. "Rilla!"

I race up the stairs. "Gram?" The air in the hall is dense with oil, the waxy air of paint.

"Rilla!" Gram's cry again. Her voice is hoarse, as if she's struggling to make sound. Adrenaline rushes through me, filling my ears with its dull weight.

"Gram! I'm coming!" I push into her room, but she's not there. Behind me, the attic door slams.

"Gram!" I throw myself against the attic door, twisting the locked doorknob. "Gram! Let me in!" I pound on the door with an open palm. Thunder booms outside. "Open the door!" The door gusts open, its panel smacking me in the face. My back slams against the opposite wall.

The door shuts again.

Opens.

It swings wildly, a tornado of movement, pushingpulling, pushingpulling.

"Gram! Where are you?" The door stops in midswing, as if halted by someone.

But there's no one.

I take a step toward the attic stairway. I place my foot on the short, narrow tread. A crackle of lightning beams its white light. I wait the length of a breath for what? To test the stair's strength? To listen for Gram?

"Gram?" This time my call is a whisper.

I walk slowly up the attic's bare wood treads, each one creaking as my footfall forces it to bear my weight. *Creee-eeee.* Thunder ricochets outside. And then silence. Except for my breathing, the groan of the stairs. Gone is the wind that burst the door open, then shut.

"Gram?" I let the question fall into the cushion of quiet. The total quiet. Silence pulls me up the stairs. The air turns colder with every ascending step. Paint, so palpable in the air now. I fumble at the wall when I reach the third floor but can't find a switch. There's a tickle at my face, a light brush. I reach for it and my fingers find string. I pull the cord, and light invades the attic.

I expect to see my gram.

I don't expect to see Agnes.

But she is everywhere. On canvas. Her painted face.

One painting of Agnes at the shore, washing a tub of white linens against the rocks. Another painting of Agnes training tomato vines up sturdy sticks within her garden. Agnes in her open boat, oarless and drifting. Agnes in her open boat, rowing through a storm. Agnes flying over the sea, her arms stretched eagle-wide, her dress floating behind her. Agnes sleeping, her eyes closed, peace drawn over her every feature. Agnes soothing a swaddled infant at her chest, the sun high behind her.

Her large eyes stare at me from the walls, the ceiling. Images of Agnes are stacked ten, twelve deep on the easels, each one holding as many versions of her as they can bear. I turn slowly in the space, surrounded by Agnes. My heart skips and I remember my gram, the way she called for me. I scan the floor, looking for where she's fallen, but the floors hold only stacks and stacks of Agnes.

"Gram?" I whisper.

Silence.

I reach out for the nearest canvas, and I want to trace the long line of Agnes's jaw, the full spread of her mouth. My fingers hover just outside of her image before the canvas jumps, swatting me across the face. I fall back. Another canvas smacks at my head. A painting whirls at my legs. The air is stirring now, the attic a tunnel of whirling wind. The canvases fly at me, hurling themselves like discs. A *thwap* to my skull. A cut to my ankle. The corner of a frame digging at my arm. I bring my elbows high, my arms crossed at my face. I try to see my way back to the stairs, but the hard wooden edges of the canvas portraits stab at my sides, jab at my flesh. I drop to my knees, crawl to the opening of the stairwell. A print soars at me, throwing me off-balance, pitching me down the stairwell.

The stairs thud at my back, my head. Pain sears my backside, my shoulders, my pointed parts rattling over the steep stairs, the unforgiving steps.

Gram appears at the bottom of the stairs, her chest heaving, her face washed of color. She gathers me to her arms as I break across the bottom step.

"You're all right," I croak.

The attic settles to a still quiet above us. Rain pounds at the roof, the only sound.

"Of course I'm all right. But, Rilla." She looks me over, her thumb brushing across my cheek. She clears my hair from my face. "What happened?"

"I heard you calling for me."

"I wasn't calling for ya. I heard ya yelling for me."

I bend to sit up, press my fingers to my temple. My one knee screeches with pain, as if a hammer smashed it—the first tumble. The crease of the stair. I gather my leg to my chest and push down the pain. I hobble to a stand, and Gram steadies me as my body adjusts to the wounded parts of me.

"Why were ya up there?" Gram says it like an accusation, like it's my fault I fell.

"I thought you needed my help. I was worried about you."

"I'm right here."

"Gram." I look her in the eye, see the love I've always known. The woman who has been my grandmother and mother and everything in between. "You know her."

"Know who?"

"Agnes."

Gram's face wrinkles. "I don't know any Agnes, Rilla." She puts the back of her hand to my head. "Are ya sure you're okay?"

I brush her off, move slightly so that I'm standing by my own might. "The girl in your paintings."

Gram's face pales, her eyes searching mine. It is a minute,

maybe longer before she speaks. I watch her try to make sense of what I might be saying. I watch her wrestle with the notion that I might know her girl. "Ya know her?"

"I do." I take Gram's hand and we walk upstairs together.

The paintings are gone. They are shredded canvas, sprawled over easels, broken pieces hurled into the attic's corners. Shreds of Agnes hang from the windowsill. Agnes litters the floor. Her eye. A part of her mouth. Locks of her hair.

Gram throws her hand to her mouth. "Did ya do this?"

"No, she did."

"Who?"

"Agnes."

"How?"

It's a question I can't answer. I don't know how any of this is happening, what force tore the canvas to scraps, but I know Agnes has been haunting my grandmother for years. Visiting her paintbrushes, in the room above mine, all my life. I think of how Gram told me my mother's mind deteriorated so terribly while she was pregnant with me and know that Agnes has been trying to reach the women in my family for too long.

And I know all the things I have to tell my grandmother.

CHAPTER TWENTY-TWO

I make tea. Chamomile, lavender, linden, skullcap, and rose petals. I don't know a recipe that can calm a haunting, so I throw it all in there. Anything to help the mind.

"Why did you paint her? Only her?" For years. "There were hundreds of paintings of the same girl. Why?"

Gram looks down at her hands, palms flat against the kitchen table, her cup between them. "She lived in my fingers. When she wanted to come out, I would put her on canvas."

"She's real, Gram. That girl you paint. She lived when you were very young. She lived out on Malaga before the islanders were evicted. Our family knew her. Your mother knew her. She laundered our family's wash. She came to this house."

"How do ya know this?"

The bees pollinating our stories.

The sea carrying a song.

"I've met her. The girl," I say, and my gram's face washes with white.

"That's impossible. Ya said she lived on Malaga. That girl would be older than me now."

"She's real. Well, maybe not real, but she's here." I tell her the story of the island girl and her song, how she sang to me at the shores, how she sang to me underwater.

"What ya saying sounds like a ghost, Rilla."

"I can't say what she is, Gram, but she's here. She can scratch messages into the wood on my windowsill and she can leave a flower in her wake. She can come to you so strongly that you need to put her to canvas. I can hear her song. That song can pull me to the sea, speak to me when I'm underwater." I don't tell her how she took me back to the past or how I know her name. I think too much might be too much for Gram.

"Rilla. The way ya are talking . . . ya sound like . . ."

I know who she's comparing me to, just like I know she'd never make the comparison out loud.

"I know I do. At least, I think I can imagine."

"Ya can't imagine, Rilla. Ya can't know how much you're scaring me."

"I don't want to scare you, Gram." I reach for her hand, sandwich it between mine. "I want to be done with being scared."

"Tell me how ya do that, Rilla, and I will help. I promised your mother the same thing a lot of years ago."

"I think something happened to that girl a very long time ago." I remember the way her head was indented when she was waiting on my pillow, the seaweed caught in her curls. "Something terrible. She needs our help. I think she's been trying to reach out to our family for a long time."

"Why?"

"Because I think she's kin."

"Kin?"

"I'm pretty sure."

Static churns on the VHF downstairs. I hear Sam's handle scratching through the wavelength, calling to me.

"Go," Gram tells me.

I head to the downstairs hall and pick up our VHF receiver. "Fairtide to USM research craft. Switch to channel sixteen. Over."

I turn the dial, wait on channel sixteen.

The rain has thinned now, bouncing off the ocean. I watch raindrops play at Malaga's beach, its granite mound. The drops turn to sparks as they hit the ground. These wet, trailing rains make fire as they connect with the soaked earth. Just a spittle, enough to drag at my sanity. I pop the receiver off its base and run outside. Rain flutters onto the lawn around my feet. Cool, wet rain. Until the raindrops ignite as they pluck against the grass. Each with a small pop of fire as if the grass and rain are stones rubbing sharply against each other. Sparking.

I radio Sam again and listen as static comes across the channel. The only response. Then it's not static in the air, but the sound of fire sizzling against the waves. Thousands of crackles, each one a dancing flick of flame. Smoke from the snuffed sparks rises gently along the ocean, coats the water with a thickening fog. No, not fog. Smoke. Smoke from a fire that cannot possibly sit on top of a salted sea. The hot raindrops turn to rain again, the regular kind. I radio for Sam as I bend to the earth, press my hand against the wet grass. The soil holds heat, too much heat. I have to pull my hand away before the burn penetrates my skin. There's no mistaking the thick charred smell that lifts from the ocean, carried on the current, lifted by the air. Smoke and fire mixed with salt.

And that smell of death holding its breath.

Then a light. The spotlight from a boat just off Malaga's shores.

I know it's Sam. I fear it's Sam.

I run to the *Rilla Brae*, turn on her VHF. "This is the *Rilla Brae* to USM research craft. Over."

Sam's light illuminates the back of his boat, brightening its entire deck. I watch him, fearing the worst. I am a child again, watching my father go to sea without me. I am my great-grandmother watching her husband brave the ocean for fish, for lobster, for food to put food on their table. I am six watching my mother try to give herself to the Water People. I am Gram watching me come home that day with Dad in the wheelhouse, his slumped body too heavy for me to move from where he'd fallen. I am grief and hope and generations of fishing people, all tied around one beating heart.

I crank my key, push my engine hard.

The spotlight on Sam's boat casts a spray of white onto the black waves and spins around him as if the bulb is set to rotate. I set my binoculars to the bridge of my nose, squint my eyes to separate the dark sea from the dark night. It is then I see that the bulb isn't rotating; it's the boat that's spiraling.

Sam's boat whirlpools in circles, whirling and twisting.

The boat doesn't move from the exact spot where it spins off Malaga's shores. Has Sam dropped anchor? In my years at sea I've never seen a boat twist in a circle like this, and the impossibility of it stuns me. My suspicions jump to Reed or Old Man Benner. Could they have sabotaged Sam's engine in some way that Sam wouldn't know how to fix? Or maybe another family that doesn't want the story of Malaga to be unearthed? I know for certain it's not Agnes. Agnes isn't interested in Sam. Only me and Gram. Possibly, my mother.

Then Sam blows the emergency horn, and it doesn't matter what's wrong, only that everything is wrong. The bleat of his air horn hangs in the air, bellows over the roar of my engine, over the thundering spasm of my heart.

When I near Sam's craft, I call to him, "What's happening? Is it your engine?"

"No! Everything's shut down. I—I think I'm stuck." His voice strains over the distance. "Is this a riptide?"

The Under Toad, the mysterious creature that lives under the water and pulls you down into his world, holds you there, all so he can have a playmate.

Sam's boat spins and spins, slowly, playfully. Cruelly.

This is no rip.

The water here taunts Sam's boat, swirls it, controls it. There's only one creature I've met in the deep that could do these things. But I don't want it to be Agnes.

"Sam!"

He comes to his rail, though I lose sight of him as the craft makes another round. Then I can only see the back, the engine. The motor's turned off, sleeping, and yet a spark pops from its plugs. My body goes cold. Sam runs to the rear of the boat and another spark jumps out of the engine's lines.

"Sam! Can you swim?"

"Yes!"

"You need to abandon your boat. Jump off! Now! Dive and swim as far as you can as quick as you can!" Two sparks leap now, partners in their crime. "Can you hear me?"

"You want me to jump?"

"Now, Sam! Get as far from your boat as possible. Swim to shore." I know he's struggling to hear me through his fear and my own engine, but I can't turn it off. I can't take the chance of not being able to rescue him. "Dive now!"

Sam climbs to the front deck and flies into the night, a straight dive away from his boat, away from me. I nudge my throttle forward and maneuver past his craft, which is now spitting sparks in a waterfall. I can't be too close when one of those sparks finds his gasoline engine. Or my deck. And just as I think the thought, Sam's boat fires with a wall of flame rising from the motor, running along the broken lines of gas that spurt as his boat turns.

The red glow of light shows me Sam in the water, his head bobbing. He throws one arm up to call me to him. A wave smashes over him. I lose him to the crash of the black sea before he resurfaces and my heart restarts. I motor to him and slow when I get close. Close enough for him to climb aboard but not so close that I make the waves bigger around him. He is struggling already, his muscles surely tiring in the swells.

"Climb up! You're going to be all right!" I need to believe

this promise. I head to the back of the boat, readying my hand at the ladder.

He swims toward the *Rilla Brae* but stops. He struggles as if he doesn't know how to swim, or can't move.

The flames rage upon his research boat, the smoke rising in clean red stacks of blaze. The boat is engulfed and the water is freezing. I want Sam safe, onboard. "You need to hurry! I know you're tired, but you need to swim now!"

"I can't, Rilla." Sam's voice is muffled with something that sounds like confusion.

I know how exhausted a body can get from treading water in the ocean, but he has to try. "You can. Just a few more strokes. I'm here. I'll help you up."

"Rilla, I can't. I can't get closer." Sam raises one hand, and his palm flattens against the nothingness that separates us. Except his hand is too still. It doesn't move with the sway of the water. It's as if he's pressing his hand against an invisible glass wall, too similar to the invisible man who pinned me down.

"Sam?" This time his name moves over my lips with almost no sound. Why is this happening?

"Rilla!" Sam yells. The flames that engulfed his boat jump now. They spark on the surface of the ocean, one leaping ember and then another. The hot specks of fire don't extinguish when they hit the water. They shimmer with coal-red heat.

"Sam." I force my voice loud. "Can you swim to the island?"

Sam twists toward Malaga. He takes a few strokes and hope grows in my chest. Embers pop from Sam's boat. Too many embers. I watch Sam slowly making his way toward Malaga, watch as the fire builds on the sea. "Sam! Swim faster!" The fire chases after Sam, each popping ember marking a trail along the water, pursuing him with its fiery length. Worry rattles within me. Then the fire on the water bursts, as if seawater itself is flammable. A wall of fire surrounds Sam, traps him.

Sam will die. He'll be burned to death or drown. I am horrified and helpless.

But then.

The girl is on Malaga's shore. Watching us. The fire around Sam. Agnes stirs the flames, building their intensity with her gaze. The same way she burned me when she rose from the deep with the seaweed in her hair and the fire in her touch.

Like that first day, I arc my arms above me. I call to her. "Agnes, stop! I'll do anything! Anything you ask! Just leave him alone! He has nothing to do with this!"

The fire around Sam closes in. I can't see him behind the height of the reaching flames.

I scream my bargain. "Save him and I will save you!"

The fire doesn't cease. I search my brain for anything. Everything. The attic, her portraits, her calling to me underwater, waking next to me in my bed . . . and scratching her words into my sill: FIND ME. Find her. Find the girl who doesn't show up on census records, whose name was never registered at the state asylum. The girl who has slipped from history's memory.

"Save him and we will find you! I need his help! Please, I promise you! I promise we will find you!"

The fire quells, softens into soft orange liquid before churning into the cool sea black of the waves. Impossibly, the sea becomes the sea once again. I know the sea.

I maneuver the *Rilla Brae* as close as I can to Sam and throw him a life float. He fits the ring over his head and uses his remaining strength to force his exhausted limbs to climb the ladder to my deck. He collapses there, a puddle of fatigue.

Agnes waits for us on the shore. For a split second I consider leaving, racing my boat all the way to the edge of the horizon and beyond, but I couldn't leave Gram behind, and a part of me knows that Agnes would find me, follow me. Or she would haunt Gram in a new and terrible way that I can't allow. Sam coughs up seawater as I edge us closer to Malaga. I help Sam into the dingy and row the small boat ashore.

I glance back at Fairtide, fearing this is the last time I'll see my home. The lawn is quiet, dark. Sleeping. All the homes on the peninsula are dark. Too dark. I squint, trying to find light along the shore, among the trees, but the homes are pitched into a blackness that feels wrong. Around us, the air is as dark as death.

Agnes reaches for my hand. She cradles a bundle in her opposite hand. I think it is the baby, but the infant is too quiet. Whatever she holds is wrapped like a package, a gift. Agnes pulls me up the open-air stairs that connect the beach to the highest part of the island now. Sam follows, his steps stumbling from exhaustion.

There are homes on the island. Fishing shacks with small front porches. The same ones from the photographs. There are vegetable gardens, plants reaching for the sun that will rise with tomorrow. We pass the school with its straight lines and shingled roof. I turn to Sam. "Do you see? The homes everywhere?"

"No."

"Take my hand." Sam wraps my grip with his, and something electric passes between us. He squeezes my fingers as we step onto the beach.

He gasps. "I see it now."

"You see her?"

"I see everything."

I hold tighter to him, Agnes leading us both now. I don't want to break our connection. I need Sam to see what I see. What Agnes needs us to see.

The island is asleep, the homes visible only because of the

spray of moonlight casting Malaga in a soft glow. There are no lights in any of the homes, no candles burning in the windows. Only smoke lifting from the chimneys, small rivers of gray rising up to the clouds.

Then there's movement behind us, a sound.

Footsteps crunching shells.

So many footsteps.

Silent men slip up the beach. Agnes stops when the men and their quiet feet reach the top of the island. Three men stand in front of each home. The men are coordinated, this whole night planned. Then the island fills with bursts of light as torches flame in front of the homes. Each man lights his torch, a *whoosh* of fire against the night. There's the smell of burning hay. Then the men and their flames duck inside the meager houses.

All at once the screams fill the air. Women. Children. Their screeches so loud they burn my ears. But I can't block it out. I can't put my hands to my ears. Agnes wants me to hear the cries. It's why she holds my hand so tight. And I don't dare let go of Sam, because he needs to be connected to me. I can't survive this alone.

The way Agnes has had to survive this alone.

Terror sweeps across the island as the men move through the houses like a storm, tearing the residents from their beds, setting fire to the emptied shacks. Each home is set ablaze. The fire burns too close to my skin. Sam grips my fingers as if he's trying to hold on to my bones.

Men order barked calls. "Get up!" "Get out!"

A woman pleads. Children call for their mothers.

Agnes pulls us across the island, and the voices rise, the cries of panic drowning out all words. She wrenches us past the house with a rocking chair ablaze in the front yard, the red reaching flames rocking backandforth, backandforth, backandforth. The old woman, already gone.

"Tell us how we can help you," I beg, even as I fear Agnes won't tell. She drags us farther across the island, the night lit by fire and terror and the ghostly cry of islanders.

I want to run to the men with their torches and drown their flames and their hate in the sea. I want to talk to Agnes. I want her to tell us her story, all the reasons why we are here. And then we see her.

Agnes is at the south side of the island, on a dark pocket of granite. So far from us now. Yet Agnes holds my hand still. She is more real than ever and she watches this other Agnes so near to us.

The Agnes at the water settles her bundle into an old skiff. The skiff from that first day, the dory with its flaked paint and sturdy lines.

The bundle cries. The same cry as that first day. It starts as a stutter at first, as if the infant is not sure what sound to make. The cry grows to a howl. Loud enough to drown out the shrieks from the other side of the island, the wretched screams that rise into the night. Agnes unties the boat from its hitch and drags the dory into the sea. She lifts her white dress around her ankles and raises her foot into the boat. She sings to her baby, trying to soothe her screeching child. *Come here, come here, my dear, my dear, won't you co—*

Agnes has one foot in the skiff, the other raising. But she's ripped back from the edge of her dory, and it is only then that I see the hulking man nearly two times her size. His shoulders are wide and strong, and he snaps Agnes out of the water as if she is no heavier than a flower.

Agnes struggles but doesn't scream. She kicks at him, flails her one free arm. The man drags her up the shore. He pins her to the earth, his hands locked over her wrist. My body blazes with the same memory. The man on top of me. His smoky smell. His weight. His rage.

"Ya filthy thing. Trying ta escape, were ya?"

He claws at her hips and arms and legs. I feel the attack in my bones. I remember the attack in my bones.

He tries to bind her arms with the rope he pulls from his waist. She struggles; her dress rips.

The man reaches to tie her arms and his weight shifts.

Agnes wrestles free. She scrambles to the shore, her feet tripping from her speed. She reaches the water. The infant in the open boat. "I am here," she says. "Do not worry, my dear. I am here."

The man is at the water in seconds, his fine shoes soaked with the sea. He yanks Agnes by her long braids. He tosses her to the shore as if she is weightless, as if she is nothing. The boat slips deeper out to sea, and the child wails louder for her mother.

The man pushes Agnes to the ground, her skull splitting against a rock. I hear the crack, see the way her head spills to the side, her eyes rolling to watch her child disappear with the currents.

I want to scream. I want to rescue the child. Sam feels me tug away from him, and his grip tightens around my hand. *Stay,* it tells me. *There is nothing you can do,* it tells me.

We watch the blood drain from Agnes's wound as life leaves her eyes. She is dying. She reaches toward the sea with her raw, clawing fingers. They are bloody, caked with dirt. She sings a song, *Come here, come here, my dear, my dear,* but the boat is caught in the current, drifting from the shore, drifting to the open black sea.

Blood pools around Agnes's head, crawling into her braids. Light washes from her face.

The man tosses Agnes over his shoulder, her lifeless body no different from a sack of grain. The man kicks at the ground, driving his heels against the grass until he's unearthed a large slice of stone. His adrenaline rakes the stone along the earth, digging away the soil and removing hunks of stone until he has formed a thin pocket of earth. He drops Agnes into the hole. Her hair cascades around her face, seaweed gathered in the tangles of her hair.

The man kicks dirt and stones over Agnes.

And he turns on her shallow grave.

He runs. Toward the burning homes, the islanders imprisoned on boats.

I say her name. "Agnes." It's the only word that seems big enough in this moment. No other words will do.

I turn to tell Agnes that I'm sorry, that I finally understand what she needs, but she is gone. The hand that brought me here has vanished.

As are the fires that consumed the island only moments ago.

The screams have disappeared.

There is only one small voice that rises out over the waves. The small cry of a small voice. A child. Set to sea alone.

Eleanor.

I look to Sam. I want him to tell me this has all been a dream. He shakes his head, and I know this wasn't a dream.

By the time we return to Fairtide, I'm not willing to let Sam go. We sit on the dock and hold one another through the entire night. We watch Malaga. We listen to the waves lick the shore, the water flowing toward us but then retreating, as if it decided it would rather be at sea. We sit under the all-seeing moon.

We say all the words that pass between us, all the words that could never change what happened.

Before the sun rises, I stand. "I need to talk to my gram."

He nods. "I'll be here if you need me."

"I'll need you." I stand, face him. I'll need him to process all of this. To make sure I always remember this story. To make sure it always lives in the world. "I'm certain of it."

Sam kisses my forehead. He stamps his warmth there, and it feels electric. Like the buzzing of bees.

I go inside and throw on the light in the stairwell. I walk slowly up each step. I study my ancestors to see their resemblance passed down through generations to Gram, me, my mother. But the old photos are grainy and will never tell me what I need to know.

I kneel next to Gram's bed and watch her sleep. The sun begins to rise outside, and the soft light spills across her room. It is when I see Gram's face in its purest calm, lost in the depths of sleep, that I see Agnes. The shape of her mouth, her high cheeks and soft jaw. Gram's skin looks so brown in the hesitant light. Dark like Agnes. And that is when I know for certain.

The baby in the boat.

Agnes haunting the women in my family for decades.

The screaming infant was Gram.

Her unmanned boat made it to the shores of Fairtide that night. Brought by the currents that always deliver the sea to our door.

I can't know if my great-grandfather discovered the bundle when he went out to sea the next morning. Or when he came home from the raid that night. I'll likely never know how much my family knew of—or participated in—the attack on Malaga residents.

I'll never know if Gram was legally adopted. I'm fully aware of the disappointing practice of record keeping in those days. I do know that Gram hasn't lived a life of shame. She wasn't locked away in an institution. She was lucky.

Lucky that the Murphys took her in, chose her. Lucky, like Sam. To find a home and a family. Our roots are as deep and proud as I'd always thought. Only different. Now our story is richer.

Gram breathes in and out, in and out, her lungs' rhythm so delicate.

I'll never know the story my great-grandparents had to conjure to raise Gram as their own. But their story is wrapped in my story. Gram is my family, and our family is so much more. I am so much more.

Gram opens her eyes, soft at first, and then a startled look comes over her.

"It's okay," I tell her. "Everything's going to be okay."

AFTER

Sam holds me as we sit on Fairtide's wharf. We share one of Gram's old wool blankets while we watch the University of Southern Maine researchers arrive for work on Malaga. The morning is cold for late August. Fall tugs at the leaves on the trees, its chilly breath already weaving a nip through the wind. Six boats arrived at the island the day after Sam and I witnessed the raid. Members of the university. The county coroner. Me and Sam. Many more reporters showed up but were banned from coming ashore.

Sam and I led the USM team to the burial site. Twenty-two people sifted at the place where Agnes was forgotten. The earth she was buried under had thickened with time, the winds kicking dirt over her as if to protect her for us.

When the head archeologist excavated the dirt around her skull, Sam and I were asked to leave. It was time for the police and officials and a murder investigation.

"Thank you for this discovery." It was the professor. The lead archeologist. I forgot his name in the whirl of introductions, but I wouldn't forget the round of bone I saw in the earth, the way Agnes's skull was turned toward Fairtide, watching us. The way her jaw was open just a little. Enough to slip a Flame Freesia bloom through the space there. As if a song were still on her lips. I stood quickly then. I didn't want to see anything more. Sam took me home, the only man to ever captain the *Rilla Brae* besides my father.

My dad used to say that he loved my mother unconditionally, even after she left both of us. They were bonded, he said. He brought me into the world with her and they would forever be attached, the way Agnes brought her child into the world. I understand it now, sitting with Sam. I helped to bring Agnes back to the world because she and I have always been forever connected.

It's strange to be at the dock without Dad, without the *Rilla Brae*. She's pulled from the water now, her season cut short by the University of Rhode Island's orientation, which begins the day after tomorrow. My boat's in dry dock, her fuel lines already prepped for winter storage. Hoopah promised to give her a new coat of bottom paint. She'll be ready when I need her. And the pettiness of Old Man Benner's threats seems like nothing in the wake of all that's happened.

I wish my dad were here to see the work on Malaga unfold, to see me off to school. I wish for a lot of things that will never be. Maybe that's just all part of getting on with the business of living, as Gram would say.

Sam convinced me and Gram to have our DNA tested by an online service. He'll have access to the DNA they gather from Agnes once he returns to school, and he's promised to tell me if they're a match. I know they will be. I don't need a lab to tell me where my grandmother came from, where our family's roots are set deep.

I can feel the settledness of Agnes in my bones. Gram feels it too. She paints in the living room now, the oils and her cooking raising up competing smells. We are both proud to be descendants of Malaga, the hardworking community of people who should never be forgotten. We are glad the shame is lifting from this tragedy, that other Malaga Island descendants are using social media to come forth, to claim their heritage. Even people with family members who went to the state asylum, the ones labeled "feeble-minded." The news of the body found on Malaga has reached far beyond Malaga and our peninsula. I've been messaging with other descendants. They are my family. The same DNA lives in our bones, and I'm proud to claim this new heritage. I think of the fiercely independent Eliza Griffin, the child who couldn't identify a telephone, the old woman in her rocking chair. I carry them with me. In me.

I will likely never know the name of the man Agnes was married to. I can assume only that he was white because of his Irish ancestry, and the color of his skin was a trait he passed to Gram, something that helped her find safety in the aftermath of a brutal attack.

I hope Agnes will be buried on Malaga.

I hope all other island residents buried at the former Maine School for the Feeble-Minded can be returned to Malaga, put to rest under stones with individual names. The islanders buried their dead on Malaga so they would forever be part of the soil. I hope the state of Maine will finally do right by Malaga's people, my people, and bring them home one day.

Agnes's grave won't say that she was a wife or a mother. The grave will probably not bear her name. These are things that Sam and I know because they are part of the most private thing we share together. And today, next to the water, with Agnes and Malaga and the history of the island in capable hands, that seems like enough.

It's like our whole world has let out a deep breath. The peninsula is quiet, focused on the hard work of getting by.

My sleep has been dreamless.

Maybe the quiet will reach all the way to my mother, bring her peace.

I find I miss messages on the windowsill.

I find I miss my dad less some days. More on others. I think he would have been proud of my great-grandparents for bringing an orphan under their care, giving her family. Taking Gram in would have been an enormous risk in the days and years following the men with their torches.

Gram was chosen, in the same way Sam was chosen, and that still feels like something more than a miracle. And Agnes was no different from me. A fisherman's daughter. I hope I will be a fierce mother the way she was a fierce mother. Someday.

I hope Agnes can know peace now.

Sam and I head inside the kitchen, where Gram has made entirely too many cupcakes for my going-away party, as if she couldn't decide which flavor to bake. I pull up one that I think is butterscotch under its chocolate frosting. Gram gives me the evil eye, but she can't swat my hand away from the dessert since she's busy lugging her record player to the deck. Brenda Sherfey is right behind her, a stack of The Who records in her arms. Sam helps them with their loads.

I lick the frosting and my mouth floods with the sugary wave. The house is covered in balloons and streamers, and Hattie's still not done plastering the kitchen's thick, low beams.

"I'm going to miss this." Hattie's intent on the end of the

streamer she's taping to the ceiling and doesn't meet my eyes.

"You and Gram can throw me a send-off party next year too if you like."

"So you're definitely going, then?" She jumps off the wobbling chair and unrolls a few additional feet of the crepe paper.

"Ha-ha."

Hattie winks. "Just don't forget about us little people."

She doesn't know about my family's connection to Malaga. I visited the graves at Pineland without her, those five lonely stones nearly disappearing into the earth and grass. I walked the grounds and saw the large, recent memorial marker acknowledging the plight of Malaga residents. But the marker, the bodies. They're still in the wrong place. Too far from Malaga.

"I'll visit," Hattie says. "Check out all the cute guys with the big brains."

"I'll expect it." I know Hattie won't be down to Rhode Island. More than half the families on this peninsula will never leave the county we live in, the county they were born in. Still, it's good knowing Hattie wants to come. And who knows? Maybe she'll surprise me. It wouldn't be the first time.

I move the chair next to Hattie and stand on it as she hands me the crepe streamers. She rips off a piece of tape, and I affix the decoration to the ceiling. "Four years is no time at all, Hattie. And it's really just ten months if you think about it. Hell, its two months till I'll be home for Thanksgiving and then again for Christmas. Then spring break, then summer. You'll practically be sick of me by then." I jump down.

"Not possible."

We move to the next random spot, and I tape up another loop of paper streamer.

"It's hard knowing that you won't be coming back."

"But I wi—"

"I mean, I know you'll be *here*. You'll physically come back, but you'll be different, Rills. You know it. Like how we always talked about the ways we wanted to change the world." She hesitates, and then, "And how we wanted the world to change us."

Hattie and I would often dream of a train station in Anywhere, Europe, and how the songs of a dozen languages would dance around our ears. How we'd walk streets where no one looked like we did. Visit a village in the Andes and let the newness of food and thin air wake our senses.

"It's the way it's supposed to be, Rills. College will change you. You'll come back thinking our tiny peninsula is backward and tired. You'll hate that we have no diversity. You'll miss the foreign foods."

"I'm only going to Rhode Island, Hatt."

She lowers her eyes before drawing them up to meet mine.

Her gaze is wet, already mourning. "You know what I mean."

I do. Everything will be different once I leave because leaving a place always changes a place.

Hattie hugs me then, holds me for longer than she's ever held me. We press together, all eleven years of our laughter, our tears, our fears, and our dreams. They melt between us, our stories.

There's a knock at the door.

"You go ahead and get that. I'll finish up." Hattie waves me off and I open the door to guests. The house fills quickly, and our company overflows to the grass, the deck. Reed hasn't showed, and I'm not sure he will, despite my invitation. It's strange to love someone so deeply and then not be a part of their lives. Still, his love is in me, like each of my gathered stories.

Gram comes to stand beside me as I step outside. The sun is high, and the breeze is chilled. The long green lawn fills with people from all over the peninsula with drinks in their hands and Malaga in their sights. It's hard not to hear a group chatting about the discovery out there last month.

"People will be talking about Malaga for a while."

"Only seems right." Gram takes my hand. "It's the forgetting that's wrong."

I lean against my gram and her strong shoulder, the way she stands still and straight and as dependable as a lighthouse. "I'm gonna miss you."

"I'll miss ya too, Rilla. I can't think of a finer feeling than loving someone so much that ya miss them."

I smile and let out a small laugh. My gram. "You're one of a kind."

"I should hope so. How boring would a world full of Eleanor Murphys be?"

Not so boring, I think.

After everyone left last night, the peninsula returned to its quiet rhythms of the sea lapping, the gulls calling. I wrote a letter to my mother. I told her about the girl discovered on Malaga, but I didn't tell her my role in any of it. Instead, I wrote about going to school, how good Gram is doing. Keep it light—that's what kept going through my head. Maybe because I hope we'll have time to talk later. Or maybe we'll exchange letters for a while. Exchange stories.

Gram meets me in the driveway, hands me a small box of bottled herbs, which I settle onto the middle of the bench seat in my dad's old truck. For strength, for adjustment. Gram, watching out for me always.

Gram hugs me, short but sweet. I know she's not big on good-byes. "See ya soon," she tells me.

"Can't keep a seal from the sea."

She smiles then, her full smile.

It's a good smile.

"This is the last one." Sam places the final cardboard box into the Chevy's bed.

"You sure you're up for this road trip?" I ask.

"Haven't got anything better to do." He winks and goes around to the passenger side. The creak of the pickup's old door is as familiar as my father's voice. Sam has so much work to do when he gets back, has school of his own to return to. Even though the USM boat fire was deemed an engine malfunction due to exposed wiring meeting with gasoline, I know Sam feels obligated to work twice as hard to try to repay the university for the craft that was destroyed.

He'll drop me off at my freshman dorm and return Dad's truck to the peninsula. Next year I'll be allowed a car on campus and I'll take Dad's pickup with me, as planned. "The closest I'll ever get to college," Dad used to joke.

I get in the driver's seat, behind the wheel, and turn the key. The motor coughs out its dependable rumble.

Sam has his phone out, scrolling through tunes for our long drive down the coast. He puts on "Won't Get Fooled Again" loud enough for Gram to hear. She stands in her garden, her hands on her hips. She raises an arm and waves. I press my hand to the glass for what seems like a long time.

When I put the truck in drive, we bump along Fairtide's gravel driveway. In the rearview mirror I see Gram surrounded by the bulging blooms of white hydrangea bushes, the sea at her back, Malaga behind her.

I turn onto the highway that stretches along the coast, heading due south, straight for my future.

A bee darts across my windshield, carrying a story.

Acknowledgments

I am so grateful for the village of readers, writers, family, and community that made this book possible.

Thanks first and foremost goes to you, dear reader. For picking up this book. For your dedication to so many books. For supporting authors everywhere. You are passionate and tireless and my craft would mean nothing without your love of the written word. Thank you.

A ridiculously huge thanks goes out to authors Kali Wallace, Kathleen Glasgow, Amber Smith, Adrianna Mather, Sarah Glenn Marsh, Lilly Richardson, Tayler Warren, Rebecca Podos, and Karen Fortunati—for your early reads of this book, your keen insights, and your gorgeous endorsements.

Many of the details for this book were gleaned from the hardworking women and men who serve as stewards of Maine's working waterfront. I'm grateful for all the support I received from the women and men fishing the Atlantic. Thank you to Maine Coast Heritage Trust for protecting the island of Malaga and the Phippsburg Historical Society for protecting Malaga's history. Thank you to the Damariscotta River Association's Archaeology

ACKNOWLEDGMENTS

Field School. My great thanks and gratitude go to the students, authors, and researchers working to tell the real story of Malaga.

I'm beyond grateful to so many authors who have supported me in my writing journey. To Marci Lyn Curtis, Laurie Elizabeth Flynn, Carrie Firestone, Kerry Kletter, Elly Swartz, Bridget Hodder, and Lindsay Currie for being the purest forms of lovely. To Ashley Herring Blake, Sonja Mukherjee, Meghan Rogers, Chris Bernard, Jenny Bardsley, Estelle Laure, Catherine Lo, Brooks Benjamin, Victoria J. Coe, Nicole Castroman, Michelle Andreani, Natalie Blitt, Jennie K. Brown, Erica Chapman, Jill Diamond, Jennifer DiGiovanni, Julie Eshbaugh, Emily Henry, Meg Leder, Kathy MacMillan, Kerri Maniscalco, Jennifer Maschari, Jenny Moyer, Kathryn Purdie, Erin Summerill, Laura Shovan, and so many more! Your brilliant novels are only a shadow of your supportive, brilliant spirits.

Thanks to Darcy Woods for being sunshine and laughter—much needed ingredients when cooking up a novel! To Shea Earnshaw, Marisa Reichardt, and Janet B. Taylor for being the most hilarious support group any girl could ever wish for. You make me wonder how I got so lucky.

The hugest of thanks goes to Marisa Reichardt. Your keen eye and rad reader instincts helped give this book its beating heart. Thank you for the countless texts, emails, DMs, phone calls. You are my first laugh most mornings and my most precious person. Thank you for always being there. For being you.

A unique thanks goes to Rilla Brae for allowing my protagonist to borrow her beautiful name. To my fabulous agent, Melissa Sarver White—thank you for always championing my work. And to my editor, Nicole Ellul, thank you for your endless cheering, your tireless devotion, and all your beautiful exclamation marks!!!

Final thanks goes to my family. While you are mentioned here last, you are always first in my heart. You are my whole heart.

Author's Note

As a storyteller, I am at home in the heart of a story. I ache for stories. So when I came across a radio and photo documentary named "Malaga Island: A Story Best Left Untold," I was immediately intrigued. The untold stories are often the most important ones.

While this book is a novel, Malaga Island is a real place, located just off the coast of Phippsburg, Maine. I have tried to stay true to the ecological—marine and land—environments that reflect life on Malaga and life fishing Maine's coast today. Any errors in representation are completely my own.

Malaga's history of forced eviction and forced institutionalization is real. The orchestrated cultural erasure took place in 1911 and 1912, though I have moved the historical occurrences to 1931 and 1932 respectively for the sake of this novel's contemporary storyline. In 1912 Governor Frederick W. Plaisted evicted forty-five innocent people from Malaga Island. Plaisted had eight residents committed to the Maine School for the Feeble-Minded. The schoolhouse was moved to another island. Malaga graves were dug up and seventeen bodies were interred in five graves at the Maine School for the Feeble-Minded.

James McKenney is mentioned in this novel and by all accounts served as "the king" of Malaga, as he was regarded as one of the best fishermen along the coast. He was the island leader during the eviction. Eliza Griffin lived on Malaga in a sea captain's wheelhouse and left behind traps that are helping researchers understand the evolution of fishing. Agnes, as well as all contemporary characters in the novel, are a creation of my imagination.

My research was intended to gather historical facts but it also illuminated a pervasive and enduring legacy of shame that is still suffered by many of the descendants of the Malaga Island community. It is my hope that my work of fiction has explored the events surrounding Malaga Island and its residents thoughtfully. I hope this story will help to inspire a generation of teen readers to research the full scope of factual events that occurred on Malaga Island. I hope that a collective effort to bring the story to light will help to lift the enduring shame of islanders being falsely labeled "feeble-minded" and "immoral."

I am grateful for the ongoing academic and cultural interest in Malaga Island's history and the recent articles that have appeared in Maine's *The Working Waterfront*, *Bangor Daily News*, and *Maine Sunday Telegram*. These articles, along with the research being conducted by the University of Southern Maine—and the exhibit at Maine State Museum—are helping to tell the real story of the Malaga Island fishing community in a way that newspapers from the time did not.

While recent Maine governors have apologized to the families of the Malaga Island victims, it is still unsettling to know that deceased Malaga Island residents remain buried in combined graves on the grounds of the former state institution. Malaga's families were proud fishing families whose ancestors had populated the islands throughout Casco Bay since the 1700s or earlier. It seems time to return the deceased home to Malaga, to the shores where their familial and cultural roots run deep.

Notes

1. Adrienne Heflich et al., "Malaga Island: A Brief History Compiled by the Students of ES 203 Service Learning Project," Typescript, Bowdoin College (2003).
2. Holman Day, "The Queer Folk of the Maine Coast," *Harper's Magazine* (September 1909), 521–530. http://www .unz.org/Pub/Harpers-1909sep-00521.
3. Rob Rosenthal and Kate Philbrick, *Malaga Island: A Story Best Left Untold*, (Salt Institute for Documentary Studies, Portland, Maine, 2009). http://malagaislandmaine.org.
4. Colin Woodward, "Malaga Island: A Century of Shame," *Portland Press Herald* (May 20, 2012).
5. Burke O. Long, "The Children of Malaga Island." (Bowdoin College, Summer 2015). https://research.bowdoin.edu /children-of-malaga-island/essay. "What a blood endowment for the youngsters" quoted directly from source.

Sources

Barry, William David. "The Shameful Story of Malaga Island."
Down East Magazine, November 1980: 53–56, 83–86.

C-SPAN.org. "The Evictions of Malaga Island, Maine."
(Video.) September 10, 2012. http://www.c-span.org
/video/?308505-1/evictions-malaga-island-maine.

Corson, Trevor. *The Secret Life of Lobsters: How Fishermen and
Scientists Are Unraveling the Mysteries of Our Favorite
Crustacean.* New York: HarperCollins, 2004.

Day, Holman. "The Queer Folk of the Maine Coast." *Harper's
Magazine,* September 1909, 521–530. http://www.unz.org
/Pub/Harpers-1909sep-00521.

Dubrule, Deborah. "Digging for Truth Malaga Excavation
Reveals the Lives of an Island's Evicted Residents." *The
Workings Waterfront,* October 1, 2006.

Dubrule, Deborah. "Evicted: How the State of Maine
Destroyed a 'Different' Island Community." *Island Journal*
16 (1999): 48–53, 90–91.

Heflich, Adrienne et al. "Malaga Island: A Brief History Compiled by the Students of ES 203 Service Learning Project." Typescript. Bowdoin College, 2003.

"Poverty, Immorality and Disease." *Bath Enterprise*, March 1902.

Long, Burke O. "The Children of Malaga Island." Bowdoin College, Summer 2015. https://research.bowdoin.edu /children-of-malaga-island/essay.

Rosenthal, Rob and Kate Philbrick. *Malaga Island: A Story Best Left Untold*. Salt Institute for Documentary Studies, Portland, Maine, 2009. http://malagaislandmaine.org.

Woodward, Colin. "Malaga Island: A Century of Shame." *Portland Press Herald*, May 20, 2012.

Woodward, Colin. *The Lobster Coast: Rebels, Rusticators, and the Struggle for a Forgotten Frontier*. New York: Viking, 2004.

About the Author

S. M. Parker lives on the coast of Maine with her husband and sons. She works as a literacy advocate and holds degrees from three New England universities. She can usually be found rescuing dogs, chickens, old houses, and wooden boats. She has a weakness for chocolate chip cookies and ridiculous laughter—ideally at the same time. *The Girl Who Fell* was her first novel.